By Swati Hegde

Love Beyond Reasonable Doubt

Can't Help Faking in Love

Match Me If You Can

For Teens

As Long as You Loathe Me

Love Beyond Reasonable Doubt

Love Beyond Reasonable Doubt

a novel

SWATI HEGDE

DELL
NEW YORK

Dell
An imprint of Random House
A division of Penguin Random House LLC
1745 Broadway, New York, NY 10019

randomhousebooks.com
penguinrandomhouse.com

A Dell Trade Paperback Original

ISBN 979-8-217-09203-1
Ebook ISBN 979-8-217-09204-8

Printed in the United States of America

1st Printing

Book Team: Production editor: Jennifer Rodriguez • Managing editor: Saige Francis • Production manager: Samuel Wetzler • Copy editor: Jennifer Prior • Proofreaders: Liz Carbonell, Claire Maby

Book design by Alexis Flynn

The authorized representative in the EU for product safety and compliance is Penguin Random House Ireland, Morrison Chambers, 32 Nassau Street, Dublin D02 YH68, Ireland.
https://eu-contact.penguin.ie

For Anshuman

Thank you for loving me then and loving me now.

I'm so glad we took a chance on each other again.

Love Beyond Reasonable Doubt

Chapter ONE

Bangalore, October 2026

Everyone at work knew Naina Shetty was the queen of confrontation. No one could be a good lawyer without easily facing things head-on, and Naina was the best junior legal associate on the Akhtar, Kumble & Co. team.

But right now, as she crouched under her perfectly tidy desk, hoping the two short walls of her cubicle hid her from view, confrontation seemed like the most terrifying thing in the world. She peered through the glass windows of her boss's office in the distance, recognizing the handsome not-at-all-a-stranger shaking Iqbal Akhtar's hand, and whispered, "Shit."

"What are you doing?"

Naina didn't stand. Instead, she turned and gestured for Anil to crouch down beside her, then put a finger to her lips.

Anil quirked a brow, but as her work bestie of five years now, he did as he was told, no questions asked. He got down and looked in the direction of Iqbal's office. "Why are we spying on our boss?" he asked.

"I'm in trouble," Naina said softly. She pushed her glasses up on her nose and sighed. "And it's all your fault."

"My fault?" He jostled her shoulder as he shifted in place. The cramped space under her desk was too small for his gigantic gym-bro frame. When Naina said nothing, he pressed, "Can you please tell me what is going on?"

Naina finally tore her gaze from the glass windows and locked eyes with Anil. "Remember when I went to Goa in May last year and had that"—she winced—"summer fling?"

Anil snorted. "Oh, yes, the sexy stranger with the cliché nickname. I mean, he called himself Prince Charming? Anyway, that fling was probably the only time you took my advice."

"Well . . ." Naina jutted her chin in the direction of the private office. "It seems like Prince Charming is the firm's new client. Don't look," she added hastily as Anil gasped.

He didn't listen. He gripped the desk and pulled himself up to his full six-foot-five height, training his wide eyes straight ahead.

Naina grumbled and stood up too, just as the office door swung open and Iqbal walked out with Prince Charming—his real name was Tejas—in tow. She had never referred to him as anything but Prince Charming when telling Anil about him, but she'd moaned his *actual* name enough times last summer to have it imprinted in her memory, along with the searing-hot touch of his hands on her bare waist and the roughness of his stubble between her thighs.

And here he was now, presumably the anonymous high-profile client her boss Iqbal had been in talks with for the past week. It didn't make sense. If Tejas was rich, why had he shared a bunk bed with her at the youth hostel last summer?

"Folks, can I have your attention?" Iqbal called out, and everyone in the office looked up at the sound of the managing partner's voice.

Naina wanted to hide under the desk again, but Tejas had already spotted her. For a brief second, she hoped maybe he wouldn't make the connection. After all, since returning from Goa seventeen months ago, she'd let her beachy brown waves grow out into her usual straight black hair, stowed her contact lenses away in the drawer under her bathroom sink, and dumped her sundresses at the far end of her closet, opting for business casuals instead. Her hot girl summer phase had ended as soon as the plane touched back down in Bangalore.

But she wasn't that lucky, because Tejas's dark eyes widened a fraction, and his chest rose and fell deeply underneath his lime-green collared shirt. He opened his mouth, then shut it and looked elsewhere, hands in his pockets. Yep. He remembered her.

Shit. Naina was gripped by the sudden fear that this super-important case might slip through their fingers, all because of the stupid summer rebound idea Anil had put into her head last year. And if they lost this deal because of her, she'd never get promoted to senior associate and be on track to eventually make partner.

Iqbal put an arm around Tejas and grinned. "This is Tejas Rajput, one of my childhood neighbors from Jaipur, and"—he beamed—"our newest junior associate."

Naina reached for Anil's arm instinctively, and he shot her an alarmed look as Iqbal's words hung in the air.

Junior associate.

Not client.

Junior *fucking* associate.

Just like Naina, Anil, and three others at the firm.

She swallowed the bile rising in her throat and plastered a smile on her face to match those of her colleagues. Some people clapped, while others walked over to Tejas to greet him. Naina, on the other hand, sat back in her revolving chair and refreshed her inbox on her laptop.

Anil nudged her heel with his boot, an exasperated sigh on his lips. "What are you doing, Nay?"

"Working," she answered in a monotone. "Like we're supposed to?"

He closed her laptop and ignored her squeal of protest. "We should go say hi, like everyone else in the office, or it'll seem weird. Do you want to draw attention to the fact that you and he—"

Naina glared at him, and he said, "Come on, then," and mimed zipping his mouth shut. He led the way to the group of people still talking to Tejas and Iqbal. Naina followed behind, wiping her clammy palms on her beige A-line skirt.

"Oh, there you both are!" Iqbal drew them closer as the rest of the group dispersed. "Tejas, Anil Puranik is the coolest guy at work, and he's a born-and-bred Bangalorean. If you need anything from anywhere in the city, just ask him."

Anil held out his hand. "Nice to meet you, buddy. Welcome to the office."

"Glad to be here." Tejas smiled, eliciting the faintest of dimples on one cheek, and returned the handshake firmly. Naina recalled smothering that almost-dimple with kisses late one night when they were both drunk off their asses on coconut feni, the local liquor in Goa.

Her heart thudded when Iqbal gestured to her next. "And this is Naina Shetty, the smartest gal on the team, especially when it comes to criminal law. She'll help you get acquainted with some of our current cases, won't you, Naina?"

Naina nodded in lieu of saying anything more. She kept her hands clasped firmly behind her back so she wouldn't have to touch Tejas at all. Fuck, this was disastrous. She'd seen her newest colleague naked.

Multiple times.

Thankfully, Tejas didn't extend his hand. He simply ran his fingers across his dark stubble, the beginning of a smile on his lips. "It's a pleasure, Naina Shetty," he said, and she'd have been lying if she said her name from his mouth didn't make her shiver. Well, whatever. She bit her lip and nodded again, deciding it was better to play it cool than reveal her cards.

Iqbal put his arm around Tejas. "Come on, catch me up on everything you've been up to until IT logs you in!"

Tejas turned back once to grin at Naina before letting Iqbal steer him away.

"Wow." Anil whistled once the two men were out of earshot. "Did you see the way he smiled at you? He's—"

"He's going to stir up trouble." Naina clenched her jaw, hoping her blush had faded. "I won't let him get to me. Especially not after how we ended things. Or rather, how *he* did."

Anil tugged on her arm so she'd face him. He shook his head at her, looking morose. "Are you kidding me? You were so—dare I say it—*happy* in Goa. Smiling like a fool every time we FaceTimed and you went on and on about Prince Charming." He chuckled dryly. "You haven't smiled like that since you came back."

Naina pulled her glasses down an inch, batted her eyelashes, and smiled widely and sickeningly at her best friend. "Are you satisfied now? I'm smiling."

"You know what I mean." As they headed back to their cubicles, Anil lowered his voice. "Nay, maybe this is a sign that you should get back out there."

"And hook up with my new co-worker?" She turned on her laptop again, while Anil took his seat behind her desk. "Not a chance."

Tejas walked by, holding some reports in his hand. Naina ducked down before he could grin at her again, and when she resurfaced, Anil laughed. "If you don't hook up with him," he said, smirking, "I will. He's gorgeous."

"Shut up," Naina admonished, though her cheeks colored anyway.

Anil's lips quirked. "Look, if it was me in your situation, and Tejas and I had done it a whopping twenty-one times over the course of two steamy weeks—"

Should have never told him that, Naina thought.

"—then I would at least ask him how he's been in the year and a half since we last saw each other. Maybe, just *maybe*"—he booped Naina on the head—"I'd offer to show him around town and bring that number up to twenty-two."

"Anil, you can't blame me for avoiding him," Naina said, her jaw clenched as she swatted his hand away. "It's scary to know your past has caught up with you."

"If my past looked like him," Anil said, "I would have done the catching up myself. When fate brings two hot people back together, there's something to it."

"This isn't one of your favorite K-dramas, Anil," Naina snapped.

"Exactly," Anil said, gesturing wildly before returning to his laptop. "For the first time in more than a year, your life is actually interesting. Make full use of it!"

Naina ignored him and focused her gaze on her inbox, though her mind was far from work. *Interesting* wasn't the word to describe it, but she had to accept that seeing Tejas again had made her raging hormones wake up from their seventeen-month hibernation.

She wouldn't admit it to anyone but Anil, but the last time she'd gotten laid was last summer—with Tejas. Naina wasn't the most sexual woman out there, at least not anymore. And honestly, she wasn't the most romantic. After her evil ex-fiancé, Santhosh, hooked up with his neighbor and ended their two-year engagement and six-year relationship, why would she ever think romance was a priority?

Goa had been . . . she gulped. Cathartic. Anil always said the best way to get over someone was to get under someone else. Crass, but he had a point. Rooming with Tejas at the youth hostel had been pure chance—he'd actually called it *fate* before they shared their first kiss—and it was the opportunity she'd needed to stop wanting to be Mrs. Santhosh Naidu someday.

But she didn't need catharsis now, and she probably wasn't capable of romantic love anymore. She needed to be on her A game. Her eyes went to the corner office next to Iqbal's. Ramesh Kumble, the other managing partner and founder of the firm, was taking early retirement six months from now. Naina had heard through the office grapevine that Iqbal and Ramesh would promote one of the junior associates *and* mentor them on the partner track before Ramesh left. And if everything went according to plan—and Naina would ensure it did—she would be the one landing the mentorship and eventually joining the three other partners at the firm. She had been at the top of her law school class, she'd spent five years dominating at Akhtar, Kumble & Co., and she wanted this more than anything else in the world. She had it in the bag, as long as she didn't let any distractions get in the way. Distractions like . . .

A throat cleared. *Speak of the devil.* Naina didn't have to look up to know it was Tejas. Despite a year and a half going by, she clearly still had his voice memorized. "Hi, do you need something?" she said, trying to keep her voice level.

"Can we talk?" Tejas asked, and she frowned at him. "Please?" he added, a softness to his words.

"Fine." She slammed her hands on her desk, then dusted off her skirt and followed him to the watercooler a few feet away from the cubicles without looking back. Anil was probably spying on them. That was what best friends did, right?

Once they were at the watercooler, Naina folded her arms across her chest and stared Tejas down. "Are you stalking me?"

"What?" Tejas looked like he was at a loss for words. He raked a hand through his messy curly hair—which was shorter than she remembered—and shrugged. "I didn't know you worked here. I didn't even know you were a lawyer. Wrong answers only, remember?"

Naina shifted her gaze to his shoes. Shiny, dark mahogany leather, glinting with polish. So unlike the slippers and sneakers he wore during the two weeks they spent together. "Yeah," she said, swallowing, "I remember." That had been their deal that summer. Save for first names, they'd shared almost no other personal information. Everything else had been a lie.

Except for the feelings she'd forced herself to push down.

"Hey, look at me."

At that, she raised an eyebrow.

"This doesn't have to be a bad thing, us meeting again." Tejas gestured to the air between them, smiling with what looked like fondness. "Maybe this is—"

"Do not say *fate,*" Naina rushed to say. Oh shit, now the memory of their first kiss was running through her mind. Their bodies pressed together at the loud, chaotic rave, the air heavy with anticipation, until he'd touched his mouth to hers, one hand fisting in her hair and the other cupping her jaw—

Tejas's smile quirked, and his eyes fell to her lips as though he too was recollecting the memory. Then he dared to laugh. "Destiny," he finished, shoving his hands into his pockets. He tilted his head the slightest bit and went on. "Join me for a beer after work? I bet you know a good place."

Ignoring the strong sense of déjà vu, Naina shut her eyes, letting herself breathe fully like Appa did during his morning yoga sessions, then promptly opened them. "No thanks," she said, turning away. "I have to get back to work. Welcome to the office, Tejas. I'll email you with an update on our caseload."

"Naina, don't go," he murmured, and she felt the soft grip of his fingers on her arm, tugging her back.

She ignored the tightening of her core and instead glared at him. "Why not?" she snapped. "I thought you were all for leaving."

Tejas swallowed and looked away, his face paling. If Naina tried hard enough, she could almost smell the salty tang of the ocean air, hear the sound of violins, and taste the sweetness of Tejas's champagne-stained lips from that final night. A perfect moment, until it wasn't anymore.

Finally, he said, "I . . . I thought that was the right thing to do."

"You thought wrong," she replied, sighing.

With that, she left him there by the watercooler and raced back to the safety of her desk. She set a trembling hand on her closed laptop, then wiped a line of dust from the framed photograph of her father. Appa smiled his hundred-watt grin at her, and she ran her fingers over his face. She wished she could run straight home and tell him about this drama—she knew he'd have words of wisdom to impart—but she doubted her dad would want to know anything about her summer fling. Anil would have to do, for now.

Lips pursed, Naina turned in her chair. "He asked me out," she whispered.

Anil kept typing away on his laptop, but his shoulders straightened. "What did you say?" he mumbled from the corner of his mouth.

"That I had to get back to work."

He side-eyed her. "You never say that to a hot guy."

"No, Anil, *you* never say that to a hot guy. I say whatever I want."

Anil chose not to respond.

Naina huffed and returned to the report she was working on. Tejas passed by again, probably searching for Iqbal or tech support, but she didn't dare look away from her laptop.

How could this be happening? Tejas was *here*. Not in a fever haze, not in a daydream, not in her confusing fantasies—but here, in the office that had become her respite from every conflicting emotion she'd felt in Goa.

A beer with the best sex she'd ever had might sound appealing to some, but Naina's life wasn't about what she wanted anymore—her life was about what she needed. And that was to become partner at Akhtar, Kumble & Co. one day.

Nothing more, nothing less.

Chapter TWO

Goa, May 2025

The wind whipped Tejas Rajput's curly hair around as he stared out the open car window, his face breaking into a smile for the first time since his best friend's wedding.

As the taxi turned around the bend, now steadily moving across a bumpy seaside road, he caught glimpses of coconut trees, sandy beaches, and tourists clad in bikinis and shorts—all of whom were drinking, smoking, and dancing like they had no care in the world.

Well, they probably didn't. They were in Goa, after all.

"First time here, sir?" the balding taxi driver asked, catching Tejas's eye in the rearview mirror and grinning.

"Yep," Tejas answered. He leaned forward in his seat, eager to make conversation with someone local. "I took the bus from Mumbai. Any must-see places near the hostel you're taking me to?"

"Too many to name, sir." The driver laughed and wiped the back of his neck. It was sunny and humid, and the stench of sweat permeated the air inside the small taxi. May in Goa was not the best time to visit—summer was no joke here—but Tejas had packed plenty of sleeveless shirts, shorts, and flip-flops. He'd make the most of this desperately needed vacation, regardless of the scorching heat.

"You need to visit Baga Beach, of course." The driver took out a piece of paper from his shirt pocket. "Here is a list of the best parties happening in North Goa this week. Whatever you need, be it hash, grass, shrooms, or acid, you can get it there with the phone number listed at the bottom. Here, take a photo." He slowed the car and handed the paper to Tejas before returning to the steering wheel.

Tejas swallowed, considering it. He wasn't in Goa to get high, but . . . parties were definitely on the agenda. He snapped a picture with his phone camera, then handed the paper back to the driver with a quick thanks. He continued staring out the window, watching the trees and shrubbery fly past, the gray-blue waves cresting and troughing in the distance, until his phone chimed with a text.

Rahul

hope you reached Goa ok?

Tejas almost scoffed before letting his phone screen fade to black. He wouldn't reply. He had every right to be mad at stupid Rahul. So what if Rahul was his best friend? Rahul was also his secret ex-boyfriend who was now married to some woman his parents picked out for him. Why? Because according to him, being queer in India was too difficult and this was just a simpler, easier way to survive life.

On some level, Tejas got it. He didn't flaunt his bisexual identity, either. It was hard to be out in many parts of the world, but especially India. His parents still didn't know, not that he talked to them anymore; he'd only told a few friends and his sister, Latika.

But what Tejas wasn't okay with was Rahul insisting he come to said wedding and then dance alongside the other guests in the baraat—the groom's wedding procession with all his guests—as they headed to the wedding venue. Tejas had had no desire to celebrate Rahul's marriage to a woman he didn't love, a woman he'd only met two months ago at his parents' behest. Rahul was supposed to love Tejas, his boyfriend of three years. They were supposed to end up together, have a big fat Indian wedding when the government legalized queer marriage (with their small circle of progressive friends in attendance, family be damned), and drive off into the sunset with two adopted kids sitting in the back seat.

Tejas gritted his teeth as another text lit up his screen.

Rahul

thanks for coming to the wedding btw. meant a lot to me ☺

Rahul is typing . . .

we're boarding the plane to the Maldives now. i know you said you wanted space but i'm always here for you ok?

Sighing, Tejas picked up his phone and started typing. Enjoy the honeymoon, you asshole. Then he shook his head, hit backspace, and simply added a thumbs-up reaction to Rahul's last text. That would have to do. Not just for right now, but forever.

Rahul's parents were conservative, old-fashioned, and traditional enough that they would start pushing their son's new wife for grandchildren soon enough. If Tejas stayed in touch with Rahul, he'd probably become the kids' godfather. Doing the work of the unofficial best man at the wedding, welcoming the bride and groom's extended family to the hotel, and being introduced to the guests as "Rahul's best friend" was enough self-inflicted pain for a lifetime.

Tejas had tortured himself far too much this past weekend at the wedding. The solution? Partying in Goa, the one place he'd always wanted to visit since moving to Mumbai for law school. And it was finally happening. He'd had his dark moment, and now there would only be sunshine.

And alcohol. Tons of it. And maybe Tejas would even make use of the jumbo pack of condoms in his suitcase.

The taxi slowed to a halt in front of a three-story white building with multicolored accents along the walls—red, orange, blue, yellow. A sign out front proclaimed it to be the GoGoa Youth Hostel. Grinning, Tejas thanked the driver, paid the taxi fare, and entered the hostel with his suitcase in tow.

"You've opted for the semiprivate room, yes?" the woman at the narrow front desk in the hostel lobby asked. When Tejas nodded, she handed him a yellow key that said 202 on it and directed him to the second floor. "The communal bathroom stalls are three doors down from your room," she added.

There was no elevator at the hostel, so Tejas dragged his suitcase up the staircase. There were at least fifteen rooms on the second floor, all numbered weirdly. For instance, room 213 was across from room 207, next to which was room 201. There were no directions in sight. He pursed his lips and looked at the yellow key again.

"Can I help?"

Tejas lifted his head and smiled at a friendly-looking short woman with a thick, long braided hairstyle, wearing a kurti and jeans. "Uh, room 202?" he asked.

The woman gestured for him to follow her down a narrow corridor. "Down here," she said. Once they were in front of room 202, he said, "Thanks. I'm Tejas."

"Raziya," she replied, then smirked and jutted her head toward the door. "Huh, 202? Interesting."

He frowned at the closed door. "What do you mean?"

Raziya laughed. "You and your roommate have really different vibes. She's downstairs talking to the others—I'm sure you'll meet her soon. See you!"

Tejas stared at the door in confusion for a full ten seconds after Raziya left, then shook himself out of it and unlocked the door.

More color greeted his eyes. The air-conditioned room, painted a cheerful yellow, had a blue cupboard off to one side, a small desk and chair in the corner, and a white wooden bunk bed with a laptop on the top bunk. There was also a tiny balcony off on the side, the curtains partially open to let some sunshine in.

He dumped his stuff on the bottom bunk, wondering when the roommate Raziya had mentioned would be back. Her things were already scattered around the room: the laptop on the top bunk with zero stickers on it, a towel hanging neatly on the back of the door, a makeup bag full to the brim . . .

Guess he'd have to get acquainted with the mysterious roommate some other time. He decided to take a quick shower in the communal bathroom, then returned to his room, which was still empty. Shrugging, he settled into the bottom bunk and FaceTimed his sister.

"Hi," Latika said, smiling widely. Her short black hair was pulled into a ponytail away from her face. "How's Goa? And the hostel?"

"Good." Tejas set two fluffy blue pillows against the wall and settled in. "It's hot. Like, really hot. Thank goodness I picked a hostel with AC. But anyway, I didn't call you to talk to *you*. Where is she?"

Latika smirked and turned the phone to the right. A furry white paw appeared on the screen, followed by the face of the cutest cat in the world. Green-yellow eyes blinked at Tejas before Astrid let out a meow and snuggled into Latika's chest.

"My baby." Tejas tried to hold back his tears. It had been four days since he last saw his cat, and he already missed her. "Is she eating and sleeping okay? What about her poop? How's her poop?"

"All good, don't worry. Astrid loves her auntie, doesn't she?" Latika moved the phone so it was closer to Astrid's beautiful gray-and-white face. "Give your old man a kiss, Astrid!"

Astrid meowed again before hopping off Latika's lap. Her footsteps had always been loud—Tejas distinctly heard the sound of her paws thudding against the floor as she ran into a different room.

He exhaled, his heart aching, as Astrid's footsteps faded. He'd adopted Astrid a year ago when she was a mere three-month-old kitten, and he hadn't ever been away from her for longer than a day or two until now. Yes, Latika often took on the role of the dutiful cat-sitter, since she lived thirty minutes away from him in Mumbai, but surely Astrid missed having her papa around?

"Relax." Latika rolled her eyes. "It's only two more weeks. And you deserve a vacation after . . . everything." She lowered her gaze and added, more hesitantly, "Are you still talking to him?"

"He texted me, but I'm not going to reply." Tejas bit the inside of his cheek. "I can't move on without space, and if he doesn't seem to understand that, then it's his problem."

She nodded. "Love sucks. I'm here for you, bhai."

He cracked a smile. "I know."

Latika was still nursing a broken heart. Her arranged marriage had gone awry last year because her ex-husband had pressured their families into making a decision quickly, giving the Rajput family no time to do a thorough background check. Mere weeks after the wedding, she found out he was unemployed with a mountain of debt, a drinking problem, and no desire to ever work again. Her job as a budding psychotherapist, fresh out of college, couldn't pay the bills.

Both sides of the family had opposed the divorce, because "What will people say?" Latika and Tejas hadn't spoken to their parents since.

Tejas shook off these thoughts and got up from the bunk bed to give his sister a tour of the room. Latika oohed and aahed over the colorful décor and furniture, as well as the modest but beautiful view of Goan streets from the small attached balcony in the room. Tejas came back inside a minute later, missing the air-conditioning, and as he was sliding the balcony door closed, a woman came in, holding a half-eaten apple, her AirPods in as she grooved to whatever she was listening to. She saw him and lurched to a stop. "Oh."

Tejas didn't miss Latika's eyebrows shooting up at the sight of her. "Hey," he said to the woman, smiling even as his cheeks flushed red. Fuck, this woman was hot. She looked about his age—late twenties—with long, wavy brown hair that fell to her waist as she regarded him curiously from the doorway. She was tall, perhaps five foot nine to his six foot one, with legs that went on for days beneath her short floral red dress.

He flipped the camera back to his face and said into the phone, "Uh, I guess that's my roommate."

The woman frowned as she stood at the doorway and took a bite of the apple. "Are you on the phone?"

"I'm talking to my sister," he said, then addressed Latika. "I'll call you soon, okay?"

"Wait—" Latika started, a glint in her eyes, but he hit the end call button and slid his phone into the pocket of his shorts.

Tejas shook out his curly hair and smiled at the woman, who was still by the door. "Sorry about that, roomie! I'm Tejas." He kept his distance but held a hand out, and the woman walked up to him, raising an eyebrow as she sized him up. With how she folded her muscular arms and stared at him, stone-faced, Tejas knew right away that she was not someone to mess with.

Her mouth parted, her tongue darting out to lick her bottom lip as her eyes fell to his outstretched hand. Tejas's face flamed again, and he wondered what she was thinking. Finally, she dumped the apple core into the trash and returned his handshake. Her grip was solid and confident; this woman was probably a badass at work, and yet her touch sent shivers down his spine. "Naina."

A shadow fell over the room as clouds settled in place of the bright sun. Tejas glanced at the balcony and the slowly darkening evening sky before hooking a thumb at the room door. "Looks like it's getting cooler outside. Want to grab a beer or something?"

Naina thought for a moment, looking him up and down, her eyes lingering on the bulge of his muscled legs and the coarse chest hair peeking out from under his sleeveless shirt.

Tejas scratched the back of his neck. He wasn't often self-conscious, but with a hot girl presumably checking him out, he had to wonder what was on her mind.

At last, Naina said, "If you're trying to make a move on me, just know I'm not looking for anything serious. I'm"—she exhaled—"taking a break from relationships."

Tejas laughed. Were all women this honest in Goa? "I wasn't making a move. *You're* the one checking me out."

Her nostrils flared. It was a cute look on her. "One beer," she finally said. "I know a good place two streets away." She grabbed her purse from her bed and left the room.

"Okay, then," Tejas said, chuckling as he followed her. This was going to be a very interesting two weeks.

Chapter THREE

Bangalore, October 2026

Naina rubbed her eyes beneath her glasses and stared blearily at her laptop screen. It was past ten P.M., and she was, like on most days, one of the last people still at the office. Tejas had left around six-thirty. He'd spent most of his time getting to know his colleagues and catching up with his dear former neighbor Iqbal. Naina had emailed him a long, detailed list of their current pending cases so she wouldn't have to talk to him in person. Thankfully he hadn't approached her again.

As for Anil, he always left at six P.M. sharp, chided Naina for "working too much," and often suggested she "get a life—and maybe get laid, hmm?"

Pssh. Naina scoffed at the thought. She had a life, thank you very much. It just involved planning for her future as senior associate, then partner, and she couldn't do that without hustling and taking time off from dating. She brought her coffee mug to her lips, but it was empty. Sighing, she leaned back in her chair and checked WhatsApp, deciding a short break was in order. She hissed at all the unread messages from her father.

Appa (8:03 pm)

Putta when are u coming home? Have dinner at home pls 😔

Appa (9:17 pm)

U work too much . . . don't make the mistakes ur mother made.

The last message was from three minutes ago.

Appa (10:09 pm)

If u are not home by 11 then I'm telling all ur aunties that u are ready to be set up with someone. It's ur call . . .

Naina jolted upright and cursed under her breath. She didn't need a whole troupe of desi aunties ganging up on her and shoving matrimony profiles of so-called compatible matches in her face. With Bangalore traffic as bad as it was, she'd take at least forty minutes to get home even at this hour. She'd be cutting it close.

Naina typed out a message: Be home soon, order Subway for me please, the usual! And NO AUNTIES!!!!! As she hit send, her least favorite person at work spoke up. "Still here, huh?"

She turned in her seat to wince at her rival, Dhanush Kumble, who was frowning at her, briefcase in hand. He had always been one step ahead of her at work. They'd both joined AKC five years ago as entry-level lawyers, but his promotions often preceded hers. He became junior associate three months before her—three! And Naina knew he was vying for the promotion too. Considering he was a man, not to mention Ramesh Kumble's nephew, he'd probably be their top choice.

Nepotism ran rampant at law firms.

"About to leave," Naina said, her lips thinning. She turned off her laptop and got up. "Good night."

"See you tomorrow." Dhanush started away from her desk, then paused and said, "You know that new guy? Tejas?"

Her back went rigid, and her eyes widened. Thankfully, she wasn't facing Dhanush. "Yeah, what about him?" she replied calmly, grabbing her bag and putting her things inside.

"He was asking about you."

She finally turned to him. Slinging her bag over her shoulder, she asked, "Um, what do you mean?"

Dhanush smirked. His sharp, small teeth glinted in the semi-dark office lit only by Naina's desk lamp and the dim bulbs in the hallway outside. "He was asking how long you've been here, and what you're like. Oh, and he told me you caught him up on our caseload by email, and if it's normal for you to be this unapproachable."

Naina's jaw clenched. "And what did you say?"

"So I told him I wasn't surprised at all." With a snort, he added, "You're not going to get promoted with that personality."

"Excuse me?" she snarled.

"If you don't know how to schmooze and make people like you, no one's going to be on your side. And right now? I think apart from Anil, nobody is. Least of all my uncle." He sneered up at her from his shorter frame as he walked away, that smirk still on his face.

Naina balled her hands into fists, holding back the tears that had sprung to the corners of her eyes. She waited in the dark office for a few minutes to compose herself, then booked an Uber, hoping there would be a juicy turkey and chicken marinara sandwich waiting for her at home.

After the day she'd had, she deserved a good meal.

WHEN NAINA UNLOCKED HER FRONT door and greeted her father with "Good evening," Appa glared at her from his rocking chair and hit the pause button on the TV remote.

"It's well past evening *and* my bedtime," he said thickly.

Naina kicked off her shoes and noticed he was watching *Suits*. She groaned. "Appa, you know that show is wildly inaccurate, right? That's not how corporate law works."

"It's fun," he grumbled, but he turned off the TV and stood up to crack his back. "Your sandwich is in the kitchen. I'm going to bed now. God help me, it's nearly midnight."

"It's five past eleven," Naina corrected him. She walked up to him and tapped her finger on his nose. "You don't have to stay up every night, you know."

Appa nudged her finger away but chuckled. "I worry about you. I bet you'd live at that office if I weren't around to remind you to leave."

Naina grinned, knowing he was probably right. She made enough money to move out and get her own place, but it was nice knowing she could come home to someone. Even if that someone was her frustratingly nosy father. Honestly, he annoyed her to death fifty percent of the time, but he was also the only man in her life she could blindly trust with anything. Not to mention, he made the best dosas for breakfast every morning.

Naina shrugged, returning to the conversation. "If living at work would make me partner, then why not, right?" She turned to go into the kitchen, but Appa gripped her arm and gently pulled her back. His eyes were grim.

Dread pooled in Naina's stomach. Appa joked around a lot about her workaholic tendencies, which she'd definitely inherited from her mother, but something else seemed to be on his mind tonight. She swallowed and asked, "Appa, is everything okay?" Was it his blood pressure? An unexpected bill? Or did this have something to do with Amma?

He sank back into the rocking chair, evidently unable to meet her gaze. As he leaned his head back against the thin gray fabric covering the wooden chair, he said, "I was speaking to Kapil Bhosle today, my client from when I was still working at the bank. Do you remember him?"

"I do." Naina crossed her arms across her chest. Kapil Bhosle, the industrialist, whose company was represented by her ex's dad.

"Well, he was invited to Santhosh's wedding." Appa exhaled. "To, um, the girl he . . ." His voice trailed off, and he tugged on his mustache instead of saying the words. *The girl he cheated on you with*.

Naina sucked in a breath. She hadn't even known they were engaged. "Oh." She blinked back tears. She'd met Santhosh while interning at a law firm her senior year, and though their relationship wasn't perfect, he'd loved her. He was consistent, he showed up to their dates on time, and he was as ambitious as she was. He was—on paper—perfect for her. Despite the fights about Naina's long hours and his insecurities about not being a junior associate like her, she had vowed she'd make the relationship work.

Until he cheated on her, because—in his words, "I can't see you as the mother of my children, Naina. Especially when you're not willing to make compromises for our marriage." The compromise in question? Quitting her job and becoming a stay-at-home wife so she could take care of their future family.

Moving on from her first and only relationship had been easier than Naina had thought, which likely proved that they had been the wrong match despite dating for six years, but moving on from the certainty that her future had held? It still weighed her down, low in the pit of her belly like a tight coil she couldn't unwind, a heaviness in her shoulders that persisted despite countless spa massages. Now some other girl was living the life she'd thought was going to be hers.

Naina swallowed. She wiped her shaky, clammy hands on her skirt and stepped away from the rocking chair. "That's fine. He's getting married. So what? I have my career, and that's all I need—"

"Naina, putta." Appa stood and let out a ragged breath. "Don't you think there's more to life than just your career? Do you really want to sacrifice so much for your job?"

Not this again. Naina's father wasn't as traditional or patriarchal as some other Indian dads she knew. After all, he hadn't suggested a quick arranged marriage to "save face" after her broken engagement, and except for being nosy about any and all men in her life (except for Anil, for obvious reasons), he'd left her relationship status alone. And yet he seemed fixated on this silly notion that Naina was going to miss out on life because of her career pursuits.

Appa and Anil ought to start a club, honestly.

"I'm not 'sacrificing' anything," she corrected him. "I'm prioritizing my career over a romantic relationship, and that's okay."

"Do I need to remind you how that turned out for our family, after your mother left both of us?" Appa's eyes shone. Seven years since the divorce, and he hadn't gotten over it. Not that Naina thought it was either his or her mother's fault. Yes, Amma had walked out on them, putting a career opportunity before her marriage, but she now worked as a backing vocalist for an American pop star, and it was all she'd ever wanted. For all Naina knew, Amma was happier now than she'd ever been as a mother or wife—and that wasn't necessarily a bad thing.

"Well, it gave her the life she'd always dreamed of." The answer left a bitter taste in her mouth, because she knew it wasn't what Appa wanted to hear. "It wasn't the right marriage for either of you," she went on.

Appa tugged at his sparse hair, evidently frustrated. "She could have asked me to come with her. You were already in law school anyway. But she didn't even give me the option. She just chose to leave, like our marriage meant nothing compared to her career." He sat back down in the rocking chair with a huff and added, "You're thirty years old, Naina, and you were so excited to be a wife. I just don't want you to numb your loneliness, simply because you think your mom's happier single. We don't know if she is. God knows she doesn't tell us."

Her eyes stung, but she forced herself to smile instead. "But I'm not alone, Appa." She pulled him up from the chair and into a hug. "I promise, if I ever decide I want a relationship again, you'll be the first one I tell."

"I'll hold you to that promise." Appa hugged her back, his shoulders finally loosening, then turned the TV back on to his show.

"As you should," she replied. Then she jerked her head toward Harvey Specter's smug, frozen face on the screen. "Now, shall we get back to watching this ridiculous show you're obsessed with?"

He beamed at her. "Yes, please."

Naina grabbed her Subway sandwich from the kitchen, and once they settled onto the couch, Appa pressed play. His eyes focused on the screen, his lip curling at the heated exchange between two of the lawyers, but Naina quietly tore into her turkey-and-chicken sandwich, ignoring the voice in her head—a cross between Appa's and Anil's—telling her to admit that maybe, just maybe, she was lonelier than she let on.

After all, most of her colleagues' lives didn't just revolve around work and their parents. Ramesh Kumble had been married for decades; he even had grandchildren. Iqbal doted on his wife at every office party. Anil lived with his aging grandmother, but he spent most nights with whichever guy he was casually seeing.

As for Tejas . . .

Who did he live with?

Naina crumpled up the sandwich wrapper and threw it into the trash. Then she said good night to her dad, who only mumbled out a grunt, too occupied with the salacious plotlines of unrealistic legal dramas.

Sighing, Naina went into her room and face-planted right onto her bed, ruminating on the roller coaster of emotions she'd felt all day. Naina Shetty didn't like emotions. But it was hard to keep them in sometimes.

She rubbed away her tears and swiped through her phone gallery until she got to May 2025. Goa. Multiple photos of beaches, fruity drinks in cocktail glasses, and dark neon-lit clubs filled her screen. And there it was, the only picture she'd taken of him: at the beach club, early on in the trip. He was dressed in a sleeveless T-shirt and grinning with his little dimple out as he told her about his cat and her antics. Naina wasn't a cat person, but she'd loved every word he'd said. It might have been more about the sound of his voice and less about the cat.

Naina tossed her phone aside and changed into her pajamas. She hadn't looked at that photo since she'd come back from Goa; she'd forced herself to forget every single minute of the trip, especially after the way it had ended. And it worked. She'd almost forgotten that Tejas's picture was still in her phone gallery. It brought up beautiful memories of sun-kissed beaches at dusk, wild evenings spent partying and having adventures, and steamy nights cradled in his arms.

But that was all they were—memories. And unlike what Appa and Anil believed, Naina didn't need to re-create them. Not when her whole career was at stake.

Chapter FOUR

Goa, May 2025

Goa had looked beautiful enough in the day and a half since Naina's plane touched down at the airport, but like the fine wine she'd taken far too long to acquire a taste for, the place aged better with time. As she walked side by side with Tejas to a nearby outdoor pub for drinks, the sunset plunged the beach into every shade of orange and pink, the gray sea glittered as though made of diamonds, and the sand shone like powdered gold. That, plus the sight of Tejas's muscly arms and that little dimple in his cheek as he smiled back at her, almost made up for how uncomfortably warm the weather was. Or maybe it was his hand accidentally brushing hers every now and then that had cranked up the temperature another notch.

Tejas must have had a similar thought. "Do they not have AC here?" he asked, wiping a bead of sweat from his forehead when Naina looked back at him.

She headed over to a table on the deck facing the beach and sighed. "Get used to the heat. Very few places in Goa have air-conditioning, since everything is usually outdoors."

He sat down across from her at the table, shoulders slumped. "You've been here long, then?"

"Just got here yesterday, though I'm staying for about two weeks," she admitted. She turned her gaze to the horizon, now fading from orange to deep blue, and exhaled as reality caught up to her. "I'd already researched and planned a vacation here months ago, but I decided to stay at the hostel last-minute because, well, I needed a different experience."

She toyed with the unopened menus on their table, nearly scoffing at the words coming out of her own mouth. *Different experience* didn't begin to explain it. Sure, she could have checked in to the honeymoon suite at the Taj Hotel as planned, but lying on a bed of rose petals by her lonesome self and chugging the complimentary bottle of champagne wouldn't have fixed her broken heart.

Tejas shuffled his chair closer to hers and chuckled. "You're trying to escape reality too, aren't you?"

Naina forced herself to smile; it was better than sobbing her guts out to her new roommate, handsome as he might be. She leaned back in her chair and tied her hair into a messy bun. Then she spoke. "I was supposed to come to Goa for my honeymoon."

Tejas's big brown eyes zoomed in on her bare ring finger and the tan line that would probably take months to fade. He hesitated, then set his warm hand on hers and squeezed. "I'm sorry. Love sucks," Tejas said, and it was the genuine hurt in his voice that made Naina squeeze his hand back. Maybe he needed the comfort too.

Shoulders straightening, she said, "Seems like you speak from experience."

"Yeah." He stared ahead at the sea, his chest rising and falling. He rubbed the base of his neck. "It's a long story, but shit happened back home. I needed to leave for a bit, figure out what I want from my own life."

"Goa's a good place for that," she agreed. "New places, new experiences . . ."

"New people," Tejas finished, which elicited a laugh from her.

A server greeted them, and they perused the menu, looking through the list of craft beers on tap. While Tejas flipped through the pages, Naina tried and failed to keep her eyes from raking over him again. This man was fit. From his burly arms rippling in that sleeveless shirt to his broad chest, dusted with dark hair, he was so unbelievably . . . masculine. Naina had only slept with three men her whole life, none of whom looked this strong. Her ex had barely been able to handle one round in the bedroom without tiring himself out. Tejas, meanwhile, could probably lift Naina with one arm and pin her to the wall with the other.

"Why do they have a gunpowder masala rye ale?" Tejas said, frowning at the menu. "Isn't that a South Indian spice?"

Naina swallowed, blinking away her scandalous thoughts. What was wrong with her? She'd been single for a month. A month! And this man was a stranger. Maybe Anil's stupid advice to have a hookup was clouding her judgment.

"I tried the ale here last night," she said finally. "It's great, and trust me when I say I have good taste."

Tejas looked up from the menu, his lips twitching. "I bet you do."

Blushing, Naina cleared her throat and called the waiter over. She ordered the kokum beer while Tejas asked for the gunpowder ale, giving her a quick grin.

Once they'd had a few sips of their chilled drinks and had made some small talk about the other guests at the hostel and the weather, Naina asked, "So what's the verdict?"

Tejas lifted his glass in the air, making the beer shimmer in the light of the setting sun. "It's delicious. You were right—you *do* have good taste."

If only her taste in men were as good as her taste in beer.

Naina decided a topic change was in order. "Are you hoping to do more outdoorsy activities in Goa, or just go pub-hopping?"

He stretched his arms above his head, making his shirt rise up an inch over his abs, not that Naina was looking, of course. Although this vacation was about reclaiming the things she missed in her life. Maybe this feeling could be one of them?

Tejas sipped his beer. "Anything. Everything. I just want to live for myself for these two weeks. Not for anybody else."

"Hmm." Naina thought for a moment, picturing her anti-honeymoon bucket list. Some of the items on it were forcibly put there by Anil, hoping to bring out her "wild side," as he'd called it—the side of her she'd repressed ever since the start of her relationship with Santhosh, which, in hindsight, was doomed to fail—but something about the gorgeous man sitting in front of her, straight out of a beer commercial, made her want to do everything on the list anyway.

As Tejas set his mug down to wipe sweat from his brow, Naina tugged on the side of her ear. "Hey, I need your help with something, if you're up for it."

He narrowed his eyes. "What exactly do you need help with?"

She took a piece of paper out of her handbag and smoothed it out on the table before them. "I need a partner with whom I can do everything on this list."

Tejas bent forward to read the big, bold letters at the top of the page. "Um . . . 'Naina's Anti-Honeymoon Checklist'?"

Naina swept a strand of hair from her face, eager to tell him about her master plan. "Yes. Every single thing I couldn't have done if my horrible ex was still in my life. It's the perfect way to get over him—by reminding myself just how much he was limiting my experiences."

Tejas's shoulders shook with laughter. "Oh my God, are you serious?"

Naina held back a sigh and jabbed a finger at the list again. "Just read it and tell me your thoughts."

NAINA'S ANTI-HONEYMOON CHECKLIST

1. Stay anywhere but a hotel. ✓
2. Kiss a stranger.

3. Try any kind of drug.
4. Go to a rave.
5. Eat way too much seafood in one sitting.
6. Get shit-faced drunk.
7. Go on a real adventure.
8. Go skinny-dipping.
9. Have sex . . . outside of a bedroom.
10. Blow money on something extravagant.

"So you want my help doing *everything* on this list?" Tejas asked, biting his lip like he was trying not to keep laughing.

Naina's cheeks flamed. He was obviously referring to the two items on the list that Anil had begged her to include. "Not everything. And besides, my friends from the hostel are helping me with the drugs and the rave. But . . ." She shrugged. "I don't know, I have a feeling you're good company."

"I am." He chuckled, flicking his eyes back to the list. "What's with the seafood thing? You can do that anywhere."

"Goa is known for its seafood. Besides, Santh—I mean, my ex—is a vegetarian. And he always made me feel bad for not being one too."

Tejas chuckled. "Sounds like you dodged a bullet."

"Look." Naina leaned closer to him determinedly, catching a whiff of his woodsy cologne. "I'm on a solo trip, trying to reclaim joy. You're on a solo trip, hoping to find yourself. *And* we're roommates, so we need to have each other's back. What do you say?"

Tejas folded his arms and stared at her like he was considering it. Naina hoped she wasn't making a mistake. All said and done, he was still an unknown person she would be doing this experience with. And not just an unknown person—a witty, intriguing, dangerously attractive man who also happened to be her roommate.

Which was exactly why she would have to set boundaries, and fast. Something that would ensure her head and heart remained intact well after this vacation ended.

"I'm in," Tejas said finally. "What's first?"

"Ground rules," Naina answered. "I'm not here to make lifelong friends or fall in love. I don't want to exchange any personal information. No last names, no social media, nothing that could help us find each other after this trip."

"Nothing?" he asked weakly. "What if a personal topic comes up?"

"Well, then"—Naina clinked her beer mug with his—"we reply with wrong answers only. Like if you ask me where I'm from, I'll say . . ." She thought for a moment, then finished, "Westeros."

"Sounds fun." Tejas mulled over her ground rules and held a hand out. "Then I'm Prince Charming, from your wildest dreams."

She tried to muffle her laughter, but it came out as a squeak. Beaming, she shook his hand. "I already know your first name, but sure. I'm Naina Stark."

"So what now, Naina Stark?" Tejas returned his gaze to the anti-honeymoon list. "Which item do you want to check off the list first? My cabdriver from the bus stop gave me this." He opened the Gallery app on his phone and showed her a handwritten list of parties. "There's a rave happening every night this week."

She pursed her lips as her eyes darted to the phone number at the bottom of the photo. "I didn't realize you knew a . . . drug dealer in Goa. That's what this number is for, right?"

"I don't *know* him," he clarified. He took a big gulp of his ale, his face flushing. "I'm guessing the cabdriver gets a commission on the sales the, uh, dealer makes."

Naina opened her mouth, unsure what to say. The idea of going to a rave with a handsome stranger who had a drug dealer's phone number, while thrilling, wasn't quite that appealing to her. Besides, the others at the hostel already said they'd go with her.

"Hey, hey, come to think of it," Tejas said, lifting his hands like a faux surrender. "It might help us both to start with something easier off the list, at least until we get to know each other better."

"Yes," Naina said quickly, relief sinking into her bones that she didn't have to suggest it herself and look like a scaredy-cat. "Are you hungry?"

TWENTY MINUTES LATER, THEY CLUTCHED their plates as they stood in front of the slowly moving conveyor belt that carried more seafood than Naina had seen in a lifetime. This authentic Goan restaurant promised an all-you-can-eat dinner buffet with over seventy delicacies, and thankfully a handful of tables were empty.

Naina tried not to visibly drool as she peered at the small labels on the different dishes passing them by: truffle-butter pomfret, recheado mackerel, bacon-wrapped grilled shrimp . . .

"Well, shall we?" Tejas asked.

She nodded. Naina stacked up her plate with fish, prawns, crabmeat, shrimp, squid—not a vegetable in sight. A grin spread along her lips at the thought of Santhosh and how he'd react if he saw her plate right now. He'd have been scandalized. She snickered to herself and took another piece of prawn tempura for good measure.

They settled in to their table, clinked their beer bottles, and toasted to "new beginnings," then ate in silence, breaking it only occasionally to praise the food. "This is the best prawn I've had in my life," Tejas said, wiping his mouth with the edge of his napkin. "And that's saying something, considering I live in—"

"Nope," Naina said, swiftly pressing a finger to his lips. "We don't talk about where we're from, remember?"

Tejas exhaled sharply. "Right, of course. Did you like the tempura?"

She withdrew her finger, warm from his breath, and sucked on her final piece of prawn. "It's delicious. I'm kicking myself for never having tried prawn before."

"Because of the ex?" He shook his head. "The list is looking more and more necessary now."

"Exactly," she answered, finishing her second beer of the night, then calling for the check.

They walked back to the hostel, pausing every so often to look at the stretch of sea that flanked them on the right side, or marveling at the two or three stars in the sky. Minutes away from their destination, the darkness of the night gave way to fireworks, red and blue and green, from a loud party in the distance.

Naina stopped in place, gasping. "Beautiful," she said.

"Very," Tejas said, and she noticed from the corner of her eye that he wasn't looking up at the sky. Her cheeks flamed.

As they resumed their walk, Tejas's hand brushed Naina's, and despite all logic and rational thinking, she let herself enjoy the heat of his skin and the sparks flying that had nothing to do with the fireworks.

There were two items on the list, put there by Anil, that required someone's company in a not-so-platonic way. Maybe, just maybe, she wouldn't have to search too far and wide for that someone.

After all, the night was still young.

Chapter FIVE

Bangalore, October 2026

Tejas stood in line at the Sunstag Café at Vittal Mallya Road, which was a five-minute walk from the Akhtar, Kumble & Co. office. He rubbed the scruff of his beard with one hand as he scrolled through his unread emails. It was only his second day at his new job, and he already had an overflowing inbox.

He bit his lip to hold back a chuckle when his thumb rested, mid-scroll, on the name Naina Shetty. It was still wild to him that he'd actually run into her. A year and a half of trying to find her face in every crowd, hoping for an impossible coincidence, and now, finally, here she was. Not just in his daydreams, but in his contacts list.

"Hi, what can I get for you?" the barista asked brightly as Tejas got to the front of the queue.

He smiled back. "Can I get a caramel latte with whipped cream?"

"Sure." The barista wrote down his order on a cup and accepted his credit card, while another barista yelled out, from the end of the counter, "Pumpkin spice latte for Naina, Americano for Anil?"

Tejas turned so fast toward the other side that his neck cricked. There, just a short distance away, stood a frowning Naina. She pushed her glasses up on her nose and shook her head when the barista tried to hand her the latte, reaching instead for the Americano. Anil took the latte, snorting.

"This is why I hate ordering together," Naina fumed. "They always assume I want the god-awful, basic, overhyped coffee order, just because I'm a woman."

Tejas tore his gaze off her cute scowl when the barista said to him, "Sir, we'll call your name when the order's ready." Nodding, Tejas took his card back from her. He stepped aside and watched Anil boop Naina on the head while she swatted his hand away. They still hadn't noticed him.

"Enough about coffee," Anil said, pushing the door open as cold, drizzly air floated into the café. "We still have to talk about Prince Charming. Did he really—"

Tejas couldn't help the loud chuckle that escaped his mouth. Anil and Naina froze, halfway out the door, and Naina turned to lock eyes with Tejas. Pink dusted the apples of her cheeks as her nostrils flared, and she all but shoved a laughing Anil out onto the street.

When his name was called, Tejas grabbed his coffee and went outside. Naina and Anil were a few strides ahead of him, talking animatedly. She'd seemed so unapproachable to Tejas yesterday, and clearly his second first impression of her had been spot-on. Where was the energetic, eager, free Naina Stark he'd fallen for seventeen months ago? Was she giving him the cold treatment because of how they'd left things in Goa . . . or had something about her changed since then?

He slowed his pace, not wanting to disturb the two friends or their gossip session that was likely about him. As he walked to work, he replied to some of his sister's texts—she still couldn't believe Tejas had run into Naina—and then he checked the footage from the cat camera he'd installed so he could keep an eye on Astrid while he was at work. Sure enough, she was napping in one of the many moving boxes Tejas had yet to throw out, her vibrating snores loud and clear.

He grinned and resumed his walk as the tall office building loomed before him. Astrid seemed more at home in Bangalore. Maybe it was the weather—a healthy mix of breezy, rainy, and sunshiny, unlike the perpetual heat and humidity of Mumbai—or perhaps she liked that they now lived in a spacious one-bedroom with a small storage area and a balcony. Despite the beauty and culture infused into every Mumbai street, the rents were always tragically high. Never again would Tejas have to spend half his paycheck on a matchbox-size studio apartment that was so tiny even his cat seemed to judge him for it.

Tejas tapped his key card against the entrance and took the elevator to the twenty-first floor, heading to his cubicle. He passed by Naina's desk and smiled, but she only averted her gaze to her keyboard. Holding back a sigh, Tejas slid into his chair and greeted his cubicle mate, Dhanush. "Morning."

Dhanush grinned at him. "It's a good morning, indeed. My uncle told me we're getting assigned a bunch of new cases today. I can smell victory already."

"Nice," Tejas said, chuckling. He went through his inbox again, noting that Iqbal had assigned to him a workshop on sole-proprietorship law. The workshop was for a nonprofit that worked with domestic violence survivors, helping them start their own entrepreneurial ventures so they could support themselves and their children. Per Indian law, neither lawyers nor law firms were allowed to openly solicit business or advertise their services. Save for hosting a modest website with basic information and taking on countless pro bono cases for PR and word of mouth, law firms couldn't legally chase after clients without breaching that pesky law. Tejas had grown up watching American legal thrillers and dramas, but after his first few months at law school, he was shocked by the jarring contrast between the legal systems in the West and in India.

Akhtar, Kumble & Co. boasted an impressive roster of clients, but neither founder had strong nepotistic ties to the corporate world, unlike the law firm Tejas had worked at in Mumbai, where every other client they represented was a friend of a friend in Bollywood who'd done something horrible and now needed a lawyer, stat. Most of Tejas's nicer, hardworking, actually innocent clients had been pro bono cases.

AKC, on the other hand, seemed to have good people with good intentions doing good work. Tejas smiled to himself. He'd fit right in here.

♡ ♡ ♡

An hour later, Tejas sat in the conference room with all the junior and senior lawyers for an urgent meeting scheduled by Iqbal. It was five past ten, but Iqbal had wanted the other managing partner to be present too, and it looked like Ramesh Kumble was late.

Dhanush sat beside Tejas, his brows furrowed. "Apparently there's a really important client on the case list. I need to land it to get the promotion and the partner mentorship."

Tejas looked at him curiously. "Aren't you pretty much a shoo-in? Being Kumble's nephew and all?"

Dhanush scoffed, as though that were irrelevant. "Iqbal would never let me get it without earning it." His fingers shook as he drank his black coffee. "I have to prove myself to him."

Across the table, Naina was in conversation with Anil, their voices hushed. Tejas's eyes drank in her snug cream-colored shirt, tucked into a high-waisted pencil skirt, her toned legs crossed. Her glasses glinted in the light as she shot a glare at the door. Patience was clearly still not her strong suit. Tejas remembered that from Goa.

Finally, Ramesh Kumble strode into the room and took his seat at the head of the table, next to Iqbal. Chairs screeched and pens clicked as people sprang to attention.

"Good morning, everyone," Kumble said in his booming voice, his wrinkled hands folded on the table. "I'm sure you're all eager to take on more cases, and this first one is certainly a big fish. Iqbal, if you please?"

Iqbal nodded, straightening his collar, and went up to present the new case as the room fell silent. He flicked the remote, and a picture of a smiling old man with silver-gray hair filled the presentation screen.

Tejas jerked his head back, having recognized the man.

"Kamal Subramanian," Iqbal said, standing back and appraising the photo, "is said to be India's most ethical billionaire. He's funded hundreds of infrastructural projects to improve our standard of living, there's a never-ending Wikipedia page of his philanthropic efforts, and his companies offer well-paying jobs to millions of middle-class college graduates every year across industries."

What could this case be about? Tejas wondered. A merger? A patent? Or perhaps a pivot in his business strategy?

"Unfortunately, his PR team is going to have its hands full." Iqbal flipped to the next slide, his teeth gritting.

The gasp that left Tejas's mouth was echoed by several other lawyers in the room. The screen now showed a blurry but unmistakable picture of Subramanian being taken away in handcuffs by two cops.

Kumble stood, leaning his hands on the table. "Embezzlement and money laundering," he said. "An accusation that could destroy not just his stakeholders' careers but also India's economy."

Iqbal clicked over to the next slide. "The press has caught wind of the case as of this morning, although Mr. Subramanian has known this was coming for some time now—which is why he came to us last week."

"He knew this was coming," one of the other lawyers repeated. "So he's guilty?"

Kumble scoffed from his seat. "That's irrelevant. Our job is to prove he isn't."

Tejas bit the inside of his cheek. Well, it seemed AKC wasn't all that different from the other law firms out there. This was one of the things Tejas hated about being a lawyer, apart from the long, grueling work hours and the ass-kissing needed to get to the top of the chain: having to put his morals aside and defend the bad guys. He'd be happy to sit this one out, thanks.

Naina lifted her head and spoke, her words confident. "Sir, I'd like to take point on this case."

Iqbal cleared his throat. "I appreciate your directness, Naina, but Ramesh and I have already discussed this in private, and we've decided to go a different way."

Tejas thought that would be that, but Naina didn't seem ready to give up. "I've worked on three white-collar criminal cases in the past year and won all of them," she continued. "I believe I—"

Kumble waved her words away with a dismissive hand. "Dhanush will assist Iqbal on this," he said, giving his nephew a toothy grin. "They always make a great team, and we need that synergy for a case as high-profile as this."

Naina gripped the edge of the table with her fingers while Dhanush mumbled a "fuck yeah" under his breath. Tejas smiled and patted him on the back.

"However," Kumble went on, his eyes still on Naina, "we do have a client for you." He stood, took the remote, and opened a different presentation deck. "Preethi Acharya v. State of Karnataka. As we all know, she was arrested a week and a half ago for murdering the famous director Rohith Pai, who was once—"

Tejas spoke up, his forehead creased. "Allegedly," he said. He'd read about the case just that morning in the newspaper. Preethi Acharya was a barely C-list actress who now made a living posting exercise videos and doing fitness brand endorsements, while Rohith Pai had dozens of blockbusters in the Kannada film industry—commonly known as Sandalwood—to his name. This case wasn't going to be an easy one.

Kumble nodded approvingly. "Allegedly murdering Pai," he went on, "who was once her lover. He remained an A-list filmmaker, while her acting career flopped, and now, years later, he decided to direct her comeback film. Is this revenge? An accident? Or is someone framing her?" He shrugged. "Whatever the case may be, her former lawyers have given up; so, Naina, you're now in charge of proving her innocence."

"I can do that," Naina said confidently, but then her smile faded. "Wait, just me, right?"

Holy fuck. Tejas felt it coming before Iqbal gestured to him. "Well, we'd love for Tejas to work with you on this one, since he handled a lot of Bollywood cases while in Mumbai."

"Absolutely," Tejas said, smirking, loving that Naina trembled when his gaze met hers. "I'd be perfect for the job."

"I'd prefer to handle this one on my own, actually," Naina replied, looking back at Iqbal and Kumble.

"If you're even to be considered for senior associate, we need to know you can work as a team, Naina," Kumble said, wagging a finger at her.

Tejas bit his lip as Naina tugged on her shirt collar, visibly recoiling.

"So that settles it." Kumble nodded when she said nothing. "Naina and Tejas will handle Preethi Acharya's case. It'll be a tough one for you, Naina, so let's hope Tejas can keep the emotions to a low, yes?"

Tejas's fists clenched at the implication. He paused, wondering if anyone would speak up, or if this was just the norm at AKC to let misogyny slide. Anil let out a small, frustrated grunt, while the rest of the room exchanged glances in the stifling silence. Dhanush too looked down at his brief notes, his eyes boring a hole into the page. Iqbal hesitated from where he stood beside Kumble, like he wanted to object, but ultimately he only sighed.

Just as Tejas opened his mouth to say something, anything, in defense of Naina, Kumble dispersed them and headed out of the meeting room.

"Well, I'd best get started," Dhanush said eagerly, thumbing through his phone as he stood, but Tejas wasn't really listening. His eyes were on Naina, who was storming out of the meeting room, her face flaming. He scrambled to his feet and raced after her, then stopped her by wrapping a hand around her wrist, cool to the touch.

"I'm sorry about what just happened," Tejas said when she faced him. He put his hands in his pockets, head ducked. "Mr. Kumble was being such a—I know I should have said something, and I was going to, but . . ."

"But you owe me nothing," she said, and when he looked up at her with a frown, she shrugged, though there was a twitch in her jaw. "After all, we barely know each other."

Tejas's eyes darted around the empty corridor. Then he stepped closer, so close he could smell her familiar lavender scent in the air as her breath caught. "Bullshit. I meant everything I said in Goa, and I meant every word I left unsaid. And I'll regret leaving for the rest of my life. Naina, I—"

Footsteps thudded closer, Dhanush's voice growing louder as he pushed past them, yelling into the phone. "Jennifer, I don't care how you do it, I need those reports ASAP!"

By the time Tejas returned his gaze to Naina, she was walking backward, shaking her head at him. "I'll set up a meeting soon to talk about the new case."

"Wait—" he started, but she had already hurried back to her desk. Straightening his tie, Tejas got himself a coffee and went to his cubicle, where Dhanush was still purple-faced and glaring at his phone.

"My paralegal just doesn't understand how to do simple tasks," Dhanush said as Tejas sat down beside him.

"Sorry about that," Tejas said. He spotted Naina ahead, shoulders hunched over her desk as she aggressively typed on her laptop. As he looked around the office, Tejas realized with a lurch that Naina was the only female junior associate. When Tejas had asked the guys about Naina being "unapproachable" yesterday, they had all nodded in agreement. None of them seemed to particularly like her. Was she close with anyone at work besides Anil?

Tejas exhaled, sat up straighter, and switched tabs to his calendar, where a new meeting event had just shown up for nine A.M. the next day: *Discuss Preethi Acharya case*. The description said: *Meet at Sunstag to strategize, then head to client's house by 11*. Tejas accepted Naina's invite, nodding to himself. There was probably no chance Naina wanted to start things up again romantically, given her walls were up higher than they'd been in Goa, and that was fine by him. But no way was he going to let her push him away as an ally . . . or even as a friend.

Chapter SIX

Goa, May 2025

NAINA'S ANTI-HONEYMOON CHECKLIST

5. Eat way too much seafood in one sitting. ✓

When they returned to the hostel, Tejas was eager to hang out with Naina in their room and perhaps discuss some more of the list, but Naina dragged him over to the kitchen to introduce him to the friends she'd made.

The kitchen and dining area was cramped, with a stovetop, microwave oven, fridge, and six chairs around a rickety table, two of which were currently occupied. "Everyone, this is Tejas. That's Jonah," Naina said, nodding at the bald white man with a goatee; then she smiled at the tall, well-built blond man stroking Jonah's arm. "And that's Aleksy."

Tejas shook hands with them both. "Aleksy and I met years ago on one of my backpacking trips to Poland," Jonah said in a strong California accent, smiling. "He's a chef there. This summer, I finally managed to drag him out of his kitchen."

"Speaking of which, Raziya, let me know if you need any help." Aleksy stood, walking to the sink, where an Indian woman was stirring a large bubbling pot of what looked like stew.

"Relax, this recipe isn't that complicated!" she said, laughing. Tejas recognized her—she was the one who'd helped him find his room earlier. "Nice to see you again," she said to him pleasantly. "I'm currently working on a spy thriller set in Goa, but until writing pays my bills, I'm helping out at the hostel part-time and doing some research on the side."

"So, where are you from?" Jonah asked Tejas, gesturing for him and Naina to sit.

Before Tejas could tell them, Naina spoke. "Actually, Tejas and I came up with a fun 'wrong answers only' rule between the two of us, so you'll have to ask him personal questions on your own time."

Her friends exchanged curious glances but said nothing. Tejas sat down at the table and tried not to let his confusion show. So she only had this rule with him, not her friends here. What was that about?

Across from him, Aleksy said, his Polish accent as thick as his arms, "Did you have dinner already? Raziya's attempting to make my special hunter's stew."

Naina leaned against Tejas's chair, her long hair tickling the side of his neck. "We ate at a seafood buffet, but thanks."

Jonah rubbed his goatee. "Great, another item checked off the list."

"How do you guys feel about a rave tonight?" Naina asked.

"Finally! I've been dying to go out," Jonah said. "My friend told me about one happening right now, if you're down. Besides, I already scored us the good stuff from my friend's dealer."

Tejas frowned. "Uh, good stuff meaning what?"

"LSD, of course," Jonah said nonchalantly.

"Wait, what?" Tejas exclaimed, feeling Naina stiffen behind him.

Aleksy gave him a funny look. "What did you think we'd be doing at a rave? Smoking pot?"

"You don't have to unless you want to," Raziya said. She handed Jonah and Aleksy two steaming bowls of hunter's stew, and they accepted them gratefully. The smell of smoky meat was heavenly to Tejas's senses, but his mouth had gone dry at the mention of the psychedelic. He had never tried drugs, except for the rare moments he'd smoked pot in college. He'd definitely opt out of this one.

"Guess you'll check two things off your list in one go," Tejas said, turning in place to look up at Naina. "At this rate, we'll run out of things to do by the end of the week."

Naina tilted her head like she was considering something. "Maybe we'll find other ways to stay occupied," she said quietly so only Tejas could hear her.

Tejas tried not to blush. Was she implying . . .

No. They barely knew each other, and she'd set her boundaries already by saying she wasn't looking for a boyfriend. But her list made it seem like a fling was more than on the table. In any case, Tejas wouldn't overstep or make the first move, despite the way Naina was looking at him right now, like she was revisiting the almost-moment they'd shared during the fireworks.

While Naina went to take a shower before the rave, Tejas changed into a dressier shirt and sat down at the desk to go through his work emails on his laptop. He had taken the full two weeks off, handing over his caseload to a trusted co-worker, but he wanted to check on their progress anyway. His clients had been through hell: a small-business owner who'd been sued by a big corporation and was at risk of bankruptcy, a young woman whose landlord evicted her after discovering she was from a lower caste, and a Bollywood makeup artist dealing with sexual harassment from her boss. Being a lawyer was often depressing, but seeing his clients get justice was worth all the hard work and the blood, sweat, and tears he shed.

As he responded to an email from earlier that day, Naina's iPad chimed from the far end of the desk: an Outlook notification. Tejas frowned, his eyes on the lit-up screen. What did she do for work? Given her firm handshakes and her no-nonsense attitude, she was probably a big-shot corporate hustler. A consultant, perhaps, or CEO of a startup. Or—

The door opened, and Naina walked in, bringing the soapy scent of lavender with her. Tejas shook off his curiosity and shot her a grin. "That was quick."

She rolled her eyes and flung her towel over the drying rack in the balcony. "I can never spend longer than ten minutes in the shower," she said as she reappeared in the room. "It gets so boring in there."

"But hot water feels so good!"

"Oh, I only take cold showers," she said matter-of-factly. "It's better for your health."

Tejas laughed. "You're something else, you know that?"

"Thank you," Naina said, beaming at him, then checked her phone. "Come on, it's past ten. Let's get going.

♡ ♡ ♡

TEJAS JOINED HIS NEWFOUND FRIENDS in the parking lot, and they squeezed into Raziya's tiny rental car, which groaned under their combined weight. Raziya didn't drink or do recreational drugs, so she had volunteered to be the designated driver tonight. And, most likely, for the rest of their vacation. Tejas doubted anyone else in the group could go a night without drinking in Goa, of all places.

Aleksy, who sat in the front, tinkered with the music controls until an EDM song began to play. "Might as well get the party started," he said, and Naina cheered, fist-bumping Jonah, who started to groove in his seat.

Tejas's eyes were fixed out the window as he stared at passing cars and blurring streetlights. None of his friends back home, or even in college, had experimented with hard drugs. Neither, it seemed, had Naina. He might have only met her hours ago, but he'd agreed to help her with the list, and that meant being there for her if things went south. Would he be able to take care of her if she had a bad trip, or if cops showed up to the rave?

"Hey," came Naina's whisper, and he turned to her. "If you're feeling too anxious, we could go back to the hostel."

Tejas shook his head. "But your list . . ."

She placed her hand on his knee and squeezed reassuringly. "You don't have to try it with us unless you want to. Honestly, I'm scared too."

"Doesn't seem like it," he said, bumping his shoulder with hers.

She chuckled. "Fake it till you make it, right? Besides, I've played it safe for twenty-nine years. I don't want to turn thirty and still live in my comfort zone."

She's twenty-nine just like me, Tejas thought. He hesitated, then asked, "When's your birthday?"

Naina laughed, then said teasingly, "Wouldn't you like to know?"

His heart deflated—she didn't even want to reveal her birthday?—but he played along, forcing out a laugh. "Right, right, the ground rules."

Pounding electronic beats greeted them as they walked in, so loud that Tejas couldn't hear the movement of the frothy waves, or even his own thoughts. The beach was swarming with hundreds of people, ready to party in sexy dresses, bikini tops, shorts, and floral shirts—and they all wore neon accessories, from beads around their necks to light-up bracelets; many even sported glow-in-the-dark spray paint. The place smelled like sweat and salty seaside air . . . and Tejas loved every passing second more and more.

"We have to try the neon spray paint!" Aleksy yelled over the music, urging them to the many stalls flanking the periphery of the beach. Tejas paid for a can of pink paint that he sprayed all over Naina, laughing when she retaliated with a lime-green can. Raziya declined to "taint her body," as she put it, opting for a neon bracelet instead, while Jonah and Aleksy went a little too overboard, ending up with more color on their bodies than clothing.

Jonah gestured for them to wait while he went into the back of one stall. A minute later, he surfaced with a small packet, then led them to a quieter spot. He discreetly handed out tiny strips of paper to them, shrugging when Raziya and Tejas turned him down.

Next to him, Naina went still, staring at the tiny white strip. Tejas nudged her. *You okay?* he mouthed.

She hesitated, then politely stepped away from Jonah. When Tejas gave her a questioning look, she stood on tiptoe and whispered in his ear, "You were right. LSD is a little out of my wheelhouse too."

He gave her a thumbs-up as she wound her fingers around his arm, sending shivers down his spine.

Instead, they got themselves a tray of shots. With the vodka slowly absorbing into his system, easing his nerves, Tejas joined the crowd of drunk, high, horny strangers gyrating to the music and grinding against each other. Jonah, Aleksy, and Raziya remained at the bar, ordering beers and mocktails, leaving Tejas alone with Naina on the dance floor. Naina stepped closer and gripped his shirt with her fists, pulling herself flush against his body.

Tejas swallowed, his feet lurching to a stop. She smelled incredible, like lavender and sweat, and God, she looked stunning with her hair in a half-up, half-down style, her eyelids in shimmering gold, and a tight, low-cut black dress hugging her muscular body. *You look beautiful,* he wanted to say, but no way would she hear him over the music.

So, instead of saying it with words, he said it with his touch. He cradled her face in his hand, their lips barely an inch apart. Naina exhaled, her breath mingling with his. She looked up at him expectantly, like she wanted him to close the distance between them, but Tejas wouldn't, couldn't, unless he knew she wanted this like he did.

"Hey, Prince Charming," Naina said in his ear as her lips parted, "care to help me check another item off the list?"

He chuckled, moving his other hand to the back of her head, fisting it in her hair. "Which one?" he said.

Naina laughed; the sound vibrated in his chest, touching hers. Then she pressed her mouth to his. Tejas threaded his fingers through her hair and cupped her jaw with the other hand, deepening the kiss.

Her taste on his tongue was more than intoxicating; it was *addictive*. Her arms wrapped around his neck, her fingers tugging at his curls until all Tejas could feel, hear, and taste was her. Her skin against his, soft and hot. The moans from the back of her throat, her purrs as he pressed up against her. The sweet, sticky cherry-red gloss coating her mouth. Shit, Tejas had never felt this . . . alive before.

Naina pulled apart and said, grinning, "Where did you come from, Prince Charming?"

"Maybe it's fate," he replied before kissing her again.

She melted into Tejas, a giggle bubbling out of her lips, then let him twirl her around as the music swelled in his ears. Tejas's head spun, and his heart thudded beneath his rib cage when she planted a kiss on his wrist, leaving a maroon impression in its wake. Had his wrist ever looked better? He brought her closer, and as they danced, their limbs and lips intertwined, he didn't have a goddamn clue what the others were up to, and he didn't care.

All that mattered was this ethereal, neon-lit, supercharged moment when nothing existed but him and Naina.

Chapter SEVEN

Bangalore, October 2026

The next morning, Appa grunted at the television as he tore off a piece of uthappam and dipped it in peanut chutney. "Putta, isn't that the new client you mentioned?"

Naina looked up from her iPad, midway through reading a report for work, while her own breakfast lay untouched. On the news channel, a reporter was interviewing the protestors outside Preethi Acharya's house. An old photograph of a handcuffed, sobbing Preethi was displayed in the top right-hand corner. "Turn it up," Naina said, teeth gritted, and Appa reached for the remote.

"They'd better put her in jail for life," one man said in Kannada, scowling, while his friend continued lifting his poorly alliterated placard that said NO PITY FOR PETTY PREETHI. "Or better yet, give her the death sentence. Kill the killer!"

"Kill the killer!" another woman with him shouted, raising her fist.

Appa tsk-tsked. "These fans are feral. You're gonna have your work cut out for you."

Naina finally swallowed a bite of uthappam. "Looks like it," she said in a shaky voice, tuning back in to the broadcast.

The reporter looked between the three friends. "But what about 'innocent until proven guilty'?"

The first man let out a sarcastic laugh. "If she's innocent, why has she locked herself in her house? What does she have to hide?"

Naina grabbed the remote from beside her plate and switched off the television, her muscles tensing. "Are they kidding? Who in their right mind would step outside their house and walk straight into a mob, whether they're guilty or not? Fucking bullshit!" She stood, heading to the kitchen to discard her half-eaten breakfast.

"Putta, don't waste food!" Appa called out from the dining table. "You know the secret ingredient to my cooking is love."

"Thankfully, you have plenty more love to give," Naina teased as she washed up at the sink and wiped her shaking hands on a towel. "I have to run, right into the heart of that mob. We're visiting Preethi's house."

"Who's 'we'?"

"Uh." Naina coughed. "My new colleague."

Appa's ears perked up. "Is it a boy?"

Naina shot him a glare amid packing her laptop bag. "That's irrelevant, Appa."

"Ah"—he clapped his hands and whooped—"so I'm right!"

She ignored him and rummaged through her workstation by the corner of the living room. "Have you seen my laptop charger anywhere?"

"Underneath your journals," he said, licking chutney off his fingers. "Anyway, if you won't tell me about this boy, I'll just have to give Anil a call and ask him for the 'juice,' as you youngsters say."

"For the *tea,*" Naina corrected him. She shoved the charger into her bag, slid her feet into her loafers, and yelled as she headed out of the apartment, "And don't you dare talk to Anil!" She slammed the front door behind her, Appa's laughter carrying all the way to the elevator.

♡ ♡ ♡

At Sunstag, Naina sat beside Tejas at the corner table, and they discussed the case in low voices. Preethi Acharya was out on bail despite having a murder charge, because Iqbal and Kumble pulled some strings with their influence. But she would be taken into judicial custody next week, a few days before the trial began. Naina had asked around and discovered that Preethi's former lawyers had given up on the case after taking note of the public vitriol against their client.

"Can you believe the shit people are saying online?" Tejas said softly as they went through social media together. "And here I thought only actors had obsessive fans."

Naina shook her head and sipped her Americano. "Pai's movies might have . . . concerning themes, not that most cinema buffs have a problem with that, but he's in a league of his own as a director. Every Kannada superstar has worked with him."

"Crazy," Tejas mumbled. Next they put their heads together and went through the previous attorney's notes, which glaringly lacked any groundbreaking information. Tejas read out the pointers in a low, rumbly, *sexy* voice, making the hair on the back of Naina's neck stand, and when Tejas's fingers brushed her skin as he reached for the pen resting beside her elbow, she actually jumped. *Fuck.*

"Um, I'll be back," she mumbled, heading for the restroom without looking his way. There, she steadied her breathing and splashed water on her face. "You can do this," she told her reflection, gripping the edge of the sink. "Just because you're attracted to him doesn't mean you have to act on it. It doesn't mean you will. So—"

The door swung open, and a woman shot her a funny look before disappearing into one of the stalls. With a sigh, Naina washed her hands and returned to their table.

Tejas was chuckling at something on his phone, from which shrill meows played, louder than the pop music from the café's speakers.

Before Naina could stop herself, she blurted out, "Is that your kitten? Astrid, right?"

Tejas's neck whipped toward her, bringing the scent of pine with it. "You remember Astrid?"

"Well, yeah," Naina mumbled, giving him a quick shrug before focusing on her half-empty coffee mug. "Your camera roll was full of her videos. I bet everyone at the hostel remembers her."

"Yeah, she's memorable for sure." He smiled, then cocked his head at her. "Do you still talk to the others from Goa?"

"Uh, no." Naina tightened her hands over her mug. She wished the answer was yes, because she'd carry the moments spent with her hostel mates in Goa in her heart for a lifetime. And yet . . . she'd deleted their phone numbers the second she'd returned to Bangalore, knowing Tejas had their info too. If she'd stayed in touch with Raziya, Jonah, or Aleksy, she would have found a way back to Tejas sooner or later.

And that would have derailed her decision to never, ever, *ever* fall in love again.

She'd come so close to it in Goa. All the amazing things Tejas did for her, despite having known her for barely two weeks. He'd made her feel right at home, in that hostel, in his arms, almost upending her decision to keep things strictly casual.

Love was dangerous; love was unreliable. Unlike her career, where her efforts, diligence, and hard work took her places, relationships sank no matter how much she tried to keep them afloat.

No. Naina was better off alone.

"I don't talk to them anymore, either," Tejas said, and she returned to the conversation. "I tried staying in touch for a few weeks, but then things fizzled out. Honestly," he sighed, "Goa was a fever dream. I came back with memories, a few souvenirs, and a bunch of photographs, but somehow, it didn't feel real. Maybe because we never—"

"Goa was a long time ago," Naina said sharply, downing the rest of her coffee in one go. "I think it's best if we keep things professional now."

"Oh, you're one to talk," he fired back, a tick in his jaw. "We're colleagues who are working to stop an innocent woman from going to jail. You need to get over whatever grudge you're holding against me and stop giving me the cold shoulder."

"It's not a grudge. I just don't want to talk to a colleague about irrelevant things like my past."

"*Our* past," Tejas pointed out.

Naina hissed through her teeth, deciding to change the topic. "We should get back to the case. Can you call Preethi and let her know we'll be arriving soon?"

Tejas huffed audibly. "Sure."

♡ ♡ ♡

AN HOUR LATER, NAINA WIPED sweat off her forehead and checked her email as the auto rickshaw sped toward Preethi Acharya's house in Sadashivanagar.

Next to Naina, Tejas was ruffling his curly hair and smiling, seemingly enjoying the toxic, polluted air of Bangalore's traffic-heavy streets. He looked like he'd forgotten about their little fight at Sunstag. Was he always so . . . sunshiny? She let out a soft chuckle and returned to her phone.

He must have heard her, because he tapped her on the shoulder. "I can't get over how perfect the weather is here."

"Perfect?" She tried not to pull a face. "It's way too hot for October, and the smog from all the vehicles—"

"You think *this* is hot?" Tejas tossed his head back and laughed; Naina tried not to gawk at that small but familiar dimple creasing his cheek. "Mumbai is sticky and humid all year long, and Jaipur had the most scorching sunlight when I was a child. Pleasant weather in October is a blessing."

"Oh, right, Iqbal mentioned you were neighbors in Jaipur. I didn't know that's where you're originally from."

Tejas's face blanched. "Because of your silly rule."

"It wasn't silly—"

He scoffed as the auto rickshaw slowed in traffic. "Maybe not for you, since you never saw me as anything but a means to get over your ex."

She decided not to reply and instead turned to the auto rickshaw driver, who was chuckling at a YouTube video on his phone. "How far are we, anna?" she said, speaking to him in Kannada.

"Five minutes away," he answered as he checked the map. Then his face soured. "Madam, are you going to that murderer's house?"

Naina's eyes narrowed. "That's up to the court to decide."

The driver tutted and took a right turn when the traffic lights turned green. "Who else could it be? Rohith sir did her a favor offering her the lead role in spite of their history, and look how that turned out for him. May he rest in peace."

Despite the media and public attention, she didn't think an auto rickshaw driver with no ties to the film industry or the legal system would be so opinionated—or outspoken, for that matter. "Just drive," she snapped.

Tejas frowned, since he probably didn't know a word of Kannada. "What's he saying?"

"Later," Naina said. She flipped through the copy of the charge sheet and sighed. The evidence against Preethi wasn't ironclad, but given the high-profile nature of the murder and Rohith's longstanding reputation in the industry, the court would want to ease public pressure and wrap up the case quickly—even if it meant sending an innocent woman to jail.

The driver stopped the auto. "You'll have to walk from here," he said, pointing ahead. "There are too many people outside her house, and I'm not going near an angry mob."

Naina nodded. They paid the fare and got out, walking toward the lane that led to Preethi's house. Even from a distance, the screams and shouts of people and police were clearly audible. She rolled her eyes and filled Tejas in on everything the auto driver had said. "Can you believe his audacity? It's been a week since the murder, and he's already decided she's the killer."

"Well." Tejas kicked a pebble with his shoe as they rounded the corner. "At least this gives us an idea of public perception outside of social media. That, and the commotion up ahead."

Naina gasped; the situation was worse than she'd seen on the news. People swarmed outside Preethi's two-story bungalow, holding placards and banners that ranged from JUSTICE FOR ROHITH PAI to BURN THE BITCH in both Kannada and English while journalists and camerapeople filmed the whole thing. Two policemen stood by, keeping an eye on the protest and reprimanding the mob whenever their language turned ugly.

"You ready?" Tejas whispered.

Naina lifted her chin up, her eyes narrowing. "Ready."

Chapter EIGHT

Goa, May 2025

NAINA'S ANTI-HONEYMOON CHECKLIST

2. Kiss a stranger. ✓
4. Go to a rave. ✓

Never in her life had Naina felt this free. The pounding music, the neon lights, the alcohol in her veins . . . and, of course, Tejas's hands all over her body, his lips all over her face and neck as they slow-danced to the fast beats. Naina hadn't kissed someone out of the blue before. She wasn't sure if this was her wild side or her true side, but God, this felt good.

So very good that she couldn't wait to get out of this party and go back to their room, finish what they'd started. But even in her moderately drunken senses, she knew the only way to the hostel was Raziya's car—taxis in Goa were overpriced and, in the group's current condition, decidedly unsafe.

When their friends joined them, whooping and jeering, Naina pulled away from Tejas embarrassedly. "Took you both long enough,"

Jonah teased as he danced with Aleksy next to them. "I sensed a vibe the minute you walked into the kitchen together."

As the others laughed, Tejas spun Naina around, then whispered in her ear, "Was that okay?"

She let her hands trail down his shoulders and chest until they came to rest on his hips. "Yes," she breathed. "Better than okay."

"Good," he said, his voice rumbling. They danced close to one another, occasionally kissing or touching, and the throbbing between Naina's legs only grew with every passing minute. Was this what being brave and throwing caution to the wind felt like? Why hadn't Naina done this in forever? Her ex had never been one for PDA, claiming "affection is best saved for the bedroom," but Naina had to admit there was something incredibly sexy about being touched like this in public.

Around one A.M., after the gang had had their fair share of dancing and drinking, they piled into the car, exhausted, sweaty, and eager for a good night's sleep. Tejas slung his arm around Naina, and she rested her head on his shoulder, her eyes half closed while he chatted with their new friends. His voice was light and easy, his laughter melodious, and his touch gentle on her neck where his fingers made small circles.

Naina swallowed. She didn't know what would happen when they got back to the room, but she knew what she wanted to happen. *He's a stranger,* her brain reasoned, but her heart—no, the ache deep in her core—argued back in a voice that sounded suspiciously like the old Naina, the one who had died after life got in the way. *He won't be a stranger for much longer.*

And it was that voice, that feeling, that *need* that made her launch into Tejas's arms seconds after he shut the door behind them. She let him press her against the wall, his abs clenching at her touch under his shirt, as her mouth found his once more. When she reached for the waistband of his pants, Tejas broke their kiss, touching his forehead to hers. "You sure about this?"

Naina pulled him in closer, grazing his hard-on with her fingers until he groaned. "I'm sure," she replied.

Tejas made a noise in the back of his throat as she shimmied out of her dress, letting it pool at her feet. They crashed into the bottom bunk, a tangle of limbs and lips while their clothes fell to the floor. As she pulled him in for another kiss, his eyes fell to the tattoo on her waist, right under her ribs. "What's that tattoo?" he asked.

"See for yourself," she said, taking his hand and placing it on her cold skin.

Tejas traced her tattoo with a finger: an eye framed by thick lashes, except the eyeball was in the shape of a heart. Beneath the eye were the words *open eyes, open heart*.

"It's beautiful," he said, his mouth falling open. "When did you get it?"

Naina let out a soft sigh. "Years ago, when I was a naïve, foolish, and drunk teenager." She chose not to mention that she'd gotten it the summer after high school, eager for her real real life to start so she could meet the perfect guy in college, fall in love, and have the wedding of her dreams. Naina now knew that an open heart was a recipe for disaster.

"Why—" Tejas started, but Naina hooked her legs around his hips, straddling him, and he stopped talking. In no time, Naina was arching into him and gasping, her head thrown back, as he rocked his hips into her core.

An hour later, as Tejas's eyes drifted closed, Naina stroked his messy curls with her hand, her heart full but her mind racing. She hesitated, then kissed him on the cheek and changed into one of her nightdresses, not wanting to do something as intimate as waking up beside him. She climbed up to the top bunk and settled into the sheets, resting an arm over her head as she stared up at the ceiling.

Naina Shetty had just had sex with someone she'd only just met. The best sex of her life, in fact, with a complete stranger. This wasn't the kind of joy she'd planned on reclaiming—after all, casual sex had never been her thing. She and Santhosh had waited a whole month before hooking up. But it was joy nonetheless, and she'd made good progress on the list tonight. Smiling, she turned onto her side and let Tejas's soft snores lull her to sleep.

♡♡♡

THE NEXT MORNING, AROUND TEN A.M., Naina roused before Tejas. He was still lightly snoring on the bottom bunk, probably exhausted from the party and, well, the cardio after that.

She stifled a yawn, then checked her phone. Scrolling through her never-ending work emails, she bit her lip. She'd needed the two weeks off, and everyone at work had told her as much. Iqbal had requested she make use of her paid leave and not cancel her vacation. "Your brain needs a refresh," he'd said. "You won't be able to help your clients if you're not thinking straight."

He was probably right, but Naina's teeth gritted anyway when she noticed one of her cases had been reassigned to Dhanush for the time being. He'd also been promoted to junior associate not long before, and in all honesty, he was the only one at the office who could threaten her chances at making partner one day. No doubt he planned to poach all her clients and keep them even after she returned to the office. He was as competitive as he was competent.

Naina's phone buzzed with a text.

Anil

Why does your work status say "online"? Stop checking email and enjoy your time off, for fuck's sake

Naina

Pssh. I *am* enjoying my time off. In fact, I already checked items 1, 2, 4, and 5 off the list

Anil is typing . . .

Hold on, lemme see what they were

Anil is typing . . .

YOU KISSED A STRANGER????
WHO???

Naina laughed, then clapped a hand to her mouth when Tejas's snores paused from below her bunk. She waited for a moment, and when he didn't wake up, she returned to her texts.

My roommate lol

DETAILS!

Let's just call him Prince Charming for now

Cheesy, but ok. Did anything else happen?

She licked her lips as memories of the previous night flooded her mind. God, Tejas knew his way around a woman's body.

We may have slept together . . .

WHAT THE FUCK

Anil is typing . . .

Are you serious Nay????

Who are you and what have you done with my bestie?

Naina's stomach grumbled. She carefully got down from the bed and grabbed the homemade snacks Anil had packed for her. Then she returned to her top bunk and reread Anil's text, her insides squirming, and not out of hunger.

As she popped a murukku into her mouth, a rather concerning message popped up.

Anil

This trip is turning you into a brand-new person, and I have to say, I like it

Naina

That's not fair. I used to be wild before Santhosh, you just never saw it

It was true. She'd met her ex before she joined Akhtar, Kumble & Co., back when she was a regular at all her local college bars and clubs. By the time she and Anil became friends, Santhosh had already sapped the life out of her.

Sure, I believe you 😝

A hand rapped sharply on the bottom of her bunk. "Naina?" Tejas said, his voice sleepy. "What are you doing up there?"

She coughed, sending Anil a quick ttyl and setting her phone aside. "Uh, I sleep better alone. Good morning."

"Morning," he mumbled, then stood to face her. He was tall enough to rest his arms along the sides of her bunk bed. He smiled dazedly. "Hope you slept well."

"I did," Naina said, smiling back. She got down from the top bunk, and Tejas pulled her in for a quick close-mouthed kiss, probably worried about his morning breath—not that Naina cared about it at all. "Breakfast?" she asked, and he nodded.

Thankfully, by the time they went downstairs to the kitchen, Raziya was wearing a plain white apron and midway through making Polish breakfast for the others in the kitchen, with Aleksy supervising. He didn't seem to be able to get out of his chef mindset. "Today's special: open sandwiches," he announced, handing plates to Tejas and Naina.

They sat down, and Naina eagerly dug into the crunchy toasted sandwich, loving the flavors of smoked salmon, parsley, pickled cucumber, and cream cheese that mingled in her mouth. She preferred Indian food for breakfast—whether Bangalore dishes like dosa and uthappam with chutney, or the more traditionally North Indian options like aloo parathas—but this trip was all about new experiences, and so far, things were looking good.

Anil's text message flashed in her mind. This trip is turning you into a brand-new person, and I have to say, I like it. Naina rolled her eyes and blinked away the visual. *Just focus on the delicious breakfast,* she told herself. She wouldn't let Anil's opinions sway how she felt about last night—or herself.

As Raziya dished out some Bollywood gossip, Naina listened and made all the right sounds of shock and amusement, but her mind was still on what Anil had said: Her behavior last night had been out of character. She'd planned this vacation so she could let loose and distract herself with good company and lots of alcohol, but despite the items Anil had added to the list, she never actually imagined herself kissing a stranger or having a fling. She'd been a romantic through and through before Santhosh broke her heart.

And yet, she'd felt safe in Tejas's arms, euphoric as he'd thrust into her last night, and she didn't think it had just been the alcohol talking. Anil was right, this wasn't the version of Naina he knew, especially not the one who'd rolled her eyes when he'd added "kiss a stranger" to the list, but . . .

Maybe that wasn't such a bad thing. Right?

Chapter NINE

Bangalore, October 2026

As the crowd clamored in front of them, Tejas took Naina's hand in a gentle but firm grip, and she decided not to pull away despite the tingles shooting up her arm. The mob was mostly men who were no doubt raised on a steady diet of Pai's violent, misogynistic movies, and they wouldn't hesitate to turn on her.

They flashed their work IDs at the security guard manning the front gate and were let in. Seconds after they rang the doorbell, Preethi Acharya ushered them in. She was a tall, dark-skinned woman with a heart-shaped face and legs for days, although the shadows under her sunken eyes and her nervous, slouched posture made her look like a different person from the one Naina had seen on TV and social media.

"Thank you for being on time," she said, her hands shaking as she turned off the video display next to the door that showed a full view of her chaotic front yard. "Would you like some coffee?"

They murmured their agreement and sat on Preethi's leather couch while she disappeared into the kitchen. "Hand me the charge sheet," Tejas said, blowing air through his teeth. Naina did as told, then stood, looking around while he read through the document. Preethi's living room was fairly small, dusty, and littered with tissues and empty takeout containers. She'd furnished the place with a five-seater sofa set, a wooden coffee table, and four movie posters flanking the wall on either side of the television—the entirety of Preethi's filmography, not counting her latest movie that had led to the murder. Naina remembered the waves Preethi's debut had made seven years ago. It was an ambitious project for a nineteen-year-old actress who had zero famous connections, but the award-winning box-office hit propelled her career and landed her the lead role in thirty-five-year-old Rohith Pai's next movie—which, to this date, was her only other successful project.

After her disastrous affair with Pai, who had been in a serious relationship with his childhood sweetheart at the time, she blew up at him, accusing him of grooming and manipulation—which neither the media nor the Sandalwood film industry took seriously, instead branding her a "home-wrecker." Pai had claimed the relationship was nothing more than a gimmick to garner attention for their movie, and his girlfriend, Athira—who was now his wife—believed him, as did the general public.

Preethi slowly but surely disappeared from the limelight, only resurfacing for the occasional shampoo advertisement or single-episode cameo in a soap opera—and, more recently, fitness sponsorships on social media, including studios offering pole-dancing classes, which most people considered scandalous at best, immoral at worst. From the previous lawyer's notes, Naina knew Preethi's modest net worth was the result of her investing most of her movie and sponsorship earnings into profitable stocks, which was how she was paying AKC's legal fees.

"Here you go," Preethi said, coming into view with three mugs of coffee balanced precariously on a tray. She set it on the center table and sat facing them on the smaller couch. Her knee jiggled underneath her maxi skirt, and her eyes were red-rimmed like she'd cried in the kitchen. Naina's heart clenched with pain. She couldn't imagine what Preethi was going through.

"Well, shall we begin?" Naina asked, turning on her iPad, poised to take notes. When their client nodded, she opened her mouth to get started with the list of questions, but Tejas spoke first.

"How are you doing?" He sipped his coffee. "Are you home alone, or do you have someone taking care of you?"

Preethi's lower lip wobbled. *Maybe no one's asked her that question yet,* Naina thought bleakly. After all, she hadn't even considered asking herself. Being a good attorney didn't just mean knowing how to win a case—it meant knowing how to win your client's trust.

Tejas, clearly, was a *great* attorney.

"I'm alone, of course." Preethi gestured around the messy room with her mug, almost spilling her coffee. "I usually have a housekeeper running the place and keeping it tidy. She'd worked here for five years, but why would anybody stick around for a failed actress accused of killing their favorite director?"

"We're so sorry," Naina said, lowering her head, "and we're here to help in any way we can. And for that, we need you to be as honest as possible."

Preethi let out a shuddering gasp. "Okay. Let me start from the beginning." She got up, gulping the last of her coffee. Then she walked to the second framed poster beside the television, where she stood front and center in a dripping-wet white saree with the significantly older hero's lips pressed to her neck. "*Naanu Ninnade,* the project that changed my life. Well," she said, snorting, "maybe *ruined* would be a better word." Preethi touched a hand to the bold title printed on the movie poster, her gaze wistful. "That's what he'd say to me every night after filming, you know? *I'm only yours*. And I thought he meant it too."

Naina took a sip of the coffee, which was too sweet and creamy for her taste, and referenced her notes. "So you started dating Pai in mid-2019, during filming?"

Preethi scoffed. "Or so I thought. But I guess romancing me was just another PR stunt for Rohith. The movie came out on Valentine's Day the next year, and weeks after it became a blockbuster hit—days after he told me he wanted me forever, mind you—I got dumped, and he convinced the world it was a fake relationship." She turned to Tejas, who was listening with rapt attention, no iPad or notebook in hand, and added, "Wanna know what happened then?"

"He married someone else," Tejas said, his jaw clenched.

Naina's stomach churned, remembering that Tejas's ex-boyfriend had done the same thing.

"You said it," Preethi declared, arms folded. "I was sobbing into my tequila-spiked ice cream when I saw the wedding pictures on social media. You'd think he'd have explained himself, but no, I was just the immature nineteen-year-old actress he wanted to fuck in secret before settling down with his age-appropriate high school sweetheart."

Tejas rubbed the stubble on his chin. "It sucks being cast aside like that by someone who seemed to have loved you back. I'm sorry, Preethi."

"And after that?" Naina asked, her voice sharp, though she already knew the whole story—or at least the tabloids' version of it from six years ago. But a change in topic was needed so she wouldn't think about whether Tejas was referencing his own life—if he meant his ex, or if he meant Naina.

Preethi wiped her eyes with a handkerchief. "I was an emotional and mental wreck, and I could barely get out of bed. It was only after months in therapy that I realized what he'd done was grooming. Maybe I shouldn't have been so vocal about it, given his influence and popularity, but I was barely nineteen years old with no media training . . ."

"We're not going to judge you," Tejas said softly, urging her to continue, and set his empty mug down.

"I went on record calling Rohith a predator, not that anyone cared. I sent his wife screenshots and pictures of us together, hoping she'd believe me, but then Rohith reached out threatening legal action, and I backed off, though my career was already ruined by that point." Her lip trembled. "Look, I might still be traumatized by what happened, but I'm not a murderer. I would never hurt him, or—or anyone!" She let out a loud, aching sob, then stood, stacking the empty mugs on the tray. "P-please excuse me."

Once she was out of earshot, Naina leaned closer to Tejas. "How did no one think the alleged PR relationship was still problematic? He was pushing forty, and she was a literal teenager when they first got together."

"Bollywood romanticizes this shit, and people lap it up." Tejas sighed sadly and opened his notebook to a blank page. "Plus, sometimes red flags only show themselves in hindsight."

Naina bit her lip. That was how things had turned out for her too. Santhosh was never the best partner to her in their six years together. They'd had nothing in common besides both being lawyers, and there were so many moments where instead of congratulating her on her achievements, he'd pointed out the ways in which she could improve. Back then, Naina had thought he was merely encouraging her to aim higher and be better, and it was only after he cheated on her and told her she wasn't wife or mother material that she realized he was obsessed with comparing his successes to hers—and that he would always need to put her down in some way or other.

Preethi returned, her eyes noticeably puffier, and sat back down with trembling limbs. "Okay. I guess now I should talk about . . . that night. The reason you're both here."

"It's all right if you need more time," Naina assured her. "We're not going anywhere."

In her peripheral vision, she spotted a small smile on Tejas's face as he nodded, and her heart almost warmed. Almost. Thankfully, she was in control of the damn organ, not the other way around.

"No, let's get it over with." Preethi shook out her shoulders, her foot tapping against the floor. "When Rohith reached out to offer me the lead role of the young warrior princess in *Yoddha Yash,* I agreed on the spot, even though we hadn't talked since the breakup and my accusations. It was the only promising job offer I had gotten in years, and my brand deals don't pay nearly enough. I had to say yes."

Tejas finally jotted something down. "Did you think something would happen between you and him?"

Preethi opened her mouth, then shut it, looking from him to Naina helplessly. Naina reached over and placed a hand on Preethi's. "We're your lawyers," she reminded her. "We need all the facts."

"And all the feelings," Tejas added, quirking an eyebrow.

"Yes, but not in the way you're thinking." Preethi interlaced her fingers in her lap as another tear slid down her cheek. "I know he is—he was—married, and it'd been years since we were together, but I also needed closure. I wanted a conversation between us—nothing else."

"The night of his murder," Naina said, noticing how Preethi twitched at that word, "what happened?"

Preethi tilted her head back against the couch as though to suppress her emotions. "It was six weeks into filming, and we were on location miles away from Bangalore, in the hills for a specific action sequence. He hadn't mentioned our past, and his wife was often around . . . I figured I'd never get a private conversation with him. But then"—she blinked, more tears trickling down her lashes—"he texted me, saying he was thinking of me and wanted to meet in his trailer. Alone."

Naina rested her fingers on the edge of her iPad keyboard, waiting patiently until Preethi continued. "I knocked on his trailer, but nobody answered. The door was ajar. I went in, and . . . and I saw him on the floor, face down in blood." She clapped a hand to her mouth as more sobs took over. "I screamed. Ran to him, turned him over, begged him to wake up. There was a knife sticking out of his stomach. I . . ."

Tejas spoke up. "You touched it."

"I—I know I shouldn't have, but if you saw the man you once

loved bleeding to death, you'd have tried to help him too, regardless of how it ended!" Her voice was loud now, high-pitched; her face was purple and her eyes wide as saucers. "I was going to pull the knife out, then I thought maybe I shouldn't, that might make him bleed more, and it would hurt him, and then—then our producer Jagannath walked in. I guess he heard my screams, and he found me there. Drenched in Rohith's blood, my hands all over him. He flipped out, started yelling, then Gopal Krishnan, the lead actor, rushed in and called the cops. And that was . . ." She wiped her cheeks. "That was it."

As the silence stretched on, Naina looked at the notes on her iPad, swallowing hard. Preethi was found at the scene of the crime by the producer and the lead actor with her fingerprints all over the victim *and* the murder weapon. The prosecution would say this was a scorned woman taking revenge on a former lover, and the judge would agree.

Then Naina jerked her chin back. "The texts he sent you," she said slowly. "They'd have time stamps. How long after those texts did Jagannath find you?"

Preethi's eyes went back and forth. "Maybe twenty-five, thirty minutes? I only saw the messages after I finished my nighttime skincare routine."

Fuck. That was more than enough time to commit a murder.

Tejas coughed. "There's one more thing." He placed Preethi's mug shot on the table between them, which showed her wide-eyed in a skimpy, bloodstained pink camisole under a silk dressing gown. Then his eyes darted to Naina. Clearly he didn't want to be the one to ask this question.

Naina spoke. "Preethi, do you normally sleep in lingerie?"

Preethi scowled. "It's not lingerie, it's sleepwear. I like to be comfortable while I sleep, and in my haste to get answers from Pai, I decided not to change."

Naina held back a sigh. With the public already seeing her as a home-wrecker endorsing "provocative" pole-dancing classes, her attire at the scene of the crime wouldn't help their case. She exchanged glances with Tejas, tilting her head to ask if he had anything to add.

Tejas asked Preethi a few other routine questions about the police's line of questioning, making sure she hadn't told them anything different. Finally, he asked, "Any alibis who can confirm you were in your trailer for that half-hour window?"

"No," Preethi said, ducking her head. "I didn't tell anyone about it because, well, I didn't want them to get the wrong idea. I just wanted closure from him."

Naina let out a soft sigh. "And do you think anyone who was on set that night had motive to kill Rohith Pai and potentially frame you for it?"

"Everyone hated me as much as they loved Rohith," Preethi replied bitterly. "They all thought I would sabotage filming because of our past. I wish I could help you more, but I . . ."

"I understand," Naina said, standing. "This is a tough time for you."

"We'll be in touch," Tejas said, shaking Preethi's hand as he stood up too. "Don't hesitate to call us." He ushered Naina out the door, through the angry crowd, and back to the neighboring street.

They didn't speak about the case until the auto rickshaw dropped them off at the AKC building. "She's got motive, she was found with his body, DNA evidence, and no alibi," Naina rattled off, and pressed the button for the elevator. "Oh, and his misogynistic fans are out for her neck. This won't be easy."

"You're right." Tejas smiled as they got into the elevator. "If it were easy, Iqbal wouldn't have given you the case."

The compliment made Naina's heart flutter, much to her disdain. *No distractions allowed, no matter how cute his smile is,* she reminded herself. So she cleared her throat and changed the topic. "The postmortem confirmed what she said about the single stab wound in his stomach, but the full forensic report will take another week." The elevator reached their floor, and she got out first. "I have to prepare for another case. Catch you later."

"But—wait!"

If Tejas had thought she was unapproachable earlier, she'd certainly proved it now. It was probably for the best, Naina decided, as she suppressed the urge to look back at him.

Chapter TEN

Goa, May 2025

Tejas pushed his empty plate away, rubbing his full stomach as he sat back in his seat at the hostel's dining table. "Fuck. That was the best sandwich I've ever had."

Aleksy took a bow, then gestured for Raziya to do the same. "Thank you," she said, laughing.

Jonah's eyes went to the empty seat beside Tejas's. "I hope Naina liked breakfast too. I'll be offended if she doesn't like my boyfriend's recipes."

Tejas's forehead knit. Naina had finished her sandwich in mere minutes and headed back to their room, claiming she had some work to finish. He hadn't noticed it then, but in hindsight, she'd looked a little pale. "I'll go check on her. See y'all soon," Tejas said, his chair screeching as he stood.

The room was dark, the balcony curtains drawn, and there was silence except for the faint hum of the air-conditioning. Naina sat on the top bunk, fiddling with her ring finger. She barely looked his way when he cleared his throat. "Naina, are you okay?"

"Yeah, sure," she said dimly.

He ran a hand through his hair in confusion and had just started toward Naina when his phone buzzed.

Rahul

hey, how's Goa?

Tejas swallowed. Twiddling his thumbs, he regarded the text. Rahul didn't seem to understand what *needing space* meant, and Tejas wouldn't be the one to explain it to him. He deleted the text, then looked at Naina, who was still silent.

Stomach churning, he joined her on the top bunk, wondering what had upset her. Was it something he did? Did she regret sleeping with him? Had he hurt her, or pressured her into things she wasn't ready for? He didn't want to be the bad guy . . . but maybe he was.

Tejas leaned one arm against the wall and studied her. He opened his mouth, closed it, then let the words out with a shaky breath: "Did I step over the line at the rave when I kissed you? Did I make you feel pressured in any way to have sex when we came back to the room?"

Naina shook her head. "No, it's not you. I wanted it as much as you did." She flashed him a small smile. "But I'm still coming to terms with the fact that it even . . . happened."

Tejas thought for a moment, then got down and held a hand out for Naina to join him. "Some fresh air will help. Trust me."

She peered toward the small balcony, bathed in bright sunshine, then climbed down off the bunk. Once they were on the balcony, Naina sighed and undid her bun, letting her long brown hair cascade down to her waist. Then she spoke, playing with her empty left ring finger. "When I told my best friend we had sex, he was shocked. Even though kissing a complete stranger was on my list, neither he nor I thought I'd actually do it. But now"—she let out a shaky breath—"two months after my engagement ended, I didn't just *kiss* a random guy the very day I met him, but I also hooked up with him. As much as I love adventure, I've never been a fling kind of girl. It just feels . . . different."

Tejas bowed his head. He had feared right. She regretted their night together—and she regretted *him*. "I'm sorry, I had no idea you felt this way—"

"Well, you're not just some random guy anymore," she corrected herself, "and maybe different isn't, um . . . a bad thing?"

He folded his arms and smiled, noting that her gaze went straight to the curve of his biceps. "I don't think it's a bad thing. But if you'd rather go back to just being roommates and working on the rest of your list, we can limit it to that."

She licked her lips, her gaze now traveling along his shoulders and the slight V-cut above the waistband of his sweatpants. Then it returned to his face, the hunger in her eyes evident. Her chest flushed beneath her top, rising and falling with the intensity of her breaths. Tejas felt the slightest tug in his pants, urging him to close the distance between them, but he didn't do anything except stare back at her. As much as he wanted this—wanted her—he couldn't make the first move. Not after what she'd said.

Naina stepped forward, still eye-fucking him, her cold fingers running down his front until they settled along the pockets of his pants. "But I want it to be more than just that. The sex is, um, well . . . it's something. Isn't it?" She looked up at him expectantly, her mouth open just slightly.

He chuckled, wondering how she could doubt his attraction to her for even one second. He finally let himself touch her again, though it was just to brush her wavy hair away from her eyes. "It's certainly something. And I want to do it again, if you'll have me—"

She kissed him, shoving him against the balcony door, which clattered loudly. Apologizing softly, she led the way back to the bunk bed. Her lips didn't leave his mouth until she moved to undress. Tejas only got one perfect second to drink in the sight of her body before she pulled him back into her on the bed.

Their first time had been amazing, but in a rushed, urgent, have-to-have-you-now kind of way. And Tejas didn't want that again; he didn't want a quickie before they got on with their day. He wanted to savor every inch of her with every inch of him. So he broke their kiss to trail a line down her lower body with his mouth, sucking on the skin beneath that eye tattoo, and she shuddered, her hips bucking when he got to the space between her legs. "Is this okay—" he started, but she only breathed a soft "*yes*" before falling back on the pillow and letting him feel the way she writhed and shook beneath his lips as he tasted her.

Tejas had only hooked up with a couple of women his whole life, and honestly, the last time he went down on a woman must have been years ago. He almost wondered for a second if he was doing it right, if he was pleasuring Naina in the way she deserved. But her moans and gasps, coupled with the way she gripped his hair, urging him to keep going, told him enough.

Making her come with nothing but his lips and fingers was a hundred times more satisfying than last night, Tejas decided, when she purred in contentment as he kissed her again.

"My turn," she breathed, her hands going to his waistband to undress him.

Naina wrapped her hand around him, her tongue flicking along the tip, and Tejas fell back against the pillows. Fuck, she was good at this, but the way she was teasing him . . . it was agonizing. "Naina, please," he said, exhaling. "I—please—"

She paused to smirk at him. "Please what? Should I stop?"

"No," he said, thrusting his hips closer to her. "God, no. Don't stop. Ever."

Naina hummed in approval and took him in, and the sight of her between his legs, her mouth all over him as her hair fell over her face, drove Tejas over the edge in minutes. As he came, moaning out her name over and over until he crumpled into the bed and pulled her back over him, he only hoped the walls of their room were soundproof.

Chapter ELEVEN

Bangalore, October 2026

Tejas scratched the base of his neck as he sorted through pictures of the crime scene. "Do you see how poorly lit some of these photographs are?" he fumed at his laptop screen.

Naina, who was on the video call with him, let out a loud sigh and held one picture up to the light in her room. "I think Preethi's lucky those lawyers stepped down. They clearly didn't know what they were doing. I— Tejas?"

Astrid had pranced over onto Tejas's lap to stick her face into the camera, and he cursed under his breath. "Go to bed, baby." He picked her up and set her down on the floor, but she crawled back up on the couch again, settling in beside the photos. Astrid could never fall asleep at night unless she was in close proximity to Tejas. He loved that about her.

Naina let out a choked laugh. "She seems to be obsessed with you. How do you get any work done at home?"

Tejas grinned at his cat, who meowed at him angrily before her eyes shut and she dozed off. "It helps that I'm obsessed with her too," he said, looking at Astrid fondly.

"Anyway," Naina said, biting her lip like she was trying not to smile, "the photos."

"The photos." He groaned, sinking back into the couch. "What now?"

Her eyes went back and forth, then she said, "I think we're going to have to make the trip up the hills tomorrow and investigate the crime scene for ourselves. Savandurga Hills is a couple hours' drive from the city. Shall we meet there around ten?"

Tejas laughed. This woman was unbelievable. "You live in this city, right?"

Naina blinked at him, adjusting her headphones like she thought she'd heard wrong. "Yeah? Obviously."

He leaned forward, quirking a brow at her. "It appears that I live here too. Why don't we just head to the crime scene together?"

Naina's mouth parted. She looked away, her lips moving wordlessly, like she was trying to find an excuse. "I'll be driving my dad's car," she said finally. "It's old, and the seats are worn out. You'd be more comfortable driving yourself."

"I just moved here, Naina Stark," Tejas replied, trying not to laugh. "I don't have a car."

Her cheeks turned scarlet. "Naina Shetty," she corrected him.

"Not to me." Tejas sat back again, scratching under Astrid's chin while she purred in her sleep. "Anyway," he added, when Naina's eyes narrowed, "will you give me a ride? I'm in Indiranagar, not too far from work."

She pursed her lips, considering it, as the clock across from Tejas's couch ticked on. Finally, Naina nodded sharply. "Text me your address. I'll see you at eight A.M."

"Cool, I—" The call dropped. Tejas snorted, setting his laptop aside, then bent to give Astrid a kiss on her tiny head. "What do we think of Naina, hmm?" he asked her. "Do we think she'll ever warm up to me again?"

Astrid yawned and stretched her arms out before curling up in Tejas's lap. He stroked her fur, smiling to himself. "I'll take that as a yes."

Tejas stared out the window of the car, bopping his head in time to the blaring pop music on the radio as Naina pulled off of the highway. Thanks to the morning rush hour and the slow engine of Naina's dad's car, they'd spent over thirty-five minutes stuck in traffic and another hour on the highway, and were only now entering Savandurga Hills, where Rohith Pai had been murdered. The police and forensic experts had already gone through the crime scene as well as the film set and other actors' trailers to collect evidence, but they had been ordered by the court—with some influence from Ramesh Kumble, of course—to keep everything else untouched until the case was closed.

The plan was to compare the previous lawyers' notes and photographs, blurry as they were, with the actual crime scene to see if they'd missed anything.

So far, the drive had been a quiet one, save for Naina mouthing the words to the songs as she drove. Guess she still loved music. Naina had engaged in most of Tejas's attempts at small talk, though he knew she was doing it grudgingly. She'd also rehashed the details of the case with him while she drove, but the second Tejas had run out of things to say, she'd cranked up the volume of the radio.

Tejas tapped his fingers on the dashboard as Naina slowly drove the car uphill. The leather seats were comfortable enough, unlike what she'd told him yesterday, but her dad's Honda City had clearly seen better days. Tejas knew she commuted to work by auto rickshaw or the Metro. Before the drive had started, he was going to ask her why she hadn't just bought another car for herself—she could easily afford a decent one with how much she made—but then he heard the barrage of curse words from her mouth at twenty different traffic signals and realized he'd rather take public transport than drive in this city too.

Naina let out a wince as the car struggled through a bumpy, mud-stricken road. They hadn't spoken in nearly an hour, so Tejas cleared his throat. "Uh, how far away are we?"

"Almost there," she said, looking pointedly at the Google Maps navigation on the screen between both of their seats, which said they'd arrive in two minutes. "Let's hope we find something to save Preethi."

Finally, they parked outside the film set, close to a police van next to the yellow DO NOT CROSS tape blocking off the crime scene. Tejas introduced himself to the constable-in-charge, smiling warmly and gesturing toward Naina as well, and the cop handed them gloves and masks to wear before leading them down the path to Rohith Pai's trailer.

"Where are the other cast and crew members' trailers?" Tejas asked as they walked.

The constable pointed to an adjacent mud road. "There are four more trailers about a minute's walk down from there."

Pai's trailer was surrounded by police tape; the foreboding aura and the knowledge that someone had been killed here made the hair on Tejas's arms stand. He slipped on his gloves and face mask and stepped into the trailer, right behind the constable and Naina. The first thing that greeted him was the heavy, metallic smell of iron and stained blood on the floor. The authorities had clearly left the crime scene as it was, and though Tejas was grateful for the chance to carry out his own investigation, the stench nearly made him gag through the mask.

"I'll be outside," the constable said, heading back down.

Tejas thanked him and took out the photographs from his bag, and Naina held them up to compare as they walked through the trailer.

"The forensic report should be ready soon, which should help us with the defense," Naina said, hands on her hips, as they looked from the sketched outline of Rohith's body to the dried blood spatter. "Maybe the force of the weapon will indicate the murderer had to have been a man, and then our job is done. Or there'll be too many signs of struggle for Preethi to have killed him."

Tejas rubbed his chin, studying the trailer. "Why do you think a man did it?"

Naina scoffed, and he looked her way. "Statistically, over ninety percent of murders in India are committed by men," she explained. "I'm trying to keep our morale high by being optimistic."

"So, you're still an optimist?" He smiled softly as he opened the drawer of the small cupboard in the corner. "Good to know that hasn't changed."

"Focus," she retorted as she handed him half the pictures. "You take that side, I'll take this one."

Tejas turned to the walls, examining the surfaces and checking for any drops of blood or evidence that the pictures hadn't captured. "Nothing," he mumbled, sucking in his teeth.

A kitchenette sat in one corner with a small countertop, a single washbasin, and some plates. The cutlery set was intact except for the meat knife—the one used to kill Pai, Tejas guessed.

"Tejas, look at this," Naina called out from the other end of the room. She slid her mask down and beckoned him over.

He followed her to the small window beside the bed, the curtains drawn shut.

"Do you think he had a nice view?" Naina said, and then, without a moment's hesitation, she climbed into the bed and peeled the curtains apart.

Tejas hesitated, since he was wearing shoes, but hell, this was a dead man's bed. Shoes were mandatory. As the bedsprings creaked, he joined her on the mattress. She must have been taken by surprise, because she jerked back and toppled into him, nearly pushing them both down on the bed. The top of their noses brushed together like in all the Bollywood movies his sister watched—though those didn't usually involve crime scene settings. God, he'd missed Naina's lavender perfume.

Naina let out a soft gasp that he felt on his face mask, and it brought him out of his daze. He wound his arm around her waist, over the silky-smooth fabric of her shirt, and forced them both back to a seated position. “Sorry about that,” he said, holding back the urge to flex his fingers as he withdrew his hand. He shifted away from her, crossing his legs, and peered through the window. He didn’t have to look at her flushed face to know she was as affected by that moment as he was.

Naina shifted in place before bringing one of the photographs up to the window. “That must be the Krishnans’ trailer,” she said, her voice hushed. “The assistant director and the lead actor.” The trailer sat right behind Pai’s trailer. Tejas hadn’t noticed it when they first walked in, since the canopy of trees over the trailers had hid this one from view.

Tejas thought back to the conversation at Preethi’s house. “Preethi said the producer, Jagannath, found her first, and Gopal showed up after he called for help. If Gopal and his wife were so close to this trailer, why didn’t they hear Preethi’s screams right away?”

“Let’s go find out,” Naina declared.

They left Pai’s trailer to find the constable, who had disappeared somewhere. As they looked around, they brainstormed the key witnesses they could talk to—Jagannath, the producer; the assistant director and the lead actor, who were married and had shared that specific trailer; perhaps other crew members—wondering if any of them might have information they could use.

The constable was nowhere to be found, but a maintenance worker stood in the distance, sweeping up plastic food containers and wrappers, likely left behind by the authorities during their last investigation. His forehead wrinkled when Naina asked something in Kannada. She bit her tongue and asked him, in Hindi this time, who the trailer belonged to.

“Yeah, it belonged to that married couple,” he replied.

Tejas flipped through his notes. Gopal Krishnan, one of Sandalwood’s biggest actors, had married assistant director Bina three years ago. Now they were the perfect team, churning out blockbuster after blockbuster, and they had one rule: They worked on projects together or not at all.

"Sir," Naina asked, "were you working here the night of the murder?"

The worker hesitated, then replied, his words rushed, "I'm so sorry, madam. I can't testify in court. I have a wife and children here, but we're not—" He averted his gaze. "Never mind."

Tejas's heart dropped. This man was probably undocumented, from Bangladesh or a neighboring country, and wanted to lie low. It was best not to drag him into this.

Naina must have had the same thought. She spoke again, her voice soft and kind. "We wouldn't ask that of you, sir, but if you could answer some questions, off the record, we'd be so grateful."

He bit his lip, then nodded. "All right."

Tejas put his notebook back in his bag, then clasped his fingers together. "Did you notice anything that was off, suspicious, or concerning about that night?"

"I wasn't here when the—the incident happened," the worker said. "I rent a small shack a short distance away, where I stay with my family. I only work here in the daytime. But"—he swallowed—"I did notice occasional arguments between the . . . person who passed, and the other man."

"Which man?" Naina asked, frowning. "Jagannath or Gopal Krishnan?"

"I don't know their names," the worker said apologetically. "I don't watch those movies. But it was the tall man in a soldier costume."

"Gopal," Tejas said. "Do you remember what they were fighting about?"

The worker let out a wry smile and folded his hands. "I couldn't understand them, sir. I don't speak either English or Kannada. I'm a simple man. I do my job and I stay out of conflict."

Naina smiled back. "Thank you for your time."

The worker resumed picking up the trash, and Tejas and Naina got back to work. A quick sweep of their client's trailer showed nothing out of the ordinary, not that they'd expected it to be. It matched the poorly lit photographs well enough.

They returned to the parking space, talking about what Gopal's arguments with Pai could have been about. Creative differences? Personal beef? Or something far more sinister?

Suddenly, a cat sprinted ahead of them. "Look at that!" Tejas exclaimed, just as the cat stopped in its tracks, its wide yellow eyes staring back at him. "That poor baby, it's so bedraggled and thin . . ."

Naina tsk-tsked from beside him. "What a shame. Maybe there aren't as many rats here for it to catch."

"Let's fix that." Tejas rummaged in his bag until he found the extra cat treats he carried everywhere. Unfortunately, he couldn't adopt every stray cat he chanced upon, but he could at least feed them one meal. He bent low and urged the cat forward, enticing it with the treat.

Slowly, hesitantly, the cat approached him to sniff the treat. Within seconds, it had gobbled up enough for an entire meal. "Wow," Naina breathed as the cat meowed and scampered away. "You keep cat food in your work bag?"

Tejas straightened and gave her a smile. "Yeah. Why, is that weird?"

Her face was unreadable as her mouth twitched. "No. It's not weird, it's . . . Never mind. Let's head back."

After Naina unlocked her dad's car with a beep and strapped herself in, Tejas followed suit, and she backed out of the parking area, turning on the radio again.

Tejas held back a sigh as music blasted from the speakers. He shifted toward her, hoping to start a friendly conversation, but she only exhaled, keeping her gaze staunchly on the road.

A minute later, Tejas spoke, if only to diffuse the tension in the air. "I can't believe how much cheaper the rent is in Bangalore than Mumbai."

"Uh-huh," Naina said as she made a left turn along the hilly path.

"Renting a pet-friendly apartment in a decent neighborhood would have cost me an arm and a leg back home, but here?" Tejas laughed. "Astrid is so happy with all the space—"

Naina sighed loudly, and he stopped mid-sentence. As the car barreled through the soil, she said, "We don't have to fill every moment of silence with a conversation."

"But I want to," he said. "Naina, I'd love for us to be friends, if nothing more. From what I know about you—"

"You don't know me anymore, if you ever did," she said, slowing the car as they drove down a road with particularly rough terrain. "Besides, weren't you the one who told Dhanush that I'm 'unapproachable'?"

"How did you . . ." His mouth fell open. Fuck, Dhanush must have said something. He obviously didn't like Naina. "I was just wondering about it on my first day," Tejas said finally, "and I fully expected the guys to correct me."

"But they didn't," Naina said sharply.

"They didn't," he agreed.

Then, after a pause, she added, "Look, Tejas, we've had sex. Multiple times."

Tejas let out a breath. Hearing her say it out loud, for the first time since they'd met again, brought equal parts relief and anxiety. And, of course, beautiful old memories. The slight coolness of her skin. The tug of her teeth on his lower lip. Her spunk, her energy, the light in her eyes . . . none of which he saw in her anymore.

Finally, Tejas bowed his head. "We've had sex," he agreed. "And if I don't know you anymore, I'd like the opportunity to begin again."

Naina bit her lip. "I can't be friends with someone I've slept with. Let's leave it at that."

"Then we'll be friendly," he countered, "for Preethi's sake, if no one else's."

He waited with bated breath as she considered it, his heart in his throat. They'd shared so much in Goa that was impossible to shove down or ignore, but now there was so much at stake in Bangalore. A woman's life was on the line, after all.

Finally, after the longest minute of Tejas's life, Naina turned down the radio and said, "All right, Tejas. Friendly it is."

Chapter TWELVE

Goa, May 2025

The next afternoon, Tejas awoke from his nap to the buzzing of his phone and sounds of nature from the balcony. He yawned, then realized he was once again alone in the bunk bed, though he and Naina had fallen asleep together. *Wonder why she likes sleeping alone,* he mused. Sure, the bunk bed wasn't large enough for both of their tall, muscled frames, but didn't she enjoy cuddling?

He stood up and stretched, then looked around the tiny room, bathed in sunlight. Naina was nowhere to be seen. Maybe she was in the bathroom.

His phone had received a spam-worthy number of cat photos in the past few minutes, all from Latika. Grinning, he swiped through them, zooming in on Astrid's face, paws, and bright eyes. God, she was the sweetest little thing.

Tejas

Fuck I miss her so much. What's she up to right now? Send me videos

When he saw Latika's reply, he laughed aloud. She's digging in her litter box. I think we should give her some privacy

He resumed scrolling through the photos, his heart clenching with love. He and Latika were born and raised in Jaipur, where their parents still lived, and they'd never had pets growing up, despite having a house with a front and back yard. Adopting Astrid had been a spur-of-the-moment decision. Last year, in Mumbai, he'd gone out to a new restaurant for lunch on a rainy afternoon, not knowing it was also a cat café. Two hours later, he was in talks with the café owner's sister, who was a foster mom, to adopt a kitten of his own.

Latika had been cynical, like always. "You know nothing about pets," she'd said. "This is a lifelong commitment. Are you sure you can handle this?" But he'd fallen for Astrid the second his dark eyes met her light green ones, and the rest was history.

Naina returned from the shower, her hair damp, just as Tejas's phone buzzed. "Be right back," he said to Naina, rushing out to the balcony and closing the door behind him. "Hey," he said, answering the video call.

Latika was holding Astrid, but when her video came into focus, her eyes narrowed. She set the cat down and said exasperatedly, "Bhai. You hooked up with your roommate, didn't you?"

That was when Tejas realized he was shirtless, not to mention sporting a faint hickey on his collarbone. He averted his gaze and didn't reply until Latika said "Bhai?" again.

Tejas lowered his voice. "Yeah, fine, I did."

"What's her name?"

"Naina," he answered.

"So is she from Mumbai too?"

Oh no. His sister was not going to like what he said next. "I, uh . . . I don't know."

Latika's forehead wrinkled, making her look much older than twenty-six. "You didn't ask your roommate—who you hooked up with—where she's from?"

He quickly filled her in on everything: the Anti-Honeymoon

Checklist, the "wrong answers only" policy, the rave; and by the time he was done, Latika had one hand pressed to her cheek in concern.

"It's fine," he assured her. "This is just casual."

"Except you can't do casual," she said, dropping her hand with a sigh. "We both know you suck at separating emotions from sex. Isn't that how you got your heart broken the last *three* times before Rahul?"

She was right. He'd had his fair share of situationships before Rahul—men and women who'd wanted to "go with the flow" while he caught feelings two dates in. With his ex, they had gone from friends to lovers after one kiss. Then again, given how things had ended, perhaps Rahul had seen their relationship as casual all along.

That didn't mean this thing with Naina would go the same way, though. "I've got this, okay?" Tejas said testily. A knock sounded on the balcony door, and he cursed. "I'll talk to you later."

Latika nodded. "Be careful. Bye."

He went back inside the room, shaking his head.

Naina greeted him with a smile. "Ready to go out?" she asked, popping some snacks into her mouth, then putting the container away. "The gang is off to a beach club."

"Sounds great," Tejas said, throwing the cupboard door open. *This time is different,* he told himself as he pulled on some clothes. He headed downstairs with Naina, deciding he wouldn't get his heart broken this time. No, this trip would just be a fun, sexy, exciting memory to hold on to for the rest of his life. A life that would *not* include Naina Stark.

♥ ♥ ♥

"God, this is so relaxing," Tejas said, exhaling loudly as the sunlight warmed his face. He stared up at the cloudless sky—now tinted red thanks to his sunglasses—and lifted his bare arms to stretch.

Naina, who was sharing a sunbed with him at the beach club, patted his thigh absently and flipped to the next page of her book. A romance novel, from the looks of it, which surprised Tejas—he hadn't pegged her for a romantic.

Naina's hair was up in a loose braided bun, and she wore a strappy orange bikini top with denim shorts. The outfit, coupled with that eye tattoo now visible under her ribs, made her go from sexy to completely irresistible. Tejas couldn't wait to bite that tattoo tonight.

"More drinks?" a passing server asked, an empty tray tucked under his arm. Raziya ordered a virgin piña colada, and Tejas agreed to split a pitcher of beer with the guys. "Naina?" He nudged her. "You want another Bloody Mary?"

Naina looked from her book to the half-finished cocktail on the small side table. "Probably not a good idea. I don't want to overdo the alcohol unless it's for my list."

Jonah snickered. "It's been two days since that party, and we're on vacation! Get her a refill," he said to the server, who left before Naina could protest.

Tejas sidled closer and slung an arm around her shoulder. "Don't worry," he whispered, "I'll drink it if you won't."

"Thanks." Naina smiled at him. "Although I'll have to pluck up the courage soon. I still want to have one night where I get so shitfaced drunk I can barely wake up the next morning."

"Considering we're in Goa, that's the easiest thing on the list." He planted a kiss on her cheek, then returned his focus to the sparkling gray Arabian sea in the distance and how the waves swept closer and closer to the club's private beach, where a group of white men were playing volleyball. Their cheers and jeers, loud enough to ring in Tejas's ears, reminded him of the time he'd played beach volleyball with Rahul and some guys from work. That was, what, three and a half years ago? Was it the very night Rahul kissed him for the first time, turning their best friendship into a doomed romance?

Tejas gulped, raking a hand through his hair. He had wasted so much time imagining a happily ever after with a man who was probably swimming with his new wife in their private pool in the Maldives. A man who had, in hindsight, never really loved Tejas at all.

Speaking of which . . . Tejas pulled his phone out from the pocket of his shorts. His urge to check his now-married ex-boyfriend's social media was toxic and would only bring him pain, but he had to know.

Rahul's green story ring greeted Tejas right as he opened Instagram, practically begging him to click on it. His eyes narrowed. Why was he still on Rahul's Close Friends list? They were exes in every single way—romantic or otherwise.

Changing his mind, Tejas opened his Gallery app and scrolled through the cat photos Latika had sent earlier that morning. Astrid sitting by the windowsill, soaking in the sunshine. Astrid yawning, her mouth wide and her eyes scrunched up. Astrid doing a biiiiig stretch along the floor, her paws—

Fuck it. Tejas couldn't bear the suspense. He switched back to Instagram and tapped on the Close Friends story, his stomach churning. Rahul's new wife stood at the edge of an infinity pool, her face looking away from the camera toward the ocean in the far distance. She wore a modest one-piece swimsuit and red bangles on both wrists, signifying her newly married status. The text read: What a view!

"Beer, sir?"

The attendant was back. Tejas accepted the beer and took a sip, ignoring his friends, who'd raised their mugs for a toast, but the chilled beverage offered no respite from the whirlwind of thoughts in his head. Was Rahul happy in the arranged marriage he swore he didn't want? Was he already in love with this strange woman he'd met two months ago? Was he sending some sort of message to Tejas by not hiding this story from him?

Ugh.

"You okay?" Naina asked, patting his shoulder as the attendant set her second Bloody Mary on the table beside her first unfinished one.

Tejas forced himself to smile. “Of course. Why wouldn’t I be?”

“You’re fake-smiling,” she challenged with narrowed eyes.

He frowned. “No, I’m not.”

She turned toward him, her muscly body on full display, and said, “You have this tiny dimple that only shows itself when you smile for real. I don’t see it right now.”

Tejas chuckled. “Maybe you need glasses, because I don’t have any dimples.”

Naina leaned closer to him with a twinkle in her eye, her delicious lavender perfume hanging in the air. “Did your sister share any more pictures of your cat today?”

Despite his sour mood, Tejas grinned as he showed her the photos, swiping through them one by one. “Doesn’t Astrid look so cute here with her sharp teeth showing? And this one, it’s like she’s doing cat yoga or something.” He paused when Naina whipped out her phone. Before he knew it, she’d clicked a picture of him.

“See,” she said, showing him her phone.

“Huh,” he said as he looked at the photo. She was . . . right. Something poked his cheek, and he looked up to see a triumphant Naina smirking at him. “That’s where your dimple is, when you *actually* smile.” She pressed her finger into his cheek again. “It’s faint, but it’s the cutest thing in the world, so don’t you dare let anyone make it disappear, least of all your own self.”

A funny sort of feeling tickled the corners of Tejas’s eyes. Tears? “No one’s told me I have a dimple before,” he said, his voice thick. “Nobody ever noticed.”

“Well,” she said, chuckling as she finally finished her first cocktail, “then maybe they’re the ones who need glasses.”

“Maybe,” Tejas said, kissing her briefly on the lips, tasting vodka. *It’s just a casual fling,* he reminded himself. *She’s only being sweet and nice and cute because we’re hooking up. It doesn’t mean anything—and I won’t let it mean anything.*

The others decided to head back to the hostel after sunset. When Tejas stood to follow them, Naina stopped him, coiling an arm around his shoulder. "There's this lake a short distance away. Want to go there? Just us?"

His eyebrows rose. "Skinny-dipping?"

A smile slowly formed on her lips. "Yes. It's getting dark, so now is the perfect time."

They'd already brought towels and spare sets of clothes to the beach club, so they headed straight to the lake. It was a twenty-minute walk, and like Naina had said, there was nobody around. Hidden behind a large, mossy rock, the lake's dark waters sparkled in the light of the crescent-shaped moon. Tejas's clothes clung to his body with sweat after the walk, and although the possibility of catching pneumonia—or something worse—loomed over him, he couldn't wait to shed his layers and plunge into the cold depths of the lake.

They undressed, their eyes raking all over each other. Naina tied her hair up, then took his hand in hers. "Ready?"

He nodded and inhaled deeply before they jumped in together.

"Oh fuck!" Tejas yelled, running a hand over his face. "The water is so refreshing."

Naina giggled, then sank her head underwater before resurfacing. "We did it," she said with a grin. "Skinny-dipping." She swam a few feet away, her strokes precise and well-trained, yelling for him to follow.

Tejas's gaze lingered on her toned legs and the dip of her low back as they did a few laps across the small lake.

"You know," Naina said, when they stood facing each other, their breathing shallow from all the swimming, "I might have put on a brave act, but I was really anxious about doing this."

He smiled and swam close enough that his chest skimmed the peaks of her breasts. "Anything else on the list you're worried about?" he asked as his growing arousal pressed against her thigh.

Her throat bobbed. "Not worried as much as . . . anticipating."

When her gaze flitted to meet his, adrenaline and lust surged through Tejas's bones. He dipped her head back to kiss her neck, his desire fueled by her moans. She wrapped her legs around his hips and pulled him closer, and that was when he shook his head and stepped back.

"What are you doing?" she asked.

"I don't have a condom," he said. "We shouldn't. Not here."

Naina's eyes softened, and then she jumped out of the lake without warning, giving Tejas a full view of her perfect body, dripping wet. *Holy fuck*. "Hostel. Now," she announced, tossing him a towel as he got out too.

They dried off, changed back into their clothes, and ran to the hostel, giggling and squealing like horny teenagers. Tejas realized, with a smile, that his heart hadn't been this light and happy in months.

Chapter THIRTEEN

Bangalore, October 2026

Naina settled into her cubicle next to Anil's, shaking out her stiff body and hoping she hadn't dealt permanent damage to her lower back. "God, the drive to and from the crime scene was agonizing."

Anil swiftly put his laptop on standby and turned his chair to face hers. "Too much sexual tension between you and Prince Charming?" he asked, his voice mercifully low.

She huffed. "You could have cut it with a knife." While Anil chuckled, she darted a look at her phone. It was already past two-thirty in the afternoon. Naina and Tejas had a conference call scheduled with Preethi, Kumble, and Iqbal to catch them up on their progress. Knowing their expectations, Naina should have already come up with at least five things they'd discovered that could help them win the case. Currently, with less than a half hour to go, she had . . . zero in mind.

Anil rolled his eyes when Naina told him this. "At least your partner on this case is a decent human being. Kumble just assigned a pro bono case to me and Dhanush. Five years of never having to work with him one-on-one, but I guess my luck had to run out sooner or later."

Naina made a pitying noise and placed a hand on Anil's shoulder. "I'd offer to trade, but I'd rather have sexual tension with Tejas than end up in jail for murdering Dhanush out of sheer spite, so . . . my condolences, Anil."

"Well, best get on with it." He shrugged off her hand and swiveled back to his desk.

Fifteen minutes later, Naina stared at the blinking cursor on the Word document, her mind as blank as the pages, when her inbox pinged with an email from Tejas.

RE: RE: ACHARYA V. K'TAKA CASE

Naina,

I drafted some points for our meeting at 3, and I've already shared the link below with Mr. Kumble. Feel free to edit it if you've got anything else to add. I'll see you in his office soon!

—T

[LINK: Preethi Acharya Case Notes]

She read through the Google Doc, mumbling to herself under her breath. He'd listed basic findings like the maintenance worker's account of the bad blood between Gopal Krishnan and Rohith Pai, and the Krishnans' trailer being mere feet away from Pai's trailer, but also how the proximity could have meant access to Rohith's trailer, making them key witnesses as well as potential suspects.

Another note said: *Ask the other witnesses (Jagannath, misc. crew members, Krishnans) about Gopal/Pai beef and see if it's different than what the worker said. Since the worker won't testify, we need someone else to confirm.*

Naina made a small noise of approval. Tejas was smart. It might be frustrating to work with him on account of . . . everything, but he was a competent lawyer to have by her side. And with them having talked about being friendlier, she needed to set their differences aside and win this case, not just for Preethi's sake, but also her own.

Gritting her teeth, she took out her phone and sent Preethi a quick message, keeping her dream of making partner at the forefront of her mind.

Five minutes before the scheduled call, steady footsteps that Naina recognized all too well pulled her attention from rereading the document. She looked up at Tejas and smiled. "Hi," she said. "I was just making some additions to your points."

Tejas bit the side of his cheek, like he was trying not to laugh. "More like rewriting them. I guess Naina Shetty is just as competitive as Naina Stark?"

"I'm afraid Naina Stark is no more."

"Good thing I like Naina Shetty too." His voice was buttery-smooth as he said her last name; then his gaze softened as he looked at her. He licked his lips. "Very much, in fact."

Her face flooded with heat, especially when Anil cackled next to her. "I'm doing this for Preethi," she replied quickly, and pushed her chair back so she could stand. "On to Kumble's office, then?"

Nodding, Tejas led the way. "You think Preethi's doing okay?" he asked as they walked. "She goes into judicial custody tomorrow. I hope we can ease her anxieties during the video call."

Naina's shoulders slumped. Based on her text exchange with Preethi, they definitely needed to reassure her to the best of their abilities. "I hope Mr. Kumble won't say something mean to her if she breaks down crying," Naina said as they paused in front of the managing partner's office, where Kumble and Iqbal were already waiting.

"I wouldn't put it past him." Tejas ran a hand through his curly hair. Naina tried not to glance at the way it fell across his forehead. They knocked on the glass door and stepped inside after Kumble yelled, "Come in!"

The spacious office's floor-to-ceiling walls overlooked half of Bangalore, from the skyscrapers and luxury apartments to the smaller, run-down slums interspersed between different neighborhoods. There were no photographs on Kumble's desk, no personal trinkets in this sterile white-walled office, not even his degrees or accolades framed on the wall. He didn't have plants, either. Kumble didn't care for anything green unless it was code for "money."

He sat at his desk in his revolving chair, squeezing a stress ball, while Iqbal stood next to him, thumbing through some reports.

"Good afternoon," Tejas said, straightening his tie. "How's everyone doing?"

"Fine, fine." Kumble ushered Naina and Tejas to sit across from him.

"So," he said, his voice low, giving Iqbal a quick glance, "we've just gone through the document you shared with us. These are interesting findings, but"—he sucked in a breath—"prosecution will use the scorned lover angle, which is very believable."

"She hadn't spoken to him in years," Naina pointed out, though she knew he was right about the revenge angle. "Besides, she did no wrong accusing him of grooming her. A man in his late thirties should not be doing anything with a nineteen-year-old who doesn't have a fully developed prefrontal cortex."

"Girls mature faster than boys," Kumble said. "Anyway, we're digressing."

What a reductive take. Naina opened her mouth to argue, then stopped herself. There was no use.

"Another thing to consider," Iqbal said, "is that the remote location, closed set, and lack of security could mean our killer had planned the whole thing. They might accuse Preethi of premeditated murder instead of culpable homicide."

"So that's the death penalty or life imprisonment versus ten years in jail," Tejas said. "If they find her guilty at all."

"Which they probably will," Kumble said, shaking his head, "unless we do the smart thing and pin this murder on someone else."

Huffing, Naina said, "Sir, we're not detectives, we're lawyers. Are we really supposed to solve this murder when we should be trying to defend our client?"

"You don't need to solve the murder to find a new suspect. Whether they actually did it or not"—Kumble waved his hand dismissively—"is irrelevant. We care about proving our client's innocence. Nobody else's."

Naina tried not to let her annoyance show. "Of course," she said. "Do we know how Preethi's dealing with all the media attention and the trolls?"

"Probably not great," Iqbal started, but Kumble cut in. "She was absolutely hysterical when our paralegal called her this morning to confirm the meeting. Unless she dials it down, everyone will believe she's guilty. Why else would she be so sad?"

"Maybe because she's accused of murdering someone she once thought she loved?" Tejas suggested, cocking a brow. "Don't you think people would be more suspicious if she weren't devastated?"

Naina nodded. "She's acting like a person who went through a lot of trauma both before and after the murder, and is now being tried for something she didn't do. If she were unemotional, detached, or indifferent, people would find it weird. Then again"—she glared at Kumble—"people call women hysterical if they're devastated, so I guess we can't win either way."

"Damned if you do, damned if you don't," Iqbal murmured.

Kumble sighed. "Let's get on with this meeting."

Naina and Tejas turned their chairs around to face the screen opposite Kumble's desk while Iqbal started the Zoom call. Seconds later, their client hopped on, and Naina sucked in a breath. Next to her, Tejas stiffened. This would be the last time they'd talk to Preethi before she was taken to prison.

"H-hi, everybody." Preethi looked worse than the last time they met her. She sat at a desk, her blotchy face half hidden by the three tissues she was dabbing on her eyes. Several used tissues were already scattered on the desk. Cringing internally, Naina hoped Kumble wouldn't say anything dismissive while they were on the call.

Iqbal smiled kindly at Preethi. "Ms. Acharya, how are you doing?"

"I'm—I'm terrified," she said, her voice catching on the last word. She blew her nose on the tissue. "I don't want to go to jail."

"You'll be in judicial custody for just a short while," Kumble snapped. "While we're collecting more evidence and hashing out an ironclad defense for you, we'd like you to record a video statement about how you're doing." Kumble shot a glance at Naina, his eyebrows knitting. "Let's see if your theory proves right, Naina."

Preethi's lips parted in confusion, and she looked in Naina's general direction. *Does this man not have any empathy?* Naina thought bitterly. She stood, pushing her chair back with a groan. "Sir, with all due respect, I don't think she's in the right state to record a video statement. Which is why I already worked on a written statement with Preethi before this meeting." She showed Kumble, Iqbal, and Tejas the statement, which was to the point and respectful of Pai's death and the gaping hole left in the Sandalwood film industry, and also included a kind appeal to the public to trust whatever the court found to be right and just.

Tejas scratched the back of his neck. "I think this looks good. Let's send it to the press on her behalf."

"If it comes from her in the flesh, it'll be more impactful," Kumble argued. Iqbal looked among the four of them almost helplessly, then finally intervened, laughing nervously. "A written statement is fine. Anyway, Preethi." He turned to the screen. "We're on top of things with your case, and Mr. Kumble will ensure you get the best possible treatment in prison."

"Do you hear yourself?" Preethi said, hiccuping. "Prison!"

"We're handling this," Tejas chimed in, his eyes sad, while Kumble merely shook his head. "Try not to worry too much."

"How?" Preethi looked straight at the camera, her eyes bloodshot. "I'll be on trial for murder soon. Murder! I can't sleep, I can't eat, I can't stop crying . . ."

Naina gulped and finally spoke up. "You don't deserve this. Nobody does. But you need to—"

"Be strong?" Preethi shrieked. "I can't do that. Have you seen what people are saying about me on the internet? Outside my own goddamn house?"

"You don't need to be strong," Naina said, smiling softly, "but you do need to have faith, because that's the one thing that keeps people going despite the shitstorm life throws them into. You're innocent, Preethi, and we'll prove it. I promise."

A single tear slid down Preethi's cheek, but her face softened. "Thanks, Naina," she said, then looked around her surroundings, frowning. "I . . . I'd better go. I need to clean up in here before they take me away."

Once the call dropped, Kumble gestured toward the door. "We'd all best get back to work. The law waits for no one. Especially not a murder suspect."

Iqbal smiled politely as Naina and Tejas headed out. Once they were in the corridor, Tejas spoke, his hands in his pockets, punctuating the silence left in the wake of Kumble's chilling words. "That was beautiful, what you said."

Naina bit her lip. "She needed to hear it from someone."

He cocked his head to the side. "I'm glad we're working on this together. You're a good lawyer, Naina, but more than that, you're a good person."

A warm feeling coiled low in her belly, slowly creeping up her arms and into her chest, where her heart thumped loud enough to ring in her ears. People in the legal field had called her a good lawyer countless times. Her professors, her colleagues, her bosses—even Kumble, on occasion—but no one had thought to compliment her values over her accomplishments before. She swallowed. "I . . ."

"See you around." Grinning, Tejas turned and walked back to his cubicle at the other end of the office while Naina tried to stop her twitching lips from returning that grin.

Chapter FOURTEEN

Goa, May 2025

NAINA'S ANTI-HONEYMOON CHECKLIST

8. Go skinny-dipping. ✓

Tejas pushed Naina against the glass balcony door, rattling it, his mouth moving hard and fast against hers. Her cold fingers moved to unbutton his shirt as her tongue flicked over his lower lip. He let out a moan, his hand lifting up the hemline of her short skirt, and she broke their kiss to shush him.

A week had passed since they'd started working on the list, and Naina had decided today's agenda was to check off the ninth item. Tejas had had sex outside of a bedroom plenty of times, but it was Naina's first time doing anything as "scandalous" as this—her words, not his—and though Tejas had suggested doing it in the bathroom of a pub or on the beach, she'd decided the balcony of their second-floor room was a safer bet. She told him it was "exposed" enough for the wild side of her she was slowly reclaiming without being so dangerous as to get them in trouble with the law.

"We have to be quiet," she reminded him as he pressed kisses along her neck. "It's barely dinner time, so people must still be awake."

"It's Goa," he replied, grinning when she gasped at his hand sliding in between her legs. "I guarantee nobody's counting on us to be quiet."

"I'd like to see you try anyway," she teased, clapping a hand to Tejas's lips, even as her head pushed farther back into the balcony door. He kissed her hand and took her fingers in his mouth, licking and sucking until she moaned louder than him.

"Condom," she breathed, tugging his jeans down, and he complied, pinning her against the balcony door and filling her up as her eyes rolled back.

When they finally pulled apart, both of their chests heaving, Naina's shoulders went slack, and she whooshed out a breath. "My God, why haven't I done that before?"

"Wrong timing, wrong guy," Tejas said, pressing a kiss to her forehead before he could stop himself. Hopefully, that didn't feel as romantic to Naina as it did to him.

Naina smiled, but it didn't reach her eyes. "Maybe," she said, then adjusted her skirt and went back inside their room. With a silent sigh, Tejas followed her, his mind whirling with thoughts.

Honestly, seven days into this trip, Tejas had finally gotten used to his new routine: Wake up alone on the bottom bunk after a night of great sex; say good morning to Naina, who was always scrolling through her phone on the top bunk; fuel up with Aleksy's delicious breakfast; spend the entire day with the gang drinking, dancing, and exploring Goa; come back to the room and worship every inch of Naina's body; and . . . repeat.

There was just one thing that frustrated him. He knew the individual bunk beds weren't exactly spacious enough to accommodate both his and Naina's long limbs, but he wished he could wake up with her in his arms at least one morning. Maybe he'd ask her about it again soon.

They met up with the gang for their dinner reservation at one of the best sea-facing nightclubs in town. At the club, while Raziya and Naina headed to the ladies' bathroom to touch up their makeup, Jonah shifted his chair closer to Tejas's, his voice conspiratorial as he said, "So? How's it going with Naina?"

Tejas swirled the ice around in his whiskey sour, not meeting Jonah's gaze. "Great progress on the list, if that's what you mean."

Aleksy's laughter boomed. "Man, anyone with eyes can see how you look at her. You're catching feelings, aren't you?"

"No," Tejas snapped, more defensively than needed. "It's just . . ." He hesitated, then told them about Naina's sleeping habits. "She's already told me she's not ready to wake up next to me, which is fair, except it makes me feel like a never-ending booty call."

Jonah and Aleksy exchanged glances. "But isn't that what you are?" Aleksy asked.

"I mean, it's difficult to keep things casual for some people," Jonah intoned, gesturing to himself. "I've never been good at it."

"Me neither," Tejas started, but Jonah went on.

"And maybe casual is just Naina's style?"

Tejas gritted his teeth. "But she said she's never had a fling before. Maybe," he wondered aloud, "she gets really hot at night and can't go to bed cuddling. It's just that she always waits till I'm asleep to climb into the top bunk. I wish she'd . . ."

"Look, Tejas," Jonah said as he took a big gulp of his beer. "You agreed to this weird rule. If you've changed your mind and aren't okay with it, tell her instead of overthinking so much."

Tejas was silent for a moment, mulling over Jonah's words. Then he said, "So I should tell her I want more?"

"Do you think you're ready for more, though?" Aleksy tutted. "You've both had terrible and awfully recent breakups. This is the time to be alone, heal your wounds, and look inward, not assume you have feelings for her just because the sex is fun."

"As much as I relate to you, Tejas," Jonah said, "I have to agree with Aleksy. I tried the casual route with the last guy I dated." His face darkened. "It . . . was a disaster. I've never been that heartbroken."

Aleksy slung an arm around Jonah and kissed his forehead. "But you found me, so it was all worth it, right?"

Jonah hummed in agreement, then turned to Tejas. "Based on what little we've gathered about Naina, it's clear she's here just for her list agenda. Keep your feelings in check, yeah?"

Tejas swallowed as Naina and Raziya walked toward the table. "Yeah," he said quickly. "Got it."

His friends were wrong. Tejas didn't have feelings for Naina. It was a simple crush, brought on by their proximity and Naina's mesmerizing beauty. But they'd clocked one thing: He couldn't let this crush turn into something more. He had come to Goa with a broken heart, after all. No way would he leave this place with his heart in the exact same condition.

"What were we talking about?" Raziya asked when she sat down.

Jonah coughed. "Oh, uh . . ."

Thankfully, the waiter appeared, giving them the perfect distraction: food. Goan-style lobster, fish curry, vegetable xacuti, and a chicken tikka platter, all waiting to be devoured. Naina sat beside Tejas, one hand on his thigh as she dived into her fish curry and rice. Her cheeks were still flushed, though Tejas didn't know whether it was from the sex, the humidity, or her makeup. Maybe all three.

The gang talked about their plans for the next week. Jonah and Aleksy were going skydiving, and Raziya, who had been to Goa twice before, gave them suggestions on the best places to dive from.

"You wanted to do something adventurous for your list, right?" Aleksy asked Naina as he tore off a piece of malai chicken tikka with his teeth. "Skydiving's pretty adventurous."

Naina chewed her food, thinking. "I'm not sure I want to jump off a plane," she said, "but Tejas and I can figure something else out."

Tejas smiled; Jonah's gaze immediately went to him, and he shook his head ever so slightly. The message was clear: *Don't you dare jump to conclusions*. Tejas tried not to roll his eyes and returned his attention to the delicious lobster on his plate.

Close to the end of their meal, by which time they'd all had at least three drinks, the DJ played Naina's favorite pop song, and she dragged Tejas onto the dance floor.

Laughing, he shuffled his feet to the beat while she threw her hands in the air and swung her hips, not a care in the world. Tejas grinned goofily at the sight. Naina had said the list was about finding her way back to her old self, and it was evident that she'd succeeded. This woman was a free bird; she was brave, beautiful, and most of all . . . happy.

And some of that happiness was because of Tejas.

Just as the others joined them on the floor, Tejas's phone buzzed from his pocket. His blood turned cold when he saw the text message from Rahul.

Tejas hadn't texted his ex-boyfriend back since Rahul had last reached out. In fact, Tejas had taken the extra step of unfollowing Rahul on social media so those dreamy honeymoon photos wouldn't be all up in his face. Was that what he wanted to talk about now?

Frowning, Tejas read the text message.

Rahul

hey man. look, I miss you, and I don't think what you're doing is fair. we have history as best friends and it's not ok for you to dismiss that simply because I'm married now. why don't we get on a call sometime?

Tejas's eyes narrowed even as his stomach clenched. Who was Rahul kidding? "Best friends"? Besides, after how he'd treated Tejas, that man was owed nothing.

"Hey." Tejas looked up at Naina, whose eyes flicked between him and the phone. "You okay?" she said.

"I will be," he replied, squeezing her shoulder. With a sour mood and a dull ache in his heart, he blocked Rahul everywhere—Instagram, iMessage, even LinkedIn—adamant that he would never, ever let that vile man into his life again.

When his gaze met Naina's—concerned, worried, *caring*—his resolve to let things with Rahul die strengthened. Rahul was his past; who knew what the future held for Tejas?

"Do you want to talk about it?" Naina asked as she put her hands around Tejas's shoulders and moved her body to the pulsing music.

Tejas put his phone inside his pocket and wound his arms around Naina. "I can't answer that without breaking our rule."

She leaned into his chest as tendrils of her long brown hair brushed along his skin, leaving gooseflesh in their wake. "Fine. Then break it."

He pulled away, his eyes wide. "Wait, what?"

Shrugging, Naina patted the side of her purse, as if checking for something, then said, "Follow me."

They stepped outside the club, closer to the sea, where it was relatively quieter with just the sounds of gushing waves, chirping crickets, and the occasional group of people walking by.

Naina pulled him to a more secluded corner and took out a rolled joint, a lighter, and an ashtray. "Aleksy got me this earlier," she explained. "I've never smoked pot before, so I thought we could do it together. It'll count toward the one item on the list."

Tejas's insides nearly turned to mush. "Sounds good," he said, then lit the joint and gave it to her. He paused, waiting for her to take a puff, but she only turned the joint around in her fingers, confused.

Finally, she stammered out, "Uh, can—can you show me how to do it?"

Laughing, Tejas demonstrated how to take a puff, then exhaled a cloud of smoke, his shoulders sinking. God, he hadn't smoked pot in a decade, but this . . . this was what he'd needed today. He tapped the joint on the edge of the tray to get the ashes out, then gave it back to Naina. "Now you try."

She hesitated, then lifted the joint to her lips and drew in the smoke. Seconds later, she exhaled, coughing up a fit. Tejas rubbed her back until she resurfaced, giggling. "This is such a weird feeling." She took another puff, more measured and slow this time, then she exhaled, smiled, and turned the joint over to him.

They made small talk as they smoked, chatting absently about the weather, how much Naina missed her best friend and her dad, and the remaining items on the list. Mid-conversation about what they might do for the more vague "adventurous" and "extravagant" items, Tejas paused when he heard music pouring out from the club: a sped-up remix of an old Bollywood song about first love. One of his favorites, in fact.

"God, I love this song." He put out the joint on the tray, set it aside, then held out his hand and beckoned her closer. "Will you dance with me, my fair lady?"

She rolled her eyes exaggeratedly but wrapped her arms around his shoulders. They swayed together, foreheads touching, her lips brushing over his stubble, somehow driving him crazy and soothing his nerves at the same time, until the five-minute song ended.

When the next song came on, Naina frowned, facing him. "So . . . are you feeling relaxed enough to talk about what's bothering you?"

"I am, thanks," Tejas said, planting a kiss on her forehead as she smiled lazily. Then he hesitated, his eyes raking over her face. Could he trust her not to be weird about his sexuality? Biphobia ran rampant even in queer circles, and as far as he knew, Naina was straight.

"I don't know how you'll react to this." He hesitated, then leaned against a tree, his eyes on the dark sky. "My reason for this trip was a breakup, just like you . . . with an ex-boyfriend."

When Naina didn't say anything, he took a deep breath and willed himself to look at her, afraid of what he might see—but his mouth fell open. She was blank-faced, her arms folded. "Okay, go on," she said.

He did a double take. "This—this doesn't bother you?"

A small laugh bubbled out of her lips. "Why should I care if you also date men? I know you like women"—she blushed—"and all that matters is you make me feel good. *Really* good."

Tejas heaved a sigh of relief and clutched his chest. "Thank God. Anyway, here's what happened." He summarized the devastation that was his relationship with Rahul, from start to finish, and by the end of his soliloquy, Naina was scowling.

"So he doesn't even care that you asked for space?" she exclaimed, fuming. "It's bad enough that he threw away your relationship to appease society, but to act like he didn't do you dirty? To expect you to still be his friend despite the shit he pulled? What an . . . asswipe!"

Tejas burst out laughing, his melancholy dissipating slowly but surely. "Naina Stark, did you just call him an 'asswipe'? I haven't heard anyone say that since middle school."

She chuckled. "But he is one, isn't he?"

"He definitely is." *And you're amazing,* he almost said out loud, then remembered that this thing between him and Naina was supposed to be a fling and nothing more. So instead, Tejas pulled her into his arms, planting kisses onto her cheeks while she giggled. Then, with her face still pressed into his neck, he said, "I bet it's been rough for you too. I'm here if you want to vent about your ex."

Naina took a deep breath, fiddling with the empty spot on her ring finger. "I met him during my senior year internship. And I'd dated before, but Santhosh was my most serious relationship. We both had the same job, the same level of ambition . . . and after my parents got divorced because they wanted different things, I thought Santhosh and I, being alike, made sense." Her voice broke, and she looked up at him, her eyes shining. "So I compromised, even when I didn't want to, like not singing duets with other men at karaoke, or putting off work when he wanted to spend time with me. He was so insecure that he'd rather have seen me fail at my job than be better than him at it."

Tejas's heart sank as he wiped away the first tear, then the second. "I'm so sorry," he said.

She breathed out loudly. "Sometimes I wonder if I only stayed with Santhosh for so long because I didn't want my father to see me go through a breakup. The divorce was so rough on him, and he liked Santhosh—probably because I never told him about the red flags until it all came crashing down."

"Sounds like you and your dad are close." Tejas put his hand on her wrist, his touch hot. "Are things okay with your mom, though?"

"She's why I love karaoke so much. She used to sing at weddings and parties, so I grew up with music all around me, and that stayed with me even after their divorce. I don't talk to her much now. She lives in America, singing backing vocals for a bunch of musicians. She's got her dream life. I wish we could have been part of it, but c'est la vie, right?"

"My parents are blissfully in love, which is probably why I'm such a romantic," Tejas said, laughing, "but neither my sister nor I speak to them anymore."

Naina sucked on the inside of her cheek. "Really? Why?"

"They didn't support my sister's divorce when her arranged marriage fell through. They gave her the age-old 'marriage is sacred' speech, said she was a bad person for walking away for very valid reasons and that they never wanted to see her again. So I cut them off. I mean"—he shrugged—"they probably would have disowned me after they found out I'm bi anyway. Might as well get it over with."

"That sounds horrible," Naina said. "I can't imagine having to go no-contact with both my parents. After my mom left, I helped my dad through it, and he did the same for me after my engagement ended. He's my lifeline." She sniffled, then wiped her nose on her hand. "Sorry. I don't usually cry. Must be the alcohol."

"Don't be sorry." He pressed her free hand to his lips. "Besides, you look beautiful even when you cry."

She let out a chuckle. “Thanks. Anyway, want to go someplace else that’s distracting and fun?”

He rubbed the back of his head, hoping she didn’t mean their bedroom again. As much as he enjoyed having sex with her, he loved just spending time with her more. “Uh, where?”

She grinned, a genuine, childlike smile that was so infectious he smiled back, and then she said, “Ever tried drunk karaoke?”

Chapter FIFTEEN

Bangalore, October 2026

That weekend, Naina waited for Anil at their favorite bar in town, Madeira, where their usual booth was thankfully free. Madeira was the designated watering hole for most lawyers at AKC, with its dim lighting, loud music, and fantastic beer on tap—especially on the weekdays, when the bar hosted karaoke night from five P.M. through midnight. Since it was Saturday night, the place was packed, rock music playing on the speakers, and Naina spotted three trainee lawyers and one paralegal from AKC sitting on the other side of the establishment. She smiled and lifted her hand in greeting, and they waved without smiling back, then returned to their conversation in lower voices, shifting their chairs closer to each other.

Naina let her arm fall limply to her side. She'd worked with them on several cases, and though she had never yelled at them like Kumble or Dhanush often did, she knew she was a tough boss with high expectations, and that was enough to make any woman unlikable, right?

Anil chuckled as he slid into the booth across from Naina. "Don't take it personally. They don't like any of the junior associates."

She frowned. "Didn't you do karaoke with them last week?"

"Correction: They don't like any of the junior associates who are good at their job."

Anil had only become a lawyer because his father wanted to see someone in the family get through law school and fulfill the dreams he could never achieve. Anil now lived with his ajji—his grandma—whose culinary skills he'd inherited while his parents tended to their vegetable farm in the suburbs. He hated working at AKC and would rather start a catering business with Ajji's authentic South Indian recipes, but the only thing his family wanted for him was a stable career in law and, of course, a wife and two kids.

Neither Ajji nor Anil's parents knew he was gay. He'd never brought a girl home to his family, but most people in India didn't do that unless they were ready to get married. Coupled with how Anil was perceived as masculine, well-built, and "straight-passing" based on the average person's stereotypes about queer people, nobody—not even the meddlesome matchmaking aunties he had for neighbors—had speculated about his sexuality.

At this point, Anil had made his peace with never giving his parents a daughter-in-law, but he'd told Naina once that he didn't want to disappoint them on the career front too. Naina thought him being true to himself wasn't disappointing anyone, but he never listened to her.

The server came over to their table, and they ordered their usual beers without even opening the menu. When the server left, Naina shook her head at her best friend. "Anil, you're not a bad lawyer. You just don't care for it."

Anil opened his mouth to speak when his phone rang on the table. The caller ID said DHANUSH KUMBLE. He bit his lip. "I should probably take this. It might be about that pro bono case we're doing."

"God, he won't even leave you alone on a Saturday!" Naina tutted. "Tell Dhanush you're not available today because you actually have a life, unlike him—or me."

He cracked a weak smile at that, then pressed the phone to his ear. "Hey, what's up?" he said, rolling his eyes at what Dhanush was saying. "Yep, I'll send it your way first thing Monday . . . no, I'm not working today." His lips thinned. "Because I don't get paid to work on the weekends. Look, we'll talk at the office."

Naina vaguely heard sounds of protest from Dhanush before Anil ended the call and shoved his phone back into his pocket. "I hate him," Anil seethed. "I hate all workaholics."

"Hey!" She glared at him, still smiling.

Anil bopped her on the head, his expression softening. "All right, you're the one exception."

"I really think you should ditch AKC and start catering," Naina said. "Your family loves your cooking. Hell, people at the office do too! They'd all understand if you changed career paths."

"Ajji would die of a broken heart, and besides"—Anil quirked a brow—"I can't risk losing my cushy paycheck to start a business."

"Get a loan—"

"Although given my shit show of a performance at AKC, things aren't looking good either way."

Naina tutted. "I'm sure it's fine."

"It's not fine, Nay." Anil ran a trembling hand along his face. "I've missed two deadlines this month, and given how much sway Dhanush has with his dearest uncle, Kumble will let me go unless I work really hard on this pro bono project."

He was probably right; Kumble had fired employees for far less before, but Anil didn't need confirmation from Naina. "I still think you should do what lights you up, and that's cooking," she said. "Once you get the catering biz up and running, Ajji will come around too. She's your grandmother; she'd want you to be happy more than anything else."

"Oh, she wouldn't care what I did or where I worked as long as I found myself a wife." He let out a low whistle. "And since that will never, ever happen, I'm stuck hating my job and dealing with this asshole." He gestured to his phone, which buzzed with another text from Dhanush about a financial report, judging by the short preview text.

"Here you go." The server appeared, setting their mugs of frothy beer in front of them before heading to the next booth.

"Ugh, give me a minute." Anil texted rapidly on his phone, grumbling under his breath about "goddamn workaholics."

Naina sipped her beer and looked around the room at the rest of the patrons, then stifled a laugh. A group of attractive young women sat at the bar, stealing glances at Anil in between whispers and giggles. Thank goodness his grandmother wasn't here or she would have shoved him in their direction before he could so much as take a sip of his drink.

Movement at the AKC lawyers' table caught her eye as a familiar voice rang through the pub. Naina's shoulders stiffened. Tejas, dressed in a bright yellow shirt and dark blue jeans, had just joined their co-workers, all of whom grinned and gestured for him to sit down. One trainee lawyer even thumped him on the back in greeting.

Anil, who'd noticed where she was looking, let out a low whistle. "Well, *he's* certainly not unapproachable."

Naina shot eye daggers at her best friend as she dug her nails into the table. "He's been at AKC for barely two weeks! How do they already like him?"

"Took you less time than that, from what I remember," Anil said nonchalantly, sipping his beer. When Naina scoffed, he added, "Oh, don't deny it. He's hot and funny and smart, and you raved about him every time we talked."

"Is that what happened the morning of my flight back?" Naina snapped.

Anil ran a hand through his short hair, at a loss for words. Then he smiled. "Nay, just because things ended badly in Goa doesn't mean they have to now. He's trying to make amends."

"Yes, but—" Her words were cut short when a warm hand squeezed her shoulder. Tejas bent down, his lips near her ear, the scent of his aftershave consuming her senses.

"Do you mind if we join your booth?" he said. "That table is a little cramped for all of us."

Naina turned to him; his lips were barely inches away. She blinked and faced Anil again, who was looking from her to Tejas in amusement. "Uh, but those guys never sit with us," she said, hiding her flushed face behind her beer mug.

Tejas straightened, his hands in his pockets. "And today, they will," he said. "Come on, scooch over."

She glanced toward their colleagues, who were whispering among themselves, no smiles in sight, but at least they weren't pointing pitchforks at her. "You could do with more friends," Anil reminded her when she looked his way.

"Okay," Naina said. She shifted to the far end of the eight-seater booth, and of course Tejas sat beside her. His thigh touching hers nearly burned a hole through her jeans, but she remained straight-faced as the others joined them. Awkward silence hung in the air while Tejas got himself a Budweiser, and Naina was grateful when Anil finally spoke up.

"Jennifer, I bet that, as Dhanush's paralegal, you know all his secrets," Anil said cheekily. "Care to share a few?"

Jennifer's wary eyes went to Naina, and she pursed her lips like she wasn't sure if Naina was trustworthy.

"I hate Dhanush as much as you all do; maybe even more," Naina offered weakly, and the whole table cracked a grin, including Jennifer.

Tejas lifted his hands in surrender. "Hey, speak for yourself. I don't hate him."

"Well, we don't *hate* him," one of the lawyers said, "but we're all scared of him. Working with him is like trying and failing to conquer Everest."

"Dhanush is just burned out and frustrated by work," Tejas replied, an eyebrow cocked. "He needs a long vacation, is all."

"What he needs," Jennifer said, lowering her voice, "is to get laid."

Naina drank more beer, sighing, and mumbled under her breath, "Who doesn't?"

She must not have been quiet enough, because her co-workers burst out laughing. Tejas, meanwhile, caught her eye and raised his beer bottle in cheers before lifting it to his mouth, his gaze not leaving hers. Naina licked her lips and tugged on the neckline of her top. Wow, it was getting hot in here.

The group moved on to ranting about their bosses, and Naina chimed in occasionally, encouraged by her colleagues' nods and smiles whenever she spoke. She sensed Tejas's eyes on her the entire time, his smile directed at her, and she felt the thick skin around her heart melting the slightest bit.

Maybe "friendly" wasn't such a bad idea, after all.

Chapter SIXTEEN

Goa, May 2025

NAINA'S ANTI-HONEYMOON CHECKLIST

3. Try any kind of drug. ✓
9. Have sex . . . outside of a bedroom. ✓

Naina led the way inside the karaoke bar, lifting her head and taking in the ambiance. A random guy was singing "Summer of '69" in a flat, robotic voice on the wide stage that towered over the rest of the crowded bar. The room was drenched in purple and red lighting with a bright spotlight shining over the amateur singer, and Naina's first thought, despite Tejas stiffening beside her, was *Finally, I'm home*.

Maybe it was because her mother was a singer who lived and breathed music and had infused that energy into Naina, but Naina knew that if she weren't a lawyer, she'd have ended up in the music industry too—maybe a backup vocalist like her mom, or a pop star who commanded the stage in a stadium of sixty thousand people.

Perhaps in another life. Naina snorted, then turned to Tejas to grab his hand, but he was frozen in place.

"Fuck no," Tejas said, his voice squeaky. "This is the stuff of nightmares."

Naina let out a loud scoff. "In the past week, you've done much worse."

"True, but—"

"But singing is what scares you?" She nearly cackled with laughter, pulling him over to the bar counter, since none of the booths and tables were empty. They sat down on the rickety wooden stools, and Naina grabbed the pen and sheets of paper from a box that said WHAT WILL YOU SING? "So. Pick your song."

Tejas did a double take as he shifted on the uncomfortable stool. "Wait, just me? Don't you want to sing something together?"

She sighed, considering it. Naina had never been a team player, and Santhosh had thought karaoke was "corny," so she rarely ever did duet sessions. In fact, whenever she did bring him to karaoke nights with Anil or the others at work, Santhosh would complain about the loud music and off-key singing all night. Come to think of it, it was a surprise Naina hadn't broken up with him then and there.

But hey, she was single now. She could do as she pleased. "Fine," she said, "but I'm warning you, I may end up hijacking our performance. I have really good stage presence."

"That would be great, thanks, since I've never done karaoke in my life." Tejas flagged down a rather attractive bartender. "Can we get two Heinekens, please?"

Naina tutted, then leaned forward toward the counter. "Ignore him. We'll have six shots of your special coconut feni."

"For only the two of you?" The bartender folded his tattooed arms. "It's a potent liquor, ma'am."

"I can handle it," she said, grinning at the bartender.

The bartender sized her up—his gaze fell to her off-the-shoulder top and the dip of her neckline—then smirked. "Is that so?"

Naina looked at Tejas from the corner of her eye and held back a laugh. He was glowering in his seat, his fists clenched. He cleared his throat and pulled on Naina's barstool, dragging her close enough for him to curl his arm around her waist protectively. Fuck, that was hot.

"*We* can handle it, like she said." Tejas gave the bartender a tight smile. "Six shots of feni."

Mumbling under his breath, the bartender headed to the other side to make their drinks.

"Prince Charming"—Naina placed a hand on Tejas's chest, gently tugging on the collar of his floral shirt—"are you . . . jealous?"

Tejas licked his lips as he drew circles on her upper thigh over the shorts she wore. "Maybe I just want everyone in this bar to know you're here with me."

Naina swallowed, her eyes dropping to his mouth. "Then maybe we should sing a duet, after all."

In a flash, Tejas took the pen and paper from the counter and handed them to her. "Great. Pick a song."

Tutting, Naina scribbled a song onto the piece of paper while the "Summer of '69" singer walked offstage to smattering applause from their fellow drunk patrons. The emcee called out the next person's name. As the woman sang the latest Sabrina Carpenter single in a reasonably good pitch, the bartender returned with Naina and Tejas's shots. He slammed them on the table and walked away without a word.

Tejas picked up a shot glass, chuckling, and clinked it with Naina's. "To doing karaoke together. And getting shit-faced drunk."

"Cheers." Naina downed one shot—the pungent, sharp taste of neat alcohol contrasted perfectly with the feni's coconutty, floral undertones—then the second shot, and then the third. By the time she and Tejas put down their glasses and cheered, her vision, already soft and shimmery from the drinks at the club, had turned hazy; her head felt lighter than it had in years.

As the room spun slowly, she put one hand on Tejas's knee to ground herself, and he frowned. "You okay? I hope it wasn't too much at once."

He's so caring. Naina beamed at him, then pulled him in for a kiss that he returned just as passionately. "I'm perfect," she breathed against his lips, then held up the piece of paper on which she'd written *"We Don't Talk Anymore" by Charlie Puth & Selena Gomez*. "I hope you know this one," she said as she passed it over to the emcee's assistant, who was walking around collecting requests. "Might be cathartic for both of us."

Tejas's lips puckered, but he only said, "Sounds like a plan."

The crowded bar had given Naina the impression that they'd have to wait a while for their turn at karaoke, but the emcee called them over three songs later. Normally, she'd have been thrilled, but Tejas looked like he was going to throw up as Naina followed him up the rickety steps to where the emcee was waiting.

"Listen," Tejas whisper-yelled, tugging on Naina's hand, "the last time I performed something was in high school, when I got booed offstage by my classmates. I don't think I can do this."

God, he was so cute when he was nervous. She smiled up at him. "*We* can do this . . . together," she reminded him. "I'll be right by your side, I promise."

Swallowing hard, he nodded. They accepted a microphone each from the emcee, who gave them a thumbs-up and hit play.

The song started with the guy's part right away, which Naina should have considered, because Tejas missed the first cue and cringed, apologizing while the emcee replayed the track from the beginning.

Naina squeezed his free hand with hers, reassuring him. Tejas's eyes zoomed in on the screen projecting the lyrics, and he finally sang.

His voice wavered and cracked, and he stumbled over the lyrics, but by the time he got to the chorus, people downstairs were singing and grooving along, much to Naina's relief. When it was her turn to sing, her fingers still wound around his sweaty palm, she took a deep breath and let it all out, the music coursing through her bones. The only thing that felt as good as being onstage and hearing people sing along in the crowd was winning a case for her clients. Karaoke night was exactly what she needed.

The background music swelled, and Naina pulled him closer, planting a kiss on his cheek. "Good job," she whispered.

A chuckle bubbled out of Tejas's lips, and when the final verse of the song ended, he mumbled "Th-thank you" into the mic and returned Naina's hug while the crowd below them cheered and applauded.

"Your first time?" the emcee asked, shaking hands briskly with Tejas.

He bit his lip. "Was it that obvious?"

Naina burst out laughing. They returned to their seats at the bar and ordered some feni-based cocktails, since the karaoke had sobered them up somewhat. "You were fantastic," Naina told him, rubbing his arms, which were riddled with goosebumps.

He put a hand to his heart and whooshed out an exhale. "Is it weird that I want to sing again, despite how nerve-racking it was to be onstage?"

"Weird? Not a chance." She squeezed his knee, which was warm through his jeans, before taking the first sip of her feni mojito. "As a karaoke fanatic, I think you should go for it. And"—she took another sheet of paper from the stack—"you should sing the song your asswipe classmates booed you for."

"Huh." Tejas held her gaze for a few seconds before nodding purposefully and grabbing the pen. "You're right. It's time."

Twenty minutes later, Tejas took an actual bow after not just singing but belting out the lyrics to "Boulevard of Broken Dreams," the spotlight shining bright over him. He looked so proud of himself, his smile no longer nervous or forced, and as he locked eyes with Naina and blew kisses at her, Naina's stomach fluttered with butterflies . . . and she wasn't sure if it was the feni or something else entirely.

Fuck. She gulped as Tejas walked down the stairs. *Rein it in, Naina,* she reminded herself. *This is just the alcohol talking. It can't be anything else.*

Naina went up to sing an angsty Olivia Rodrigo breakup song soon after, and despite Tejas's whoops and shouts from below the stage, as well as a flash of light from someone's camera, she didn't dare look down. She moved her hips, tossed her hair back, and walked around the stage like she owned it. No matter the weird feelings swirling in her belly, or the slurring of her words, she would use this performance to come back to reality. Love was a lie. Breakups were inevitable. And she had nobody to rely on but herself.

And tonight, she let herself have fun. Drank to her heart's content. She sang and danced while people cheered her on, and later she'd return to the hostel and fuck Tejas's brains out . . . without making it mean anything more.

Finally, Naina ambled over to her seat and flopped into it, her eyes blurry. She wiped a line of sweat along her upper lip. "Fuck, I'm so drunk," she said. "Walking down those stairs without tripping on my heels was the hardest thing I've ever done."

Tejas's brows wrinkled. "Let's get you some water. I think this qualifies as 'shit-faced drunk' enough for your list."

Naina nodded, pushing her almost-finished cocktail glass aside. She set her head down on the bar counter and smiled. "Mmm. Tonight was fun."

Tejas played with a lock of her hair and hummed along. "It really was. I can't believe we found a karaoke bar within walking distance of the hostel."

She let out a snort, then slowly straightened. "You're gonna laugh, but the main reason I decided to book the hostel was because it was near this karaoke bar."

"Why wasn't karaoke on the list, then?" Tejas asked, frowning.

"I do it every week back home," she replied, thinking back to her more memorable performances. "Skyfall" by Adele. "Dancing Queen" by ABBA. "Look What You Made Me Do" by Taylor Swift.

Tejas pulled her in for a kiss that tasted like feni and coconut and something fresh and quintessentially *him*.

Naina cracked a grin, feeling a surge of affection for him, then pecked him on the lips, then the nose, then his cheeks. “You’re so gorgeous, do you know that? I could look at you forever.”

He tossed his head back and laughed, a faint blush on his face. “You really *are* drunk. Come on.” He helped her up, and she grabbed her purse from the counter. “Let’s get you to bed after all that feni.”

“Mmm. I’d like that.” She tossed an arm around his shoulder, and as they walked back to the hostel, chatting, singing, and swaying to nonexistent music, Naina decided this vacation was better than any honeymoon she could have ever gone on with her ex.

Chapter SEVENTEEN

Bangalore, October 2026

Thankfully, Naina and Tejas's press release statement on Preethi's behalf, sharing her respect for Pai and acknowledging his loss to the film industry as a veteran actor/director, had pacified most of the gossip-hungry cinephiles and the paparazzi who'd assumed her silence meant guilt. Nobody liked the thought of saying it, least of all Preethi and Naina, but Tejas knew they had to put their own opinions aside and do what was best for the case. And it had worked: There were fewer anti-Preethi sentiments on social media now. But proving her innocence was far from over, and Tejas hoped speaking to key witnesses would help.

"Ready?" Tejas asked as he and Naina stood before the producer's front door. Wikipedia had said his last name was Gowda, but cinema fans and the media only ever referred to the fifty-year-old veteran actor-turned-producer by his fan-given name from his acting heyday: Superstar Jagannath. That wasn't the end of his résumé, since he was also making his foray into politics now.

"Ready," Naina said.

Tejas rang the doorbell, and seconds later, a short man dressed in white opened the door, bowing to them. "You must be the lawyers," he said, ushering them inside. Jagannath's house was a sprawling three-story mansion in Koramangala, one of the more expensive neighborhoods in Bangalore. Tejas had noticed the impressive front yard with a grand five-spout fountain in the center of a well-maintained rose garden, but nothing compared to the resplendent and regal interiors of Jagan Mansion. Four large chandeliers hung from the ceiling, sending sparkles of light dancing across the cream-colored walls. Sunlight streamed through the shimmery curtains over the French windows and the balcony, and the seven-seater couch faced a fifty-five-inch television. On the couch sat Jagannath and a woman who looked like she was in her mid-forties: his wife, Tharini, Tejas presumed.

"Hello, sir, ma'am," Naina said, folding her hands in namaste. "Thank you for agreeing to speak with us."

"It's my pleasure," Jagannath said gruffly, standing to shake their hands, though his tight grip and the frown on his face as he greeted Tejas said otherwise. He led them to the couch. "Please, make yourselves comfortable. Mani," he said sharply to the man who'd opened the door, "hurry up, make some coffee for our guests."

Once they'd sat down on the couch, Tejas smiled. "We're sorry to impose on your time, but we had a few questions about Rohith Pai's murder and what happened that night."

"Right, since I was the person who saw your client killing him," Jagannath said matter-of-factly. He manspreaded in his seat, his burly arms folded, like he was trying to assert his dominance and authority over them.

Nope. Tejas didn't like him one bit, and neither did Naina, clearly, because he caught her rolling her eyes as she took out her iPad, all set to take notes. Tejas simply kept his hands in his lap; he had a half-decent memory and believed a conversational approach was always better than an interrogative one in cases like these.

"How long had you known Rohith Pai?" Tejas asked.

"Decades," Jagannath replied. "We worked on a number of movies over the years, both while I was an actor and now as a producer. He was a masterful director."

"The morning of his death," Naina said, "did you notice anything off or weird between Pai and Preethi during filming?"

Before Jagannath could answer, a quiet, concerned voice sounded from the hallway. "What's going on?" A young woman stepped into the living room, looking at Naina and Tejas in confusion.

Jagannath stood, his eyes wide. "Sandhya, I thought I told you to stay in your room."

This must be his daughter, Tejas surmised. Twenty-one-year-old Sandhya Gowda, rumored to be making her acting debut in the Sandalwood film industry later this year, no doubt thanks to her good looks and, of course, her father's connections. She had been seen following Jagannath around on the sets of many of his films to get hands-on experience.

"Is this about Rohith's death?" Sandhya's brow wrinkled. "I knew him too, maybe I could answer any—"

"You shouldn't be involving yourself in these messy things," Jagannath said, scowling. He pointed toward the hallway. "Go to your room and don't come out until I say so."

Head bent, Sandhya meekly did as she was told.

"Sorry about that," Tharini said hastily once her daughter's footsteps had faded. "She really looked up to Rohith and his work, especially since our families are close, so she's been a little . . . affected by this case."

Jagannath's mustache quivered. "Let's focus on what I saw instead of going on these useless tangents," he said, steering the topic back to what they'd come here for. "It is what it is. I was enjoying a good night's sleep in my trailer after supervising a thirteen-hour shoot when I heard a woman's screams from the direction of Rohith's trailer."

"And the Krishnans' trailer too, right?" Tejas chimed in.

"Yes, that," Jagannath said, waving his hand in dismissal.

Naina paused, scrolling on her iPad. "Do you remember what time this happened?"

Jagannath let out a scoff. "No. Obviously I didn't think to check my watch. I simply rushed out to make sure everything was okay. And then . . ." He stiffened. "The trailer door was wide open, and I saw Preethi from the doorway, crouching beside a body. Rohith's body. I knew immediately what she had done; the guilt and shame were written all over her face." He shook his head disgruntledly.

Tejas nodded, as Naina jotted everything down. "And then what happened?" he asked.

"I yelled for help, and Gopal Krishnan showed up—our lead actor. He's always been quick on his feet. He dialed the emergency number. We decided to stay there so Preethi wouldn't be tempted to run, but she barely even looked our way until the cops arrived. She was just sobbing uncontrollably and hugging the body of the man she'd killed, like the good actor she is." Jagannath's face darkened with rage. "Despicable woman."

Tejas cleared his throat. They also needed to confirm what the maintenance worker had told them. "Was there anything else you noticed that might help us? Any tensions between Rohith and . . . anyone else that day?"

"Nothing of note." Jagannath shrugged. "Well, if that's all—"

"One more thing," Naina said, her eyes narrowing the slightest amount. "You're producing three other movies this year alongside Pai's, and you're also getting involved in politics, right?"

Jagannath's jaw tightened. "Yes. How is that relevant?"

"Producers don't always need to supervise filming on set, especially not when they're as busy as you," Naina said. "Was there any specific reason they needed you on location for such a small set?"

"I'm a very hands-on producer. Now, if you're done . . ." Jagannath rose, reaching forward to shake their hands. "My wife and I have some personal matters to attend to."

"Right," Tejas said, pursing his lips. They hadn't even had time for coffee yet. Why was he rushing them?

Jagannath escorted them to the front door. Just as he unlocked it, Naina stopped. "You said Gopal ran over to Pai's trailer to help you.

Where was his wife, Bina? She was on set too, as the assistant director, and I believe they were both sleeping in the same trailer?"

Jagannath gave a shake of the head. "No idea. I only saw her around once the cops arrived."

"Right. Thanks for your time."

Tejas and Naina stood by the street, waiting for the auto rickshaw that would take them to the Krishnans' residence in Richmond Town. "I can't tell if he's hiding something or if he's just an asshole," Naina said.

"Right?" Tejas laughed. "Also, good catch with Gopal's wife's absence. I wonder whether either of them could be potential suspects. If Gopal managed to hear Preethi's screams, being in the trailer closest to Pai's, wouldn't his wife have woken up too and rushed out with him?"

Their auto rickshaw arrived. Naina climbed in after Tejas, clenching her teeth. "Let's get some answers," she said.

GOPAL AND BINA KRISHNAN, IN stark contrast, welcomed them with pleasant smiles and even made small talk with them until their housekeeper brought out some coffee. Tejas had had three cups at the office already, a mandatory requirement to get through the mountain of work he had, even excluding this case; he was suddenly grateful Jagannath had driven them away before the coffee was ready. Any more coffee would have been overkill.

Gopal lamented about Rohith Pai's unexpected death and what a loss it was to the cinema industry for at least ten minutes while his wife nodded in agreement, her face ashen. Gopal's version of that night lined up exactly with what Jagannath had said. He made no mention of waking up his wife before rushing to Pai's trailer, either, but when Naina brought it up, Bina frowned, patting her husband's knee. "Oh, I take medication for insomnia, and I'm out for the night once I take it."

"Trying to wake her before morning would have been futile," Gopal said, nodding toward his wife. "I recognized the screams as Jagannath's and knew something must be wrong, too wrong for me to waste any more time."

Tejas leaned forward, resting his elbows on his knees. "But you didn't hear Preethi's screams?"

Gopal thought for a moment, biting his lip. Then he shrugged. "I might have, maybe that's what woke me up enough to hear Jagannath shouting. Honestly, I don't remember. It was a traumatizing night, and you see, trauma distorts the memory."

Tejas met Naina's dubious gaze. "Right," she said, then turned to Bina. "Ma'am, do you have anything else you'd like to add?"

Bina slurped the dregs of her coffee, then set the empty cup down. "No, I only woke up when my husband came back to update me on the series of events after the police arrived. How devastating. Thinking of Rohith's gruesome death makes me sick."

Tejas nodded slowly. There was one last thing to figure out, but he'd have to be cautious not to make the lead actor go on the defensive with his next question. "Were there any tensions or arguments on set that morning? Between Rohith Pai and Preethi, perhaps, or any of the other cast or crewmembers?"

Bina opened her mouth, then shut it when Gopal's hand pressed on her thigh. "I don't believe so," Gopal said, shrugging. "Like we said, Rohith's murder came as a ghastly shock to us all."

"All right." Tejas pinched the bridge of his nose. "I think that's all we had to ask. Naina?"

"That's all," Naina agreed. They thanked the Krishnans and returned to the office, not speaking about the case until they were inside the AKC building.

"Neither Jagannath nor the Krishnans had anything negative to say about Pai, despite what that worker said," Naina said, tapping her chin while they were in the elevator. "But if Gopal, who was in the trailer right behind the scene of the crime, didn't hear Preethi's screams, how did Jagannath? Or is he lying?"

"He's definitely trying not to make himself look suspicious," Tejas agreed. He checked his phone. "The forensic report came out while we were at the Krishnans' place. Let's go through it at our desks and update our document."

"Roger that," Naina said. The elevator doors opened, and they both started forward, nearly bumping shoulders. The familiar, delectable scent of Naina's lavender shampoo hit Tejas's nostrils, bringing back memories he really shouldn't recall at the workplace.

"I—I'm sorry, you first." Naina pressed her lips together and gestured for him to go ahead.

Tejas didn't miss the way her chest rose and fell under her pale blue silk shirt at that slight contact. "Thank you," he said. He slid past her, grazing her arm with his elbow on purpose, turning once to grin at the flushed color of her cheeks.

He plopped into his revolving chair in his cubicle and greeted Dhanush with "Good afternoon." Dhanush, who was on the phone and completely purple in the face, lifted his hand in a weak wave before returning to screaming at whomever was on the other end of the call. "Why can't you understand that this could fuck up the entire case? How can you misplace something as important as—" He scoffed. "Yeah. You'd better fix this."

"All good?" Tejas asked when Dhanush put the phone down and ran two shaky hands through his hair.

Was it a trick of the light, or were Dhanush's eyes glossy? "I—I don't know," Dhanush said, stammering. "Iqbal's been so busy with his other clients that he's asked me to take point on the Subramanian case, even though my own caseload is full already; and with all the media attention the embezzlement is getting, my phone has been blowing up nonstop with calls from journalists and the court and junior lawyers who can't do *anything right*!" His voice rose at the last two words, and he slammed his hand on his desk. "I can't fuck up again, or my uncle will fire me."

Tejas sucked on his teeth. "When was the last time you fucked up?"

"Last year," Dhanush said, his face paling. "The client's alibi was solid, but he told it to me in confidence because he wasn't . . . out of the closet yet, and he knew I was." His eyes turned sad. "His sports career would have tanked if people found out he was gay, and I of all people know how homophobic the world can be. So I—"

"You didn't tell anyone else the alibi?" Tejas guessed.

"And we lost the case." Dhanush looked down at his shoes, his eyes dampening more. "My uncle found out afterward that I kept the alibi to myself, and he yelled at me for hours. He said the only reason I even got the job here was because of him, and if he wanted to, he could fire me and make sure no law firm ever hired me again."

Tejas hesitated, then brought his chair closer to Dhanush's. "Look at me," he said, putting a hand on Dhanush's shoulder. "You're one of the best lawyers at AKC. Ask anyone at the office, and they'd agree with me."

Dhanush snorted. "Only because they're all afraid of me."

"Because they know how good you are at your job," Tejas affirmed. "Even Naina would testify to that. Although I do think if you yelled at people less, they might be willing to help you more."

"Makes sense." Finally, Dhanush let out a weak grin. "Thanks, Tejas."

Tejas thumped him on the back. "Don't let your uncle's threats scare you, all right? You're going to win this case."

Dhanush's eyes went to his phone. "You're right. I *am* going to win. I need to make some calls . . ." He returned to the phone, his words still stern and tense—though not outright mean—and Tejas smiled to himself as he checked his email for the forensic report. Dhanush would prove his uncle wrong and win his case; and Tejas and Naina would win theirs too.

Chapter EIGHTEEN

Goa, May 2025

NAINA'S ANTI-HONEYMOON CHECKLIST

6. Get shit-faced drunk. ✓

Tejas's shoulders sank with relief when he bumped into Naina outside the hostel bathroom the next morning around ten-thirty. She had fallen asleep in his arms minutes after they returned from karaoke last night, both of them drunk and exhilarated but also exhausted.

"Oh, you're here," he said, smiling. "I woke up and you weren't on the top bunk."

Naina clapped a hand to her forehead, and that was when Tejas noticed her slumped posture and the bags under her eyes. "I've been in the bathroom for a while," she said, her voice choked, probably from throwing up. "And my head is pounding. Hangovers are brutal when you're twenty-nine."

"I'm twenty-nine," Tejas said, spreading his arms wide, "and I feel perfectly fine."

Groaning, she shuffled past him toward their room, and he followed her, not caring that he had to pee. Naina paused when they were inside, looking from Tejas to the bed, then slid into Tejas's blanket on the bottom bunk. "Sorry, I don't have the strength to climb to the top bunk," she mumbled, her closed eyes scrunched up in pain.

He knelt down beside her to brush some hair off her cool forehead, and she let out a tired sigh. She didn't seem to have a fever, but the combination of beer and feni had definitely dealt some damage. "What about breakfast?" he asked her, keeping his voice soft.

Naina gave the slightest jerk of the head. "No energy. Can't go to the kitchen."

"But you won't have energy unless you . . ." His words trailed off when Naina's breathing slowed, her mouth slightly open as sleep took over. Sighing, Tejas kissed her cheek and straightened.

He brushed his teeth and took a quick shower, then beelined for the kitchen. Aleksy, Jonah, and Raziya were already at the table with one other tourist who was busy scrolling on his phone as he sat two chairs away from them. "Hey," Tejas said, eyeing their mostly empty plates. The sweet smell of maple syrup still hung in the air. "Pancakes today?"

"You just missed it." Aleksy wiped his hands on a tissue. "We finished off the batter."

"That's fine," Tejas said. He rummaged in the fridge for milk, bread, and some eggs, then lit one of the burners on the stove. "Naina's hungover, so I'm gonna make us some scrambled eggs. My sister says it helps when you're really out of it."

Jonah whistled; bits of pancake flew out of his mouth. "That's nice of you."

Raziya stood. "I could make them for you, Tejas. I'm on kitchen duty this morning."

"Nah, I'll do it." Tejas hummed as he broke four eggs in a bowl. "Naina and I had a little too much fun at karaoke last night. What did y'all get up to after we left?"

Aleksy chuckled. "Not too different from you. We got drunk off our asses and Raziya had to drive us back in our sorry state." He winced as she exaggeratedly rolled her eyes at him. "Thank you for putting up with us, Raziya."

Tejas laughed and focused on the stove. After he put the eggs and toast on two plates, he tuned back in to the gang's conversation as he wiped the countertops.

"This concert is gonna be incredible." Raziya gestured wildly, her face flushed with excitement. "I've wanted to attend some of these artists' live shows for years!"

Jonah rubbed his hands together. "Can't wait." Then he turned to Tejas, grinning at the breakfast-laden plates in his hands. "Meet us in the lobby around three. Raziya got passes to an EDM sun-downer concert for all of us."

"It's a showcase of the best DJs from around the world," Raziya said, bright-eyed. "You can't miss it."

"Text me the details. We'll be there." Tejas nodded and shuffled out of the kitchen.

Naina was still asleep, her long, dark hair haphazardly strewn across her face and the pillow. The blanket was halfway down to the floor, barely covering the bottom of her legs. Tejas cursed. He kept the plates on the desk and pulled the blanket over Naina, hoping she wasn't cold. With the Goan summer heat, the air-conditioning was on full blast throughout the hostel.

Then he bent down and pressed a kiss to her forehead, letting his lips linger until she roused with a smile on her face. "Mm. Morning," Naina mumbled. She stifled a yawn, then sat up halfway, pressing a hand to her belly, which growled loudly. "Fuck. I missed breakfast, didn't I? It must be past noon—"

"Actually, I thought we could have breakfast in bed," Tejas said. He brought over the plates, not missing the gasp Naina let out as he joined her on the bottom bunk. It didn't sound like a gasp of delight as much as a gasp of confusion. "I'm not a great cook, and I don't cook all that often," he explained as Naina frowned, "but Astrid loves my scrambled eggs, though I make hers plain without any other ingredients, obviously, because she's a cat, and . . . Sorry, I'm rambling." He cringed. Was he overstepping? "I hope you like scrambled eggs?"

Naina nodded, not meeting his gaze, then slowly spooned some egg onto the bread and took a bite. The crunch was loud; it made her silence a hundred times more anxiety-inducing. She sank against the wall and finally grinned. "Oh my God, it's delicious. Thank you!"

"Of course." Tejas leaned back, mimicking her, and breathed a quiet sigh of relief.

Tejas got Naina a painkiller from the medicines she'd packed for the trip, hoping it would help her hangover. They talked as they finished breakfast and some more of Naina's homemade snacks, sitting cross-legged on the bunk bed, their knees comfortably touching. Tejas told her about the sundowner concert and how excited Raziya was for it. "She doesn't look like an EDM lover at first glance," he said, chuckling. "I guess appearances can be deceiving."

"She's pretty cool," Naina agreed. She got up to set their empty plates aside, then crawled right back into bed, putting her head in Tejas's lap. He stroked her hair, enjoying the moment, until she spoke. "You didn't have to make breakfast for me."

His heart leaped into his throat. "I know, but I didn't want you to miss it," he said hastily. "The kitchen gets super-crowded later in the day."

"Right, of course." Naina shifted slightly, curling into a fetal position with Tejas's fingers still in her hair. "When's the concert?"

Tejas checked his phone for the details Raziya had sent. "It's an hour's drive, so they want to leave around three."

She pressed a hand to her forehead, groaning. "I hope my headache goes away by then. That bartender wasn't lying when he said feni is a potent liquor."

"I'm sure it is, you lightweight," he said, pinching her cheek until her face melted into a smile. "Don't worry, you'll be fine."

♡♡♡

Three hours later, Tejas leaned against the doorframe, shaking his head worriedly as Naina popped another painkiller. Her headache had only gotten worse after a walk around the neighborhood. The fresh, breezy air was no match for the scorching sunlight and humidity.

"I'm gonna skip the concert and go back to sleep," Naina said morosely. She climbed into the bottom bunk and flopped onto the bed, burritoing into Tejas's blanket. "Take tons of videos to show me, okay?"

Tejas swallowed as he contemplated his options. A sundowner concert sounded fun, but he'd never liked EDM enough to go someplace just for the music. He enjoyed hanging out with the gang, but he liked Naina's company more. How could he have a fun evening when he knew she was unwell and exhausted?

"I'll be fine," Naina promised, a forced smile on her lips. Tejas could tell the difference by now; her nose crinkled when she smiled for real. "Go, get ready," she insisted when he didn't move. "You don't want to make the others wait too long."

Tejas nodded slowly. "Right, yeah. Sleep tight. I'll be right back." Hands in his pockets, he walked to the lobby, where Raziya was already sitting on the tiny couch. She must have clocked his worried face, the ratty old T-shirt and faded sweatpants he wore, and of course, Naina's absence. She stood, sighing. "You can't make it?" she said, pouting.

"I'm sorry." He hung his head. "I don't want to leave Naina alone in case she needs me."

Raziya nodded slowly. "Take care of her, all right?"

"Thanks. Well, I'm off." He saluted at her, then waltzed back to room 202. Naina was asleep again, snoring softly every few seconds. She didn't rouse as the door creaked to a close. Tejas turned off the lights and changed into cargo shorts. He tucked his wallet in his pocket and headed outside into the stifling afternoon heat. Smiling, he opened Google Maps, typing in "party decoration store near me," and browsed through the results.

If Naina couldn't come to the concert, he'd bring the concert to her.

♡ ♡ ♡

THE SUN HAD ALMOST DIPPED into the horizon, drenching the streets in shades of orange, by the time Tejas returned to the hostel, holding one large bag of supplies in his hands. "Excuse me," he mumbled as he shuffled toward his room past other tourists who milled about the staircase. Then he paused, turning to address the group at large. "Hey, do any of you have Bluetooth speakers?"

Back in the room, Naina hadn't stirred at all. Tejas touched her forehead—no abnormal temperature. *Good,* he thought, then returned to the large bag he'd dumped by the door. It was time to turn this place into a concert floor. Before he opened Spotify on his phone, he looked through his camera gallery. He'd sneakily taken a picture of Naina at karaoke night. Maybe he shouldn't have, but she looked so happy, he couldn't help it.

It was time to make her even happier.

Tejas smiled, sneaking peeks at Naina in between decorating the room. He shut the curtains, strung the color-changing lightbulbs on the wall, and plugged in the rotating disco ball he'd hung by the door. He'd already connected his phone to the speaker he borrowed from the Russian tourist in room 207. Tejas put his hands on his hips and took in the space. The bulbs cast the room in delicate colors—blue, purple, pink, yellow—and refracted against the silver disco ball, scattering light across the space. He tapped play on Spotify and soft music poured out of the speakers.

"Naina?" Tejas whispered, easing her out of sleep. "You've been asleep for a bit. Wanna wake up?"

"Oh . . . yeah, it's probably late . . ." Naina sat up and stretched, her eyes still half shut as she yawned. Tejas waited with bated breath for her to notice. She blinked, then said, "Why didn't you go to the—wait. Fuck." Slowly, she stood and walked around the room, taking in the disco ball and the lights strung along the entire periphery of the room. A few seconds went by, and she said nothing.

As Tejas scrambled to join her by the desk where he'd put the speakers, she asked in a small voice, facing away from him, "You did all this?"

"I did. I wanted to bring the concert to you. With soft music, since you have a headache, and anything louder might make it worse . . ." He paused, realizing he was rambling again, then pulled her closer so her back was pressed against his chest. Winding both arms across her shoulders, he kissed the top of her head. "Are you feeling better?"

Naina didn't speak. Slowly, Tejas nudged her around, expecting the worst—anger? annoyance? dismissal?—but no, she had tears in her eyes. She started to wipe them away, but Tejas stopped her by running his fingers down her cheeks, then he kissed where they had traced. "What are you thinking?" he whispered.

Naina's lower lip trembled. She cupped his face, leaning closer so their foreheads touched. "Where did you come from, Tejas?" she breathed before covering his mouth with hers.

Fuck, he thought as he kissed her back. *She said "Tejas." Not "Prince Charming."* Adrenaline rushed through his veins—or was it serotonin, or oxytocin, or whatever hormone made people feel on top of the world? He bit her bottom lip, then grazed the spot with his tongue as she moaned against the kiss. Her hands went to his back, tracing shapes along the side, and his muscles clenched at her cool touch. Seconds later, Naina was the one to pull away. She burrowed her face into his shirt and said, her voice muffled, "I'll never forget you."

Tejas's own eyes misted. He swallowed the pebble forming in his throat and hugged her tighter. "Me neither," he whispered.

Chapter NINETEEN

Bangalore, October 2026

Naina's laptop lay open in front of her, but her attention was elsewhere. On Tejas and Dhanush, to be precise, who were having some sort of intense conversation at their cubicles across the room.

It seemed the two men had developed a real friendship over the past few weeks. Or was there more to it? Tejas was bi, and Dhanush had been out for years. When Tejas thumped his hand against Dhanush's back, almost in an affectionate "I'm proud of you" way, Naina tasted something sour in her mouth and swiveled her chair to the front. *Why should I care? Tejas can date whoever he wants*.

If only she could talk to Anil about this, but he was still off on his lunch break, and knowing him, he wouldn't be back for a while.

Chiding herself, she refreshed her email and went through the forensic report. It confirmed everything they already knew: The meat knife used to kill Rohith Pai was from the small kitchenette in his trailer, Preethi's fingerprints and DNA linked her to the crime scene, Rohith died sometime between eleven-thirty P.M. and one A.M., and his text conversation with Preethi happened a little before twelve, which was sufficient time for an argument or altercation to have happened between them before he got stabbed. *Shit*.

Then she read the next line: There were signs of struggle, like a blow to Rohith's face and mild injuries to his windpipe, and the force of the knife attack indicated the killer was likely bigger or stronger than Rohith.

"Yes," she breathed. Sure, Preethi was tall and muscular with a strict workout regimen, but could she have overpowered Rohith Pai enough to choke him, hit him, and stab him to death? As far as biology went, men were usually stronger than women, so this could work in their favor . . .

Naina opened her shared document with Tejas and typed in the findings, grinning from ear to ear. She'd just finished sending him an update on Teams when Dhanush stormed up to her, his jaw clenched. "Where the hell is your best friend?"

Her eyes went to the adjacent desk and Anil's laptop, which was in sleep mode. "How would I know?" she retorted. "I'm not his mother, and he's not a child."

"I hate working with him," Dhanush said, continuing his rant as he paced in front of Naina's desk. "He leaves the office at six every evening, his lunch breaks are over an hour long, and he takes at least twenty minutes to reply to one email."

Naina's head hurt. As much as she wanted to jump to Anil's defense, all of those things were true and generally considered unacceptable at AKC. "Did you try calling him?" she asked, forcing her eyes onto her own laptop.

Dhanush shoved his phone toward Naina, and she reluctantly looked at the text message exchange.

Dhanush

Where are you??? Pick up the damn phone

Anil

Late lunch, since I was busy replying to your 500 emails

Also FYI, I don't pick up phone calls unless I'm given prior notice

The fuck?! We're doing a case together, of course I'm gonna call you!

Aww you're so obsessed with meeee

If only the feeling was mutual . . .

"Well, that's Anil for you," Naina said, trying to keep a straight face but failing.

"Don't laugh," Dhanush snapped. "Tell your best friend to get his act together, or I'll tell my uncle what's going on."

Naina pinched the bridge of her nose, her stomach roiling. "I have to get back to work, Dhanush."

"That makes two of us," he grumbled, walking away with his hands on his hips.

Anil returned a few minutes later, looking forlorn. When Naina asked him where he'd been, he sighed. "Uh, I was at the bank . . . for a loan."

"Oh my God," Naina said, lowering her voice so nobody else would hear. "For your business?"

He swallowed. "Yeah. I thought about what you said earlier and decided to go for it."

"Why didn't you tell me?"

"I was going to surprise you and my grandmother with the news after the bank processed the loan, but they ended up denying my application." He shook his head. "Apparently, there are too many catering businesses in Bangalore, and mine didn't stand out enough."

Naina cursed under her breath, then lifted a finger. "Wait, you could ask Appa for help. He worked at the bank for nearly thirty years, and his colleagues owe him a bunch of favors."

Anil smiled ruefully, though it didn't reach his eyes. "Thanks, Nay. I might take you up on that."

"By the way, Dhanush was here a while ago," Naina added, swiveling back to face her desk, "ranting about how much he hates working with you."

"He's insufferable," Anil complained. "I can't wait to get out of this place."

She hesitated, thinking about the texts on Dhanush's phone, then asked, "He showed me your messages. Were you flirting with him, or was I sensing a vibe that doesn't exist?"

"Flirting with *that* man?" Anil scoffed from behind her, though his voice was a pitch higher than usual. "He'd probably be too clingy for my taste. You know I like the chase."

Naina's lips turned up. "You're really toxic, you know that?"

"And proudly so," he said, the clacking of his keyboard loud. "Are you still playing hard to get with Tejas?"

That wiped the smile off her face. "I'm not playing anything with him," she said quickly. "We might have history . . ."

"And chemistry," he prodded.

"Yes, that," she agreed reluctantly as she read through a report, "but we're colleagues, and no way am I changing that equation. Although I might be warming up to his existence. He's . . . a good lawyer."

Anil snorted. "This is a development I can get behind."

"This will be the only development," she said, giving him a sideways glance. "Now get to work, you."

"On it," he replied, returning to his laptop.

Naina's Teams chimed with a message while she was answering emails about another one of her cases.

Tejas

Added my own notes to the document re: the forensic report.

We make a good team, huh? ☺

She bit her lip, then typed back, a small smile on her face, Yeah. We do, actually.

"Not only did you come home from work on time," Appa said, huffing and puffing as he brisk-walked on the treadmill, "but you've been smiling ever since? Who are you and what have you done with my daughter?"

Naina chuckled from the cycling machine beside Appa's treadmill. It was nine P.M., and they were at the small gym in the basement of their apartment building. Naina usually got her workouts in early every morning while Appa did yoga at home, but the forensic report had her energized and restless enough for a second gym session with her father, who definitely could benefit from light cardio given his age. "It was a good day at work," she told him. "I think we're making some real headway on the case."

"We?" Appa slowed the treadmill as he grinned. "Care to finally tell me about this mysterious new colleague of yours?"

"It's just some guy, Appa," Naina grumbled, turning her face away so he wouldn't see her reddening cheeks. "He's a good lawyer. Let's leave it at that."

"Is he single?"

She scoffed. "I have no idea," she lied.

"Then he's either single or a cheater," Appa said wisely. "A taken man who loves his woman would rave about her to every single person he met."

Naina let out a sigh. "Good to know. How about we talk less and exercise more? You're sixty-two, Appa, you need to be active."

"Nice job changing the topic. We'll discuss this later." Laughing, Appa turned up the speed setting on the treadmill and resumed his jog.

Once Naina finished twenty minutes on the cycling machine, she went to the free weights section while Appa did his evening stretches in front of the mirror. She was on her second set of biceps curls when her phone chimed. Who was texting her after office hours? Did Anil want to grab a drink?

She put the weights aside and pulled her phone out of her leggings pocket.

Tejas

Hey 😊

Tejas is typing . . .

Despite their history, this was Tejas's first ever text message to Naina outside of Teams. She cleared her throat and snuck a peek at Appa to make sure he was still busy with his hip-opening stretches. Her eyes fell on her reflection in the mirror. The pink of her flushed face was most definitely because of the grueling workout and not Tejas's name on her phone. Yep. No doubt about it.

What was he typing? Did he want to meet? Was this a "you up?" text? No, it was barely nine-fifteen. It was too early for a booty call, but then again, what did Naina know? Maybe Tejas went to bed early on work nights.

Her thumbs hovered over the screen as she debated what to text back. "Hey" with the same smiling emoji, "Hey" with a period, or "Hey" with an exclamation point? She didn't want to copy the emoji, but an exclamation mark would be too much excitement, and a period would be too distant. "Why am I overthinking this?" she mumbled to herself. "Just say anything, you fool."

Naina

Hey, what's up?

I think we should talk to some of the crew who were on set that day. Iqbal said he could arrange a meeting with the makeup artist and Jagannath's PA tomorrow afternoon, you in?

"Huh," Naina said. So this was about work, not . . . a booty call. Good. That was how their relationship ought to be anyway. Strictly professional. Sounds like a plan, she texted back. See you at the office tomorrow

See you! 😊

Another emoji? This man had too much sunshine in him. Naina bit back a laugh, put her phone aside, and returned to her workout, keeping her focus on the weights in her hands and not that adorable smiling emoji that looked far too much like Tejas's cheerful grins.

Chapter TWENTY

Goa, May 2025

While the others had decided to give skydiving a shot, Naina and Tejas had done their research and decided cliff diving was the way to go—and, to make things a little more adventurous, Tejas suggested exploring Goa and picking a cliff that called out to them.

"What does that even mean?" Naina asked, laughing as she wrapped a sarong over her red two-piece swimsuit, right below her eye tattoo, and closed the cupboard door.

It took Tejas a few seconds to stop gawking at her muscular legs beneath the slit of the sarong. "A cliff that feels right in our hearts," he said when he finally met her amused gaze. "And one that's not too high, so we don't break our bones with the fall."

She rolled her eyes, but she was smiling as she turned to face the mirror. "Do you always play it safe?"

He pulled her closer, his fingers toying with the straps of her bikini top. "Not always," he breathed, tilting her chin up when she faced him. "Sometimes I'm too wild for my own good."

"Is that so?" She ran her cold hands down his chest, under his T-shirt, until they came to rest at the waistband of his cargo shorts. "I'd like to see this wild side of yours."

As his groin throbbed, he grazed the side of her mouth with his fingers. "Haven't you seen enough already?"

She nibbled on the side of his thumb before sucking it between her lips, sending a jolt straight between his legs. "No," she whispered, "not yet."

Tejas picked her up in one swift motion and pushed her against the locked room door, which thudded loud enough for anybody outside to hear, not that he cared. "Good," he said before capturing her mouth with his, his hand curling around her thigh.

♡♡♡

"How about that one?" Tejas asked, one hand over his forehead as a bead of sweat rolled down his neck. The sunlight scorched above them; perhaps going cliff diving at four in the afternoon wasn't the best idea. Hopefully, the waterproof sunscreen Naina had slathered all over his body would hold up.

Naina looked at the cliff he was pointing at and chuckled. "That's barely even a cliff. It's the height of the hostel swimming pool's diving board."

"Fine," Tejas grumbled, and they resumed their walk by the narrow seaside trail, their hands intertwined. Naina had already shot down the three cliffs Tejas had picked out because they didn't "feel right" in her heart. Tejas was pretty sure the real reason was that they weren't dangerous enough for her. After all, those cliffs were popular diving spots in the morning for reasonable people who feared for their lives. At this hour, though, given the searing heat, the entire rocky stretch overlooking the sea was deserted.

They walked for another five minutes in silence until the winding path gave way to a cliff that was tall enough to get Naina's adrenaline going. Thirty or forty feet, Tejas guessed. His stomach twisted when he looked down, down, down at the sea below them, and he tasted bile as he backed away from the edge. "You're going to get us killed," he insisted.

Naina had already undone the knot holding her sarong together.

"If we die, we die together!" she exclaimed, spreading her arms wide in the humid, sticky breeze.

"Yeah, I'm convinced," Tejas replied, though he had to pinch his lips to keep laughter at bay. This woman really was something else.

"Come on," she said, smiling. She walked over to him and slid his T-shirt off his upper body, her fingers exploring the ridges of his chest. Tejas held back the urge to kiss her; his heart was already pounding fast enough to induce cardiac arrest. Sighing, he unbuttoned his cargo shorts so he was standing in nothing but his swimming trunks.

They set their bags aside and walked to the edge, fingers tightly intertwined. "On the count of three," Naina said, her words determined. "Okay?"

"O-okay," Tejas got out.

"Three . . ."

Could Naina feel how slick and sweaty his palm was?

"Two . . ."

Fuck, he was going to die without saying goodbye to his cat. His sister. His clients—

"One!"

Naina tugged on his hand, and Tejas let out a loud exhale and jumped, his mouth open wide in a scream that echoed around them. Time seemed to stop, or perhaps pass in slow motion, as they fell, fell, fell closer and closer to the sea.

When they landed, creating ripples in the water, Tejas pushed his head back up, breaking the surface. He gasped for breath and blinked back the spots in front of his eyes. Next to him, Naina pressed her wet hands through her hair, slick with salt water, her chest heaving. "How do you feel?' she asked.

"I . . ." Tejas closed his eyes and took it all in. Exhilaration was one word to explain his heart nearly beating its way out of his rib cage; the feeling underneath that was empowerment. He was free, he was powerful, he was invincible. He'd just jumped off a cliff. Everything that had bothered him up until now—his aching heart,

Rahul's broken promises, the lonely life that awaited him back in Mumbai—didn't matter anymore. He had conquered this jump; he would conquer everything else.

"I feel alive," he finally said.

"Me too," Naina said giddily. She swam forward and kissed him, and their teeth clashed because they were both grinning so wide. "Another big thing checked off the list," she said, breaking free from his lips. "Thank you."

And Tejas realized that even though his feet were floating solidly in the water, he was still falling. "No," he said, kissing the top of her head, "thank *you*."

Laughing, they broke apart and swam ahead to the shore. Tejas's heart still thumped loud enough for him to hear it, but the joy surging through his veins was all he cared about. That, and the fluttering low in his belly, reminding him that he wouldn't have dared to do any of this if it wasn't for Naina. Naina, who was beautiful, and brave, and—at least for the duration of this trip—his.

As they clambered out of the sea onto the beach, their swimwear wet and heavy on their skin, Naina squeezed water from her hair. "I wish Santhosh could see me now," she said, chuckling.

Tejas led the way back up the stairs to the viewpoint, his eyebrows raised. "Oh, he wasn't much of an adrenaline junkie, then?"

Naina shook her head from beside him. "Nope, which meant I couldn't be one either, even though my mom and I tried zip-lining and bungee jumping years ago, and we loved it."

"That must have been fun." He whistled. "Is your dad the same?"

"Not a chance." She laughed; Tejas's heart swelled at how musical the sound was, and he hoped he could sear it into his memory. "He doesn't even like roller coasters," she added. "Can you imagine?"

They reached the top of the cliff, and Tejas scrambled forward to grab their towels from the bags. "I'm with your dad. Roller coasters suck," he said as he wrung the dampness out from his curls. "At least cliff diving is only one leap. Roller coaster rides go on forever."

"They're, like, five minutes long." Naina rolled her eyes in good humor and pressed her lips to his. Tejas kissed her back, tasting salt water against her smile.

She wrapped the towel around her swimsuit and looked at the sea they'd just jumped into. "Let's stay here for a bit," she said. They sat at the edge of the cliff in silence, their legs dangling and their fingers entwined. When Naina shuffled closer to lean her head against Tejas's, he wrapped one arm around her waist, over the towel, his heart content. If only he could hold on to this moment forever.

"Hey." Naina spoke up, breaking the quietness in the air. "Permission to put a hold on the 'wrong answers only' policy?"

"Again?" Tejas made a big show of looking shocked. "Fine, granted, but just this once."

She snorted, like what she was about to say was almost comical in hindsight. "I know I told you a little bit about my breakup, but did I tell you Santhosh was cheating on me for months after he got down on one knee and proposed?"

"You didn't." Tejas tilted her face up and kissed her forehead, his heart breaking at the thought of someone cheating on this perfect being of a woman. "I'm sorry."

Naina gave a half shrug, as if it didn't matter, then flipped their hands so her cold, damp fingers were on his palm. "The cheating went on for the last seven or eight months of our relationship, around the time we'd started planning our wedding. I didn't know until I caught them together two months before the big day, and that finally gave me the courage to end things. In hindsight, he was toxic from the start."

"That must have been so hard," Tejas said. Then he paused, remembering what she'd said the night they met. "You said you were planning to visit Goa for your honeymoon. So if you hadn't found out about the cheating . . ."

"I would have still been in Goa right now, but not with you. I'd have been in a honeymoon suite with my husband, clueless about the fact that he was sleeping with his neighbor behind my back."

Naina ran her free hand along the crevices of the rocky, dusty cliff. "My flight tickets were booked, my work had approved the time off, so I figured: Why not come here anyway and do all the things Santhosh would have never let me do if we were still together?"

"Well, we only have one item left on the list now." Tejas pressed a kiss to her wrist. "I can't believe how brave you are, Naina. I could have never celebrated my honeymoon solo."

She laughed sadly. "Brave? I'm terrified of so much. Of never feeling this free or powerful again. Of going back home and having to fend off questions from my colleagues, acquaintances, and extended family who RSVP'd yes to the wedding that never happened. Of getting sick and tired of being alone, then reluctantly agreeing to be set up with some guy, only to realize I don't have the capacity to fall in love ever again." She let out a huff. "You get the picture."

Tejas's head thudded. "Do you really think you'll never fall in love again?" he asked, his voice small.

Naina blinked up at him, her lips parting, like she hadn't expected him to address that part of her rant. Slowly, she loosened her hand from his grip and stood up. "I *hope* I never fall in love again," she said, massaging the side of her neck as she avoided his gaze. "I'm not built for heartbreak, and I'd rather only go through it once in my lifetime."

"Fair enough," Tejas said.

They wore some fresh clothes over their swimwear and walked back down the hill toward the hostel. When they passed a scooter rental shop, Naina excitedly gestured at a purple scooter on display. "Look, it's so cute! Want to drive around for fun?"

Tejas thought for a moment as he kicked a pebble with his shoe; it fell into the sewer ahead, disappearing from view. "I think I'd rather return to the hostel," he said finally. "It's been a while since I called my sister. She's cat-sitting Astrid, so I should check in."

A frown creased Naina's forehead, though she only nodded. "Okay."

"But you should still rent the scooter and explore the neighborhood anyway," he added. "See you later?"

"That works," she said.

Once Tejas had walked back to the hostel and was safely sitting on the bottom bunk, wearing his favorite pajamas and scrolling through cute cat photographs, he hesitated before dialing his sister's number, knowing she'd chide him for letting things go this far.

As far as Latika knew from his last update to her, Tejas and Naina were enjoying a summer fling with no emotions involved and no facts exchanged. She'd already warned Tejas that he couldn't handle a casual relationship without developing a crush, and as it turned out, she was right.

More than right, in fact. Because no matter how hard Tejas wanted to deny it, the truth bounced back and forth in his head, mimicking the somersault of his heart in his chest: He was unfortunately and undeniably in love with Naina Stark.

Chapter TWENTY-ONE

Bangalore, October 2026

Apparently, two of the crew members who were on set the night of the murder were close friends, having worked on many of the same movies over the years, and had agreed to meet Naina and Tejas at a Sunstag Café near to where their next project, another Jagannath production, was filming.

"I'm finally feeling optimistic about this case," Naina said to Tejas as she paid the auto rickshaw driver, her mood light for the first time in days. "Especially with the forensic report hinting that the killer was likely stronger than Pai, which obviously points to a man."

"Rohith Pai was five foot eight and most definitely not a gym freak," Tejas pointed out as he exhaled, "but everyone knows Pree-thi works out a lot. The prosecution will push that angle no matter what." He led the way inside the café and upstairs, greeting the cheerful baristas with a polite smile when they yelled "Welcome to Sunstag!"

Malik and Vaishnavi, the two crew members, were already seated upstairs. This side of town was chock-full of startup founders, venture capitalist firms, and tech bros, so Sunstag had built a conference room on the second floor that they rented out. Apparently, one of Sunstag's former baristas now worked in the film industry, so Malik had pulled some strings and booked the conference room for a half hour at a cheaper rate on AKC's behalf.

"Hi," Tejas said, shaking hands with each of them one after the other. "Thank you for speaking with us."

"No problem," Malik said, smiling politely. He was an average-looking guy, not older than twenty-two or twenty-three. He wore a simple T-shirt and denim shorts, though his nails were painted silver, and his short hair was streaked gold, matching his gold eyeliner; it reminded Naina of a character from The Hunger Games.

Vaishnavi, on the other hand, was a short, meek-looking woman, probably in her early thirties. Her eyes were big and round, and she kept sneaking looks at the door like she was afraid someone would barge in.

Once they were all seated facing each other with four cups of steaming hot coffee on the table, Naina spoke, one finger on her iPad Notes app. "So, Malik, you were the makeup artist on set the night of Rohith Pai's murder?"

Malik and Vaishnavi both flinched at the word *murder.* Slowly, Malik nodded. "Yes, I handled hair and makeup for Preethi ma'am and Gopal sir. They were the only actors on the call sheet those two days." His face darkened, and he drank a bit of his Americano. "Of course, the second day never happened."

"And, Vaishnavi." Naina turned to the woman, who was crouched in her seat. "You've been Jagannath's personal assistant for how long now?"

"Twelve years. His team hired me straight out of college."

"And do you like working with him?" Tejas prodded.

"He's a good boss," Vaishnavi said, smiling at last. "He takes care of the people in his life. For example, Pai sir wanted me to share a trailer with two other male crew members because of limited space, but Jagannath sir put his foot down and insisted I get my own trailer.

We didn't have any other women on set that day except for Preethi, Bina ma'am, and me."

"Good for Vaishnavi, honestly," Malik said, snickering. "But she left my yapper ass alone with the camera crew, and God, they were a snoozefest. They turned in for the night right away."

Vaishnavi rolled her eyes at him. "Like you would have wanted to yap all night. Our shoot started at five A.M., and I know you like your beauty sleep."

"Beauty sleep versus gossip?" Malik lifted his palms as though weighing the options. "Gossip, always! Since she's a PA, Vaish has piping-hot tea about everyone in the industry," he said, nodding approvingly.

Vaishnavi's face paled. "I don't gossip about Jagannath sir," she said, hurriedly sipping her latte. "I'm very loyal to him. Not that there's ever any gossip about him anyway."

"Right," Naina said, checking her wristwatch. They only had the conference room for another twenty minutes, after which the crew had to return to their set. She took a big gulp of her coffee and asked, "So, the night of the murd—"

Under the table, Tejas put a warm hand on Naina's knee, squeezing once as if to say, *Hold on, let me try something*. "Vaishnavi, were you well acquainted with the Krishnans also?"

Naina bit her lip. Tejas was trying out his strategy of making the witnesses comfortable before asking them the right questions. Well, fair enough. He was a smart lawyer, and now her friend . . . of sorts.

Vaishnavi answered promptly. "Yes, Jagannath sir has worked with them a handful of times over the years. They're good people. I especially like Gopal sir—he's a remarkable man."

"Huh." Tejas cocked his head, finally removing his hand from Naina's knee. "Why do you say that?"

Vaishnavi smiled as she set her coffee down. "He cares about everyone in the industry. Whether it's a cameraperson, PA, actor—he's there for us all. One time on set, I was struggling through period cramps, and he had someone send over painkillers."

"Definitely a good guy," Malik agreed.

"He's respectful of *all* women," Vaishnavi went on, "which is why he was so cautious with Preethi while filming the action sequence that day."

"Really?" Naina asked. "How so?"

Malik let out a sarcastic laugh. "Cautious? More like scared. The scene was supposed to be a sexually charged moment where the warrior princess teaches the novice soldier how to shoot a bow and arrow correctly, and they didn't get a good take for over an hour because Gopal sir refused to get too close to Preethi."

"Can you blame him for that?" Vaishnavi said defensively, sneering at Malik. "I'm sure he just didn't want Preethi accusing him like she did with Rohith sir."

"Whatever." Malik finished the last of his coffee, tutting. "If the movie had gone on, the editing team would have had to cut a ton of footage of Rohith sir and Pai sir's shouting match over one teensy little scene. The romance subplot was in the script, for crying out loud! Why take on the role if you don't want to touch the lead actress?"

Naina and Tejas exchanged glances. Finally, someone had confirmed the maintenance worker's testimony. Gopal Krishnan was looking more and more suspicious with every passing day, especially since he hadn't mentioned any of this to them.

"Shall we talk about the night of the crime?" When they nodded, Tejas shifted in his seat toward Naina, perhaps signaling to her that he was done with his subtle angle of questioning.

Naina looked at the list of questions on her iPad. "Where were you both between eleven-thirty and one A.M. that night?"

"In my trailer with the camera crew, asleep," Malik answered promptly. "I don't think any of us woke up until we heard sirens and saw the row of police vans parked up ahead."

"Same," Vaishnavi chimed in.

"Are either of you deep sleepers?"

"I sleep like a baby," Malik said, finishing his coffee. "The perks of working your ass off all day, I suppose."

Vaishnavi thought for a second. "I'd say it depends. I slept well that night because the hills are peaceful and quiet, unlike the city with its traffic and all the honking of cars."

Naina asked them a few more routine questions about whether they noticed anything weird or off between Preethi and Rohith Pai that night, or if they thought someone else could have done it, but the crew members didn't have anything to say in defense of Preethi. Rather, it sounded like they were happy about the arrest. *Them and every other person in Bangalore,* Naina thought glumly.

As they said their goodbyes and got up to leave, Naina tucked her iPad back into her work bag and asked one final question. "Vaishnavi, have you ever known Jagannath to oversleep or not answer a wakeup call?"

Hopefully, her answer would help them figure out if Jagannath was a deep sleeper. Naina couldn't directly ask Vaishnavi such a personal question about her boss.

Vaishnavi hesitated by the half-open sliding door of the conference room. She thought for a moment, then said, "I don't think so? Some days, he needs me to call him to make sure he's awake, but he's usually up early in time for work. Why do you ask?"

Naina shrugged, plastering a smile on her face. "Just curious."

"I have a question too," Tejas added, closing the door so the crowd outside wouldn't hear. "Did Preethi not have a PA?"

Vaishnavi's mouth curled up mockingly. "No, I don't think she was enough of a star for that."

Malik snorted, then clapped a hand to his mouth. "Sorry," he mumbled, snickering, "but it's true. She's a nobody, and I don't understand why Rohith sir chose to cast her. That's what led to his death in the end, isn't it? What a mistake." He shuddered, then gave them a polite smile and headed out.

Naina and Tejas waited for them to leave before closing the door again. They had five minutes to debrief until their time was up. Tejas sat on the long conference table, rubbing the back of his head. "Pretty eye-opening, huh?"

"Yeah." She frowned, then added, "That was smart of you, asking them simpler, unrelated questions to ease them into talking about the murder. I usually just dive right into the facts of the case."

Tejas's brows shot up. "Did you just compliment me, Naina Stark?"

"It's Naina Shetty," she corrected him, but her lips twitched with a smile. She shimmied onto the table beside him, crossing one leg over the other. "And I'm not one to hold back on the niceness if someone deserves it."

"What else do I deserve, then?" he said, wetting his lips, his eyes smoldering.

Naina pulled on the collar of her shirt as a hot red flush crept up her neck. "Let's head back to the office. It's already five P.M.," she got out, and slid off the table.

"Sure." He grinned cockily, like he knew the frustrating effect he had on her. *Ugh*. "Although I could do with more coffee." He slid the door open and added, "Americano, right? I'll buy."

She fidgeted with her hands. Another coffee sounded tempting, but she hesitated. Tejas wasn't just her colleague now, he was a . . . friendly colleague, and friendly colleagues got coffee together all the time. It didn't mean anything more.

"Yeah, why not?" she said. "I'll grab us a table."

Tejas smiled and headed to the counter, his footsteps thumping down the stairs. Naina found a table in the corner of the slowly emptying café and uploaded her meeting notes onto their Preethi Acharya Google Doc. Trial started in a week, and although they now had a suspect in mind, the evidence against Gopal was circumstantial at best and wouldn't help their defense much. There was a lot more work to be done.

"Hey." Tejas set two mugs of coffee on the table and sat down. Naina peered at his drink over her laptop when she smelled the aroma in the air. "You got a pumpkin spice latte?" she said, pulling a face.

"It's October, isn't it?" He laughed in good humor. "I usually order hazelnut lattes, but"—his gaze raked over her face—"I was in the mood for something special today."

She looked away, hating the blush that warmed her cheeks. "Um, so maybe we could review the prosecution's witness list when we get back to the office?" she suggested. "I don't think we should discuss the case in public now that we have more concrete information."

Tejas nodded, and once she had put away her laptop, he sipped his latte and asked, his voice softer, "How are you doing, Naina?"

"I think we can win this," she said determinedly. "If we can build a strong enough case against Gopal, and the judge agrees with our analysis of the forensic report—"

"I meant in general," he said, his lips twitching with a smile. "How have you been since Goa?"

Naina swallowed a gulp of her coffee; it burned her mouth. "Like I said earlier, we don't need to revisit our past."

"Fair enough," he replied, still smiling. "So tell me about your present. Is your father doing okay? Do you still enjoy karaoke?"

"Appa's fine, and we're as close as ever," she said, smiling. "Yes, I do karaoke at Madeira almost every week, and I like to think I'm their best singer."

Tejas raised his mug as though toasting her. "I'm sure. And are you . . . happy?"

Naina blinked. *Happy?* She was about to come up with some sort of joke, tell him he was talking like a therapist, but those words died in the back of her throat. It didn't make sense, but for some strange reason, she wanted to answer his question. Maybe because no one had asked her if she was happy in a long, long time.

If ever.

She blew air over the top of her Americano, making her glasses fog up. "I don't know what happiness even means."

He didn't speak for a moment; he simply stared at her, a crease between his eyebrows, like he was trying and failing to decode her. Then he said, "Sometimes, happiness is a place. A series of moments. A person."

"A person?"

"Naina, you were happiness personified in Goa." Tejas's gaze fell to his coffee as his Adam's apple bobbed. "I don't see that in you anymore. Why?"

"I . . . that was a vacation. This is real life."

"I was so lost in life after Goa," Tejas admitted, his fingers circling the rim of his mug. "I thought I'd never be happy again. I'm not saying it was your fault," he added hastily. "I'm just saying what I felt."

A soft gasp left Naina's mouth when he looked up at her with shining eyes. She reached forward to squeeze his hand before she realized what she was doing. Despite the sparks shooting up her arm, despite her brain telling her to pull away, she held on, a desperate need in her to comfort him. "You will be happy again, Tejas," she said. "God knows you deserve it."

"Thank you." A small smile appeared on his face again, and he pressed her fingers to his lips, his breath hot. "You do too."

Chapter TWENTY-TWO

Goa, May 2025

NAINA'S ANTI-HONEYMOON CHECKLIST

7. Go on a real adventure. ✓

Naina lifted her head and soaked in the late afternoon sunshine that blazed over her, loving the way it complemented the wind howling around the scooter she drove through the streets of Goa. Party music floated up from the beachside restaurants, fellow tourists dancing and having the time of their lives just like her, while locals strolled by, some walking their pets, others running errands. What a perfect contrast in this perfect moment.

She smiled. Anil, Iqbal, and the others had been right: She'd needed this trip more than oxygen.

And yet . . .

A couple drove past her on their own scooter, the man clinging on to the woman and screaming bloody murder as she attempted a wheelie. Giggling, she brought the front wheel back down and blew a kiss at the man over her shoulder before resuming the drive. Their laughter echoed long after they disappeared from sight.

Naina sighed, then turned the scooter back. She'd been driving around for the past hour, and although she usually enjoyed being by herself, exploring Goa like this would have been so much more fun with Tejas sitting behind her.

She sucked on her teeth and plugged the directions for the hostel into Maps. Everything was more fun when she was with Tejas. Dancing, drinking, doing adventurous activities, and watching Tejas fight his fears and take the leap, not to mention the kindness he'd shown her while she was hungover and sick . . .

He had such a beautiful soul. He lit up every room he walked into. That first day, when he'd said hello to her in their room at the hostel, she'd forced herself to appear standoffish even though she couldn't take her eyes off of him. Not just because he was attractive, but because he was so . . . bright, like a ray of sunshine. So radiant and warm, despite everything she now knew he'd gone through. She had a feeling that he was slowly becoming someone she couldn't forget. Someone she wouldn't *want* to forget. And that scared her more than she could say.

But you have to forget him, she reminded herself as moments from their trip ran through her mind, one after the other, and she blinked them away. Her time with Tejas would come to a close in a matter of days, after all. So she would make the most of it while she still could—soaking in his laughter, his kisses, his touch—after which it was goodbye forever.

Naina drove the scooter back to the hostel, since she didn't have to return it until the next morning. She waved hello to the gang, who were heading for a dip in the pool, then took the stairs to the second floor. As she walked up to room 202, voices sounded from behind the closed door. Tejas was talking to . . . a woman?

What the fuck? Naina was seconds away from shoving the door open when she heard the word *bhai*. *Oh*. That must be Latika's voice. Tejas's sister. She breathed a silent sigh of relief and lifted her hand up to knock.

". . . is she willing to do long-distance?" Latika was saying, and Naina let her hand drop to her side. Were they talking about . . . her?

Naina pressed her ear to the door, her heart lurching. Tejas cleared his throat. "I don't think she feels the same way." As Latika sighed loudly, he added, "Go on, rub it in my face."

Fuck. Naina blinked rapidly, trying to process what she was hearing. Tejas had caught feelings for her. But feelings could be shut down and overcome. Feelings could fade. She knew that all too well. As long as what he felt wasn't—

"Bhai, I would never do that. Has Naina said she's not falling for you, in those exact words?" Latika said.

Oh, shit, shit, shit. Naina backed away from the door and clapped a hand to her mouth as her breaths came out in loud gasps. Tejas was falling in love with her?

She walked down the hallway to the bathroom, which was thankfully empty, and locked the door. As she splashed water on her face, her thoughts raced a mile a minute. How had she not seen this coming? All those wonderful things he'd done for her . . . the smile in his eyes when he looked at her . . . the way he touched her, kissed her, pleasured her . . .

Maybe she didn't know his last name or his job or where he was from, but she knew enough about him to guess his heart wasn't bolted shut like hers. Tejas had a soft vulnerability about him that Naina would never allow for herself again. He was sweet, he was gentle, he wasn't as broken as she was.

In another life, he could be someone she'd love without a moment's hesitation. But if Naina wanted to walk away from this trip without getting hurt again, she would have to pretend that she didn't see him as anything more than a summer fling. That they didn't want each other as lovers as much as they'd needed each other as rebounds.

She couldn't give him hope.

Naina nodded at her reflection, then wiped her face with her hands and returned to their door. She knocked, then entered when Tejas yelled "Come in!"

Off the phone now, he was sitting at the desk, browsing through what looked like Outlook. Naina averted her eyes; she didn't want to accidentally find out what he did for a living. She didn't want to give herself any way to look him up online.

"Hi," Tejas said, his voice bright and cheery. "Did you enjoy the drive?"

Uh-oh. Had his sister given him some sort of hope by the end of that conversation? Why else would he sound so . . . excited?

"Yes," Naina said, swallowing back her anxiety. She bolted the door behind her and got dressed in her pajamas in silence, although her mind was still loud with questions and doubts and fears and frustrations and—

Tejas must have sensed the tension in the air, because he stood and wrapped his arms around her, planting a kiss on the top of her head. "Sorry I ditched you," he said, still holding her tight. "I just wanted to come back and plan the final item on the list."

"Oh," she said, stiffening in his grip. "And did you find anything?"

"We could book a private dinner cruise on a yacht for day after tomorrow. The prices are a bit steep, but it's a two-hour experience with a five-course meal and live music. What do you think?"

Naina forced herself to smile and turned to face him. "I'm not sure."

Tejas smiled. "It'll be fun," he insisted, taking both her hands in his. "We could dress up, have a good meal, some drinks. It'll be the perfect—"

"The perfect goodbye," Naina said quickly. She hadn't had a fun date night in a long time. As much as she didn't want to encourage his feelings, as much as she wanted to put distance between them . . . there would be plenty of time for that after she left. As long as she stuck to her resolve, she'd be safe.

With a soft exhale, Tejas pulled her closer, and they lay down on the bed. "Don't remind me of that," he said glumly. "Do you really think you'll never want to find me again? After . . . after *this*?"

Naina snuggled into his chest and tucked her legs in between his thighs. "I'll want to look you up," she admitted, "but I shouldn't. It's for the best if we keep things that way."

"Why?" he pressed.

She blinked back tears, hoping he couldn't feel them against his shirt. "Right now, you're perfect, Tejas. I haven't found a single thing I don't like about you. But if we kept talking, if we met in real life, that illusion would shatter, and we'd find reasons to hurt each other, whether we wanted to or not."

"Naina, I know you're scared"—Tejas kissed the top of her head again—"but it might not end up being that way. What if . . ."

"I never want us to hate each other, Prince Charming," she said, winding her arms tighter around him. She dropped her voice to a whisper. "Don't give me that chance. Please."

He tilted her face up and said, seconds before he kissed her, "Okay."

But somehow, Naina didn't believe him.

Chapter TWENTY-THREE

Bangalore, October 2026

As much as Naina loved her best friend, she didn't think she'd ever met a more stubborn person. "You need to have fun," Anil insisted, tugging on her hand so hard her revolving chair almost toppled over. "It's Friday night, Nay!"

She tilted her head back and groaned. "I have way too much work. Karaoke will have to wait till next week." She fiddled with her glasses, glancing around the entire office floor. A frazzled paralegal walked past them, holding a massive stack of reports. Kumble's office was empty, but Iqbal still sat at his desk and typed on his laptop, his door ajar. On the other side of the room, a few lawyers and associates—including Tejas and Dhanush—were packing their things, all chatting among themselves. As though he'd sensed Naina looking at him, Tejas flashed her a smile.

Naina smiled back, no hesitation. Since the night at Madeira and their recent conversation at the café, she'd realized she could do with another friend in the office, her attraction to him notwithstanding. Just having Anil as her work bestie didn't feel like enough sometimes.

Anil turned back and caught the exchange, then gasped. "Naina Shetty, did you just smile at Prince Charming? Shit, has something happened since the hand-holding at the café?"

Why do I keep telling him these things? she thought as she rolled her eyes. "No," she said, "I'm just trying to be . . . approachable."

"So you want him to approach you. Understood." Anil made a salute gesture, then clapped his hands sharply. "People! Attention, please!"

Even Iqbal looked up from his desk. The office chatter died down, and everyone's eyes went to Anil—and, by extension, Naina. She gritted her teeth and mumbled, "Anil, what the hell are you doing?"

"It's been such a long week," Anil said, sighing exaggeratedly as he stretched his arms, "so Naina and I are buying the first round at Madeira. Who's in for some beer and karaoke?"

People whooped. Tejas's grin widened, and he locked eyes with Naina. "Count me in," he said loudly.

"Me too," Dhanush said. A few others mumbled their assent. Soon, ten or eleven people got up from their desks, discussing carpools to the karaoke bar.

Iqbal strode out of his office, laptop bag in hand, and closed the door with a soft thud. "Do I get an invite too?" he asked.

"The more, the merrier!" Anil exclaimed, pumping his fist in the air as Iqbal chuckled. Then Anil bent and whispered to Naina, "Ready to be even more approachable?"

She gave him a weird look as she begrudgingly powered down her laptop. "What do you mean?"

"I'll be your wingman," Anil said, rubbing his hands together like a maniacal supervillain. "And we shall find you a hot guy to make Tejas jealous. Then we'll really know what he thinks about you being just friends."

Naina shoved her things into her bag with more force than necessary, knowing arguing with him would be futile. "I hate you," she declared.

Anil smirked. "Love you too, bestie."

BEER IN HAND, NAINA STOOD at the bar at Madeira, smiling politely as the man Anil had forced on her explained how his startup got funding against all odds. "And my uncle's VC firm loved the idea, but we still had to work so incredibly hard to convince them." He sipped his scotch, looking somber. "It's a tough climate for startups, whether you have connections or not."

"Mm-hmm, sounds tough for sure," Naina said. "So do you like to—"

"And let me tell you," he droned on, "we got three million in seed funding—three million *dollars*. That's really impressive for an early-stage startup."

"Absolutely," she said, taking a big gulp of her beer. She craned her neck, hoping to signal to Anil to get her the fuck out of here so she could sign up for karaoke, but he was nowhere to be found. God, he was the worst wingman. Although he'd promised not to disappear on her, he must have found a hot guy for himself.

As the man continued bragging about the funding and how nepotism was a total myth, Tejas walked past them, holding a beer. He stopped in his tracks when he noticed Naina, his eyes going wide. *You okay?* he mouthed. She gave the slightest shake of her head.

Tejas licked his lips, then joined their group. "Hey, Naina, Anil is looking for you. Shall we?"

With a hurried excuse to the man, Naina followed Tejas to the interior of the bar, where their colleagues sat drinking beers in one of the larger eight-seater booths. Naina wasn't surprised that Tejas had bluffed about Anil being around; Anil hardly ever sat in one place with his co-workers when he could instead socialize with complete strangers, a concept that was alien to Naina.

Opposites made the best of friends sometimes.

"Thanks for getting me out of there," Naina said when Tejas stopped a few feet from the booth.

"It's fine." He grinned lazily. "You didn't seem that into him anyway."

She snorted. "How could you tell?"

Her question was meant to be rhetorical, but Tejas's eyes glinted, the irises molten. "Because you don't look at him like you look at me."

Holy shit. Naina bit her lip, and when her gaze fell to his mouth, he noticed. Tejas rubbed his free hand over his messy curls, like he was contemplating something, then took one small step closer. *Uh-oh,* Naina thought, *this is definitely not "friendly" territory.* "I gotta go," she yelped, rushing back to the bar. She would take that man's soliloquies about tech over the simmering tension with Tejas any day.

Thankfully, Mr. Three Million Dollars was nowhere to be seen at the bar; he must have found someone else to bore. Naina pressed a hand to her chest, letting her shoulders loosen up before she got another beer. The first sip calmed her nerves, and the second brought a smile to her face. She went to the karaoke emcee's station by the makeshift stage—by no means comparable to the massive one she remembered from Goa—and told him her song selection. He gave her a thumbs-up and returned his focus to the person who was singing "Uptown Girl."

"Naina? Naina Shetty?"

She turned, blinking at the familiar-looking man who'd just said her name. Was that . . .

"Zeeshan?" Her heart thudded. Zeeshan was her ex's college roommate and her former friend; they'd hung out together multiple times over the years, but after the engagement ended, Zeeshan—along with all of their mutual friends—chose Santhosh's side over hers, since they'd known him longer.

"Hey!" Zeeshan said, giving her a side hug that she awkwardly returned, narrowly missing the gin and tonic that sloshed in his glass. "How's it going? Are you here with someone? A new boyfriend, I hope."

Naina smiled tightly. "My colleagues."

Zeeshan laughed louder than the final verse of "Uptown Girl"; the gin was clearly strong. "Still the workaholic we know and love," he said.

Know and love? You ditched me for a cheater, Naina wanted to say. She opened her mouth to change the topic when applause sounded and the emcee said, "That was Raju, ladies and gentlemen! Next up we have . . . Tejas?"

Naina's brows shot up as Tejas walked over to the emcee's table and grabbed the mic. Did Tejas go to karaoke nights regularly now? Naina wondered if he'd made it a habit since they first sang together in Goa. She licked her lips, wondering what song he had selected.

As Tejas ascended the stage and the opening notes of "Boulevard of Broken Dreams" played, he caught her eye in the crowd and winked.

Naina held back a smile and turned to Zeeshan again. "I thought you practiced law in Lucknow," she said. "Are you visiting Bangalore for work?"

Zeeshan's smile faded. "Uh, actually," he said, shuffling his feet nervously, "I was here for Santhosh's . . . wedding . . . uh, so I'm flying back to Lucknow tomorrow."

Naina's hand shook as she sipped her beer, the bottle dangerously slick with sweat and condensation. Santhosh's wedding. To the other woman. Right.

Honestly, Naina had moved on from her ex a long time ago. She barely even thought about that doomed relationship, or her former life, as she liked to think of it, on purpose. But knowing Santhosh was married now, definitely in love, and most likely partner at his dad's law firm like he'd always wanted . . . it made something in Naina break.

She forced herself to blink back tears. "That's nice, I'm sure it was a beautiful ceremony. Uh, if you'll excuse me . . ." Before Zeeshan could say a word, she darted away, past the stage and toward the mercifully empty washroom. Dhanush walked out of the men's bathroom, adjusting his belt, but she cut past him, ignoring him when he yelled "Whoa, you okay?" She barely even registered Tejas's singing cutting off abruptly before she locked herself in a stall and let out a sharp whoosh of breath.

Fuck. Naina unlocked her phone. She knew she shouldn't do it, but she had to. Since Santhosh was blocked on all social media, Naina looked Zeeshan up on Instagram, as well as some of their mutual friends, and scrolled through their most recent posts—all of which were about the grand Bollywoodesque wedding. A video of Santhosh, scrawny as ever, dancing to a romantic ballad with his wife at their sangeet. A boomerang on someone's story of the ceremony where Santhosh put a garland around the woman's neck as she blushed. And, of course, a frame-worthy photo of Santhosh gawking at her like he couldn't believe he was with someone that incredible.

Naina shook her head in disbelief. She remembered seeing that exact same expression on Santhosh's face during their own engagement photo shoot. Based on what she knew, he'd already been cheating on her for months at that point.

God, love was such a lie. And life? It was a colossal letdown. This time two years ago, Naina thought she'd be married by now, that she would make partner well before turning thirty. What a disappointment she was to her own younger self.

Heavy knocks rammed on her stall door, making her jump. "Occupied!" she exclaimed, wiping her semi-damp cheeks with the back of her hand.

"It's me," came Tejas's voice, laced with anxiety. "Are you okay?"

Why did those three words said by someone who cared always bring on the waterworks? Naina broke into sobs. "No," she blurted out.

Tejas let out a loud sigh. "Open the door."

Head hung, she unlatched the door and walked past Tejas to the mirror over the sink. Her eyes were red-rimmed, her so-called waterproof mascara clumping on her lashes, and her nose was redder than Santhosh's wife's lehenga. The thought of him married, successful, happy, everything she wasn't, made her double over in sobs again.

"Hey, hey, hey." Tejas nudged her away from the sink and pulled her into a hug, holding tight like he was scared she'd run away if he let go. Naina nestled into his embrace, burying her face into his neck. A year and a half had gone by since he'd held her, but his woodsy scent and sturdy, reliable arms were familiar as ever. As she cried, she dimly heard someone else's off-tune voice in the distance.

"Wait." She straightened, her eyes widening. "What happened to your song? You were singing when I . . ."

He smiled at her sheepishly. "I saw you run away from the bar looking miserable, so I followed you."

"I—" Naina gasped. "Mid-song? Tejas! Our colleagues are here!"

"So?" His hand curled around her cheek protectively. "We're in the women's restroom, Naina, where anyone could walk in on us and make their assumptions about what we're doing. You think I give a shit about that when there are far more pressing matters on hand, like what that guy at the bar did to hurt you?"

Naina closed her eyes and sank into his hold, letting the tears fall. How was this man real? She'd had this thought countless times in Goa too—when he'd gotten her breakfast in bed, the time he set up a mini-concert in their room, or the way he had been as attentive when she trauma-dumped as when he'd worshipped her body each night—but the thought was overwhelmingly real now more than ever, as the heat of his skin warmed her down to the tips of her toes. "My ex got married," she blurted out. "And all our mutual friends from law school who no longer talk to me were at the wedding. I saw one of them at the bar and he told me about it. "

Tejas's face fell. "I'm so sorry," he whispered. "They all picked his side over yours, then?"

"Yes. Did—did you have any mutual friends with your ex?" she asked softly. "Rahul, right?"

"Uh, yeah." He tugged on his collar. "But I don't talk to them anymore. It's easier this way. Plus," he said, smiling, "I've made new connections here."

"Besides Anil, I don't really have friends anymore. But maybe that's for the best," she admitted, sniffling.

"Why do you say that?"

"Because!" She laughed sarcastically. "If you let people in, they get a free pass to walk right out."

"Hmm." He cocked his head at her. "But they also get a free pass to stay."

Naina opened her mouth to argue, then closed it when his words sank in. He might have had a point, though it most definitely didn't apply to her. "Well, yeah," she said. "They stay in an ideal world. Unfortunately, that's not how reality works."

"It does," he insisted, his other hand playing with a lock of hair on her shoulder, sending goosebumps along her neck. "Look, your ex was an asswipe"—he grinned when she laughed—"and you deserve someone who fights for you as hard as you fight for your clients."

Seriously, how is he real? Naina put her hand on his cheek, grazing the scruff of his stubble with her knuckles.

Tejas let out a shaky breath. "Naina, I . . ."

"Where did you come from, Prince Charming?" she whispered, leaning into him as applause burst from somewhere outside the door.

Tejas tilted his head closer to hers, a smile widening on his face. "Maybe this time, you'll let me tell you all about it, Naina Stark."

Their lips had nearly met when the karaoke emcee's voice rang out from the speaker in the corner of the bathroom. "That was Jennifer, ladies and gentlemen! Next up, we have a regular in the house—Naina! Naina, where are you?"

She gasped, springing away from Tejas's arms in alarm. What was she doing, or rather, what had she been about to do? *No*. She couldn't kiss him; she couldn't risk falling into him again.

"I—I gotta go," she said, hoping her shaky legs would move. "They're waiting for me."

"Naina . . ." he started with pained eyes.

"I'm really sorry," she whispered, backing out of the bathroom. As the neon lights of the bar came into focus, Naina forced a fake smile and walked onto the stage, where the spotlight was ready and waiting to shine over her.

Chapter TWENTY-FOUR

Goa, May 2025

"Does this look okay?" Tejas checked himself out in the mirror in Jonah and Aleksy's room, then tugged his black tie over the collar of his deep violet button-down shirt, the sleeves of which were already rolled up to show off the forearms Naina loved.

Hopefully, she loved more than just his forearms. Well, he'd find out tonight.

Aleksy glanced at Tejas from the queen-size bed where he was scrolling through his phone. "It looks good," he said.

Jonah walked over to the mirror and adjusted Tejas's tie. "Got a romantic date planned?"

Tejas faced him with a grin. "It'll be the most romantic night of my life. And hers, I'm hoping." The cruise was on a private yacht, the most extravagant of all their activities during this vacation, but Tejas hoped the five-course dinner, live music, and cool sea breeze would be well worth the investment and not just something to check off the list.

His conversation with his sister had been eye-opening. When he'd told her that Naina seemingly had no desire to fall in love or be in a relationship anymore, nor did she want to stay in touch with Tejas after Goa, Latika had suggested confessing his feelings to Naina anyway. Best-case scenario, she'd appreciate the gesture, and it would soften her heart, allowing her to give them a real chance. Worst-case scenario? Tejas would board his bus back to Mumbai without any regrets, unanswered questions, or doubts.

He had no idea how Naina would react when he told her he loved her. Would she say it back, sealing the start of their real relationship with a kiss before her flight tomorrow morning? Or would she give him the closure he would need to move on from her?

"Have a nice time, man," Aleksy yelled, still rooted to his bed, when Tejas stepped outside, eager to see what dress Naina had picked out for their final date night. She'd wanted to go all out with her outfit and makeup, which was why she'd kicked him out of their room so he wouldn't disturb her while she got dressed.

Hands in his pockets, he went to the lobby and paced back and forth, waiting for the woman he loved.

It was already five minutes past six-thirty, and the cab sent by the cruise organizers was parked outside. Tejas was debating whether to check on Naina in their room when her voice called out to him. "What do you think?"

Tejas spun to face her. *Fuck*. His breath caught in his throat, his jaw slack. Naina struck a pose in her silky yellow evening gown that rippled with each movement. The slit up to her mid-thigh accentuated her toned legs, and when she turned to show off the low-cut back with the sleek zipper that went down to her butt, Tejas had to put a hand to his thumping heart. "You look beautiful," he finally got out. "God, Naina Stark, I'm so—" *No,* he reminded himself. *Don't you dare say the L-word yet*. "I'm so incredibly attracted to you," he finished instead.

An unreadable expression crossed Naina's face, but maybe Tejas had imagined it, because it faded the very next second. She walked up to him in her four-inch heels, which put her right on par with his six-foot-one frame, and slid her cold hands up and down his forearms. She tilted her head so her lips grazed his right ear. "Can't wait for you to take this dress off me later," she whispered, and damn if Tejas didn't get goosebumps.

Hand in hand, they left the hostel and clambered into the cab, which would take them straight to the harbor where the private yacht was waiting for them. After a few minutes of talking about what the yacht might look like and how the food would taste, Naina rested her head on Tejas's shoulder and made a "hmm" sound.

"What are you thinking?" Tejas asked, glancing down at her.

"This is the first time I'm seeing you in formal attire, and you clean up really well." She sat up and fixed a crease on his shirt. "I love this color on you. A lot of men wouldn't experiment with shades like violet or purple."

Tejas kissed the top of her head, making her squeal. "I wear all kinds of shades to work. Yellow, purple, soft pink, baby blue. I like color in my wardrobe."

Naina wound her arm around his biceps, her lips parting. "It suits you and your half-dimpled smile."

As the driver took a sharp right turn, Tejas stuck a hand out to steady himself. "I still can't believe you noticed the dimple," he said, chuckling. "I didn't, until you brought it up."

She let out a soft, barely audible sigh. "There's a lot you don't notice about yourself."

"Like what?"

Naina hesitated. "You're a good, kind person with a wonderful heart," she finally said. "I knew it the moment we met."

If Tejas wasn't already in love with Naina, this would have done it. He pulled her in for a kiss, not caring that they were in a cab in the middle of a traffic jam. Pressing his forehead to hers, he said with a half laugh, "I thought you might have found me annoying, given how you didn't smile once."

Naina nudged his nose with hers before settling into the crook of his neck again. "I wasn't annoyed," she clarified. "I guess I was just nervous at the thought of sharing a room with someone as hot as you."

He smiled, lifting her face up and cupping it with one hand. "Says the woman who takes my breath away every time I look at her."

"Oh, hold on." She pushed away from him and cleared her throat. "Bhaiyya," she said to the driver, "the traffic seems chaotic today. How far are we?"

"Madam, we're going to be a few minutes late," he replied to Naina. "You might want to call the cruise organizers and let them know."

"Right, thanks," Naina said, and rummaged in her purse for her phone.

As she made the call, Tejas swallowed, looking toward Naina, but her gaze was outside the window, at the rows and rows of cars and scooters. Was it a coincidence that she'd changed the topic? Yes, it had to be. Honestly, she had done him a favor. A second longer and those three words would have slipped from his mouth. And he couldn't do that, not in the midst of a traffic jam with twenty other drivers honking and yelling their frustrations at the red light. No, he would tell her while they were at sea, marveling at the beauty of the stars and the full moon, as soft romantic music played in the background. And she would tell him she loved him too.

Because she did. He sensed it, deep in his heart. She couldn't have shared this time with him, made these unforgettable memories with him, without calling it love, without knowing it was the kind of love worth holding on to, regardless of distance or time. They'd make it work.

They had to.

♡ ♡ ♡

THE YACHT WAS DOCKED BY the harbor, twinkling with yellow lights and gently rocking against the waves. The cruise organizer greeted Tejas and Naina politely, then ushered them aboard. Tejas helped Naina up the ladder, his hand on the small of her back, and she turned to shoot him a tight smile. When they had boarded, she said, almost tensely, "You know, I didn't need you to help me."

He rubbed the back of his head self-consciously. "Any excuse to touch you, I guess."

Slowly, Naina beamed at him. "Good answer."

Chuckling, Tejas followed behind her and the organizer, who led them to the dock where a candlelit table and two chairs were set up. "This is Martin," the organizer said, introducing them to the server. "He'll take good care of you. Enjoy your evening."

Naina sat across from Tejas and put her hands in her lap. "You comfortable?"

"Not quite," he said, smiling. "Why don't you sit next to me?"

"Uh, yeah, sure." She smiled back, pulled her chair closer to Tejas's, and sat down adjacent to him. Tejas's heart melted into a puddle as she looked up in awe at the sky lit by the full moon and a handful of stars. Her yellow dress shimmered in the darkness as though competing with the glowing moon—and it was safe to say the dress was winning. Tejas reached for her hand, and she interlocked their fingers, shooting sparks down his core.

"I'll bring out the champagne and the hors d'oeuvres shortly," Martin said, bowing before he left. In the distance, the haunting melody of violins filled the air. The live band must have started their performance.

"This is gorgeous," Naina gushed, adjusting the bottom of her dress. "I'm so glad we did this."

"Me too," he said as he took in the starry night, the beautiful music, and the most perfect woman sitting beside him. He was the luckiest man in the world.

"Sir, ma'am." The server brought over a plate of smoked chicken canapés and two glasses of champagne. Tejas and Naina had already preapproved the menu so there wouldn't be any surprises.

Tejas held up his glass. "To a night we'll never forget."

"To a *trip* we'll never forget," Naina corrected him, a twinkle in her eye as they clinked glasses.

Before she could take a sip of the champagne, Tejas leaned forward and kissed her. *I love you so much,* he wanted to say, but Naina's stomach grumbled, and he pulled away, deciding it was better to wait until they were through with the meal. "Let's try these canapés," he said.

The chicken was so tender it nearly melted in Tejas's mouth, the smoky flavor and subtle harissa seasoning adding the perfect touch to the one-bite dish. Naina hummed in appreciation. "I could have a hundred of these," she said, licking her ruby-red lips.

Tejas smirked behind his glass. "We have four more courses to go."

Naina sipped her drink. "Let's see if they can top this one."

The next four courses were just as impressive: dates stuffed with candied walnuts and cream cheese, garden salad with fresh greens and a balsamic dressing, rosemary grilled chicken with rice and mashed potatoes, and cherry amaretto tiramisu to end the meal on a sweet note.

"What's the verdict?" Tejas asked as he sat back and wiped his mouth with his napkin.

Naina rubbed her belly. "I now have a four-month-old food baby growing inside me. And I love it to death."

Tejas threw his head back and laughed. "What a coincidence," he said, putting a hand to his own full stomach, "because I seem to be growing one too." His phone buzzed—a video from Latika with the message Help she's not eating ☹. "Hold on, my sister texted me," he said, frowning as he hit play. Naina shuffled closer to watch it with him.

Behind the camera, Latika huffed. "Come on, Astrid, it's premium tuna! You loved it yesterday!" Astrid, meanwhile, was making a back-and-forth digging motion with her front left paw beside the wet food bowl: her way of saying, "This is shit." The camera then switched to Latika's frowning face. "Bhai, what do I do?" she wailed.

Tejas sighed loudly, then texted back, She's too spoiled. You can't give her the same wet food two nights in a row. Try the chicken loaf and send me another video, while Naina giggled beside him.

"You've really pampered Astrid," Naina said. "I didn't realize cats were so picky with their meals."

"She knows we love her enough to pander to her every tantrum," he replied, replaying the video for another glimpse at Astrid. "Most people think cats don't show affection, but that's bullshit. After her spaying surgery eight months ago, despite being so weak she could barely stand straight, Astrid still tried to follow me around the apartment like she does every day. God, I love her. She's the best cat in the world."

It was when Naina wiped his cheek that Tejas realized he was crying. "And the luckiest cat," Naina corrected him. "She got you for a dad, after all."

Tejas blinked back more tears. "Want to enjoy the sea breeze for a bit?" he asked, standing and offering her his hand. This was the moment, he decided. He would finally tell her he loved her.

She took his hand, and they walked to the railing around the perimeter of the yacht. The sea was a deep, dark gray, illuminated only by the silver moon; the powerful waves crashed around the hull, as loud as the music that still surrounded them. Naina rested her palms on the railing, her eyes crinkling with her smile. "Have you ever seen something this beautiful?" she said.

"I have," Tejas said breathlessly, taking her in. When Naina turned to him, a question mark on her face, he averted his gaze to the sea and put his hands in his pockets. "Uh, we have some really lovely spots back home. I'd show you pictures, but . . ."

Naina gulped. "Yeah, you probably shouldn't do that." Sighing, she tugged him closer, linking his fingers with hers. "Tejas, you don't know how thankful I am that I got to finish the list with you."

Tejas kissed the knuckles of her right hand. "Same here. Naina, I want to tell you something." He took a deep breath. "Something I've been feeling for a while now. Something I think you're feeling too. Naina, I—"

"Wait." Naina pulled her hand from his grasp and stepped away. "Stop. Don't."

One look at her pale face and trembling lips, and Tejas knew. He just *knew*.

This was a mistake.

Chapter TWENTY-FIVE

Goa, May 2025

NAINA'S ANTI-HONEYMOON CHECKLIST

10. Blow money on something extravagant. ✓

Naina's words hung in the air, in the sudden, impossibly wide distance between them, as she stepped away and ran her sweaty palms down her dress. She couldn't do this. She couldn't let *Tejas* do this. He was going to confess his love and it would ruin everything when she couldn't say it back. It would end the night on the worst possible note, making this a trip to remember for all the wrong reasons. It would leave a bad taste in both of their mouths anytime they thought of Goa in the days, months, and years to come. More than that, it would break Naina's resolve to let him go, completely, out of sight, out of mind, out of her heart.

She wouldn't allow it.

"Don't," she repeated, even as her lower lip wobbled. She let out a shaky sigh and looked at the sea, unable to meet his gaze. "These past two weeks have been wonderful. I can't thank you enough.

But . . . tomorrow, it'll be goodbye forever. Let's not make it harder than it has to be."

"Naina, I—look at me, please."

Slowly, she turned his way, her own eyes blurring at the sight of the lone tear falling down his cheek. "Let's just enjoy tonight," she insisted. "Let's not ruin these final twelve hours."

"No," Tejas said, and for the first time in two weeks, he sounded agitated, borderline angry. "Tell me your last name, Naina."

Her eyes twitched, then shut. "I can't."

"Tell me where you're going, then, or what you do for work."

"No."

"Please, just—"

She silenced him with a kiss, but before she could soak in the touch of his lips or his beard prickling her chin, she pulled away, stepping backward, away from the railing, and wiped a tear from her eye. "This would never work in the real world, and you know it. We're just two messed-up, broken people who needed each other to be their human Band-Aids so they could move on from their exes."

Tejas's body visibly deflated; he clenched the front of his shirt, over his heart. "You're not just a Band-Aid to me. You're so much more."

"We can't. We shouldn't. I—I'm sorry." She exhaled shakily through tears. "Maybe . . . maybe one day. If we met again."

He stared back at her, his chest rising and falling, then leaned forward and kissed Naina on the cheek. "Okay," he said finally, and she breathed in the mingling scents of his champagne breath and woodsy aftershave.

"Shall we go back to our table?" she suggested, taking both his hands in hers as she forced herself to smile. "It's such a perfect night. I don't want it to end on a bad note."

He swallowed, then nodded. "Sure."

They made small talk while Martin came over to clear their plates. The meal had been paid for already, Naina and Tejas had split the cost, so she handed their server a generous tip, returning his eager smile. "Thank you for a wonderful experience," she said, and Martin nearly blushed.

"My pleasure, madam, sir," he said, bowing. "Your cab is waiting to take you back."

Tejas took Naina's hand and helped her down the ladder, and she decided not to protest. She might not have let him say it with words, but she knew that wouldn't stop him from showing it with his actions. Not that it would change her mind.

The cab ride to the hostel was supercharged with tension, a heavy silence in the air, but Naina didn't let go of Tejas's fingers wrapped around hers. She laid her head on his shoulder, he let his head fall on top of hers, and they stayed that way, not talking, until she spoke. "My flight takes off around noon, and I already called a taxi for nine A.M."

"Right." He swallowed; she felt the movement against her cheek. "My bus leaves tomorrow night."

She exhaled softly. "Could you drop me off at the airport? I don't want to do a rushed goodbye in the hostel while you're still packing your things."

Tejas stiffened. "Of course," he said finally, turning his face so his lips met her cheek.

When they were back in the room and the door had shut behind them, Naina pulled him closer so their foreheads touched. "I want you one more time," she said before dragging her mouth along his stubble. She undid the buttons of his shirt and exhaled. "One last time."

Tejas didn't speak; he only pulled her closer and zipped down her dress until it pooled at her feet. In between kisses, he picked her up and pressed her down to the lower bunk bed, settling himself in between her legs while she sat up to take off his belt and pants.

"No," he said, easing her back down.

Naina stared up at him, confused. "What—"

He hoisted her left ankle on his shoulder and took her right ankle in his hands, his eyes turning molten. "If tonight is the last time," he said, trailing his tongue along her ankle as she gasped, "then I'm going to touch and taste and kiss every fucking part of you. I'm not going to stop until I have you memorized."

"O-okay," Naina said as she swallowed. She traced the inseam of his pants with her foot, and he trembled. "But only if I get to memorize you too."

"Deal," he said before he pulled her closer, letting her thighs tighten around his neck. With every passing second, Naina seared this perfect moment into her brain, never to be tarnished. The bucking of her hips as she finished, the hunger in his gaze when she pinned him down and dropped her mouth to his bulge, the urgency with which she rolled the condom onto his length and straddled him, and every single thing they'd left unsaid as she came undone.

His arms slid out from over her hips, and he stood. Naina hated how every nerve and fiber in her body screamed in protest; she hated the knowledge that despite wanting to let go of him, she would never forget what it was like to have him, kiss him, touch him.

What it was like to *know* him.

But she didn't know him, not really. After tomorrow, she never would. Time had run out on their story, if it had ever even begun at all.

She got up, pulling her hair into a messy bun, forcing herself to keep it together. "Wow," she said. "I think that was our best yet."

"Yeah," he replied. "Definitely."

She smiled weakly at him, then tugged on her pajamas. "I'd better finish packing."

"Do you need help?" Tejas asked, his eyes sweeping across the room.

"I don't think so," she replied, dragging her suitcase out from the corner and unzipping it. "You should get ready for bed. We'll have to be up early for the cab."

Tejas went to the bathroom, his toothbrush in hand, and Naina got to work stuffing her suitcase with her folded clothes and the trinkets she'd bought for her loved ones back home. She took her towel off the door hook, stowed her iPad and chargers in her carry-on, and packed her toiletries.

When she was done, the half-empty room looked alien, as if the spirit of her alter ego—Naina Stark—had never existed at all. *Good,* she thought. Her eyes fell on the bottom bunk bed, where she and Tejas fell asleep cuddling every night, and she hesitated, her legs urging her to nestle into the sheets that smelled just like him.

Then she shook her head and climbed to the top bunk, closing her eyes and willing herself to fall asleep before Tejas came back. After the conversation on the yacht, he wouldn't ask her why she was sleeping there instead of in his arms, but she didn't want to see the look of disappointment in his eyes either way.

The door opened just as the heavy weight in her chest pushed her into a deep slumber.

♡ ♡ ♡

Naina's alarm blared out a serene melody at eight a.m. the next morning, and she roused, stifling a yawn. She sat up in bed and stretched, then tapped the wooden frame. "Morning," she called out. "Did you sleep well?"

Silence.

She frowned. Maybe it was the aftereffects of the champagne and the fact that Tejas was a deep sleeper. *Or maybe it's something else,* she thought, her stomach squirming as she took in the completely barebones, empty room. No laptop on the desk. None of Tejas's clothes on the messy floor. Not even his suitcase sitting by the door.

"Tejas?" she said, her voice trembling as a shiver crept down her spine.

No answer.

She scrambled down to the ladder, her breath heavy, and found the bottom bunk empty, the sheets and blanket neatly tucked into the corners. "No," she whispered as the first tear slid down her cheeks.

Naina left the door swinging on its hinges and her feet still bare in her haste to get to the kitchen, which was empty this early in the morning. Who in their right hungover mind would bother getting up before nine A.M. while on vacation? She headed to Aleksy and Jonah's room and pounded on the door, then paced back and forth, biting her nails as she waited.

After five knocks, Jonah answered the door with messy hair and half-closed eyes. "Hmm?" he said. "Are you leaving now? Have a safe flight."

"Where's Tejas?" she exclaimed, trying to peek into their room. Aleksy was still sleeping on the right side of the bed, lost to the world. "Is he here?"

Jonah yawned. "Why would Tejas be here?" He rubbed his eyes and returned to his bed, forgetting to close the door. Naina pulled it shut and walked back in a daze. She got into the bottom bunk, pulling the blanket that still smelled like Tejas over herself, and let her face crumple with tears and her body shake with never-ending sobs.

Why was she crying? Wasn't this what she wanted, for them to walk out of each other's lives without looking back? Why was she grieving something she didn't want to have, someone she would never meet again?

Maybe it was for the best that he'd left without a proper goodbye.

This is fine, Naina decided as she sat up and wiped her tears. This was proof that she shouldn't let someone in again. Never again would she cry over a man. Never again would she give someone false hope only for her own heart to betray her. Never, ever again.

Chapter TWENTY-SIX

Bangalore, November 2026

Tejas stifled a yawn as he walked through the hallway with quick strides toward Ramesh Kumble's office. He'd had a sleepless weekend, not only as a consequence of that almost-kiss in the pub washroom, but also because he'd spent hours working on the Acharya case, doing background checks on Pai, Gopal, and Preethi. He'd assumed fixating on the specifics of a murder case at four A.M. would make all thoughts of Naina disappear, but unfortunately, she'd been online too, adding notes to the shared Preethi case document. Tejas had made his own changes minutes later, crossing out many of her points and rewriting them, even though they hadn't needed edits.

So what, though? He had every fucking right to be antagonistic with her. She was the petty one, having ignored his texts about what happened in the bathroom all weekend, refusing to admit there was something real between them. Just like she'd done in Goa.

The clicking of heels sounded behind him, and he knew it was her before she even spoke. "Listen," Naina said, her steps hurried as she caught up to Tejas, "can we put karaoke night behind us and just be professional?"

He stopped in place and whirled toward her, ignoring the heady scent of lavender. "Professional? Are you kidding me?" Then he looked around the office and lowered his voice. "We almost kissed. You wanted to kiss me too, don't you think I know that? I'm tired of you stringing me along, Naina."

"I'm still processing what happened," Naina said, wringing her hands as she frowned.

"You've had over a year to process what happened." He paused as Iqbal brushed past them, heading to Kumble's office up ahead for their catch-up meeting. Then Tejas added, his jaw clenching, "This is exactly why I left for the bus stop without telling you, back in Goa. Because I didn't think I could watch you walk away from me without it completely shattering my heart. So I did it myself. But guess what, Naina?"

Her lip wobbled as she stared up at him. "W-what?"

Despite his anger, Tejas had the sudden urge to interlock his fingers with hers, to kiss away the lines on her forehead, to press her to his chest and remind her of everything they'd once shared. Everything they could share again, if only she'd take a chance on them.

But she didn't need to be reminded. She knew it already; she just didn't care. So he only scoffed. "On Friday night, at karaoke, you walked out on me and shattered my heart anyway. I guess that was inevitable."

"Tejas, I—"

"Anyway"—he tipped his head toward the managing partner's door—"I'm going to head in there. You should too. A woman's life is on the line."

Head bowed, she nodded, and they knocked and entered Ramesh Kumble's office. They'd already sent him their notes, and he seemed to be perusing them as he gestured for them to sit. Iqbal stood beside Kumble's chair, his eyes on the laptop too.

"So . . ." Kumble looked at Tejas and Naina, rubbing his chin. "Four days before trial, the only lead we have so far is that the actor had a beef with Rohith Pai?"

Tejas felt Naina straighten beside him, like she was going to speak, but he cut in, his jaw set. "Yes, because he refused to get close enough to Preethi while filming the action scenes. Probably because he thought she'd accuse him of something, given everything that happened with Preethi and Pai years ago. Maybe he was scared she would sabotage the film—and his career."

"Your sources?" Iqbal asked as he flipped through a copy of the latest forensic report.

"The crew members we met know a lot of industry gossip," Tejas explained in quick words so he could beat Naina to it. "The on-set makeup artist said Gopal and Pai were arguing the entire shoot, and Pai refused to budge on altering the scene. Also, it's suspicious neither he nor his wife heard Preethi's screams, but they heard Jagannath's cries for help. In any case, we're meeting with Preethi day after tomorrow to find out if she knows more about Gopal's dynamic with Pai. I'm certain we'll have some evidence against Gopal soon; he's our strongest suspect. Plus, the forensic report's findings might work in our favor."

Kumble and Iqbal exchanged glances, then nodded as one unit. "Good job," Kumble said, his approving eyes on Tejas. "Let us know what Preethi has to say. In the meantime, make sure to check our case files for any precedents we can use. Speculation and rumors won't be enough to save Preethi Acharya." Then he returned to his screen without one look at Naina.

Tejas's stomach squirmed. He himself had every right to ignore Naina—she deserved it after what she'd pulled on Friday—but why was Kumble doing it too?

Iqbal must have noticed the tension in the air, because he smiled at Naina specifically and said, "You've got this."

"Thank you," she said, her chin up.

"Back to work," Tejas said, gesturing toward the door. "We don't have time to waste."

He led the way out of Kumble's corner office without another word and strode over to his cubicle to a rather unfamiliar sight:

Dhanush hunched over the desk, no ringing phone in hand, his laptop on standby.

Tejas sat in his chair and poked Dhanush on the shoulder. "You okay?"

"No," Dhanush replied glumly, rubbing his eyes. "I was distracted all weekend, and I'm so behind on my cases. Plus, the prosecution found more evidence against Subramanian, and the stock market's already crashed in anticipation of his arrest. Court is going to be a nightmare this week . . ." He turned his eyes to his keyboard and pressed a random button on it. "My uncle's going to fire me."

Tejas scoffed. "Look at me, man."

With a heavy sigh, Dhanush did as he was told. Tejas pressed a hand to his back and smiled. "You're not the only lawyer on this case. Is Kumble going to fire Iqbal too?"

"Obviously not, he's a partner," Dhanush grumbled. "I'm the scapegoat, the one they'll blame if this case goes under. Which it inevitably will."

"There isn't a single lawyer out there who's guaranteed to win all of their cases," Tejas reminded him. Then he brought his voice to a whisper. "Do you remember the Bollywood drug trafficking case from two years ago?"

Dhanush's eyes widened. "Yeah, that producer who was arrested for selling cocaine to his actors? Isn't he serving ten years in prison?"

"I was one of the lawyers representing him," Tejas admitted, shifting in place. "And as much as we wanted to win the case, we also knew sometimes a guilty person can't be saved, no matter how good their lawyers are. It's . . ." He shrugged. "It's just how the universe works."

"In that case, I hate the universe." Dhanush's shoulders slumped.

Exhaling, Tejas said, "You and me both."

Dhanush didn't answer. His distant eyes were on Anil, who sat in his cubicle next to Naina's. There was an emotion Tejas had never seen on Dhanush's face before—something Tejas couldn't place. "Dhanush, is something else on your mind?"

Dhanush jumped. "Oh, nothing," he said quickly, wiping his face with a trembling hand. "Need to remind Anil to work on the pro bono case. I'll email him."

Tejas lifted his hand in Anil's direction. "You could just go up to him. He's right there."

"Email would be quicker," Dhanush replied, turning away.

"Okay, then . . ." Tejas returned to his laptop, but not before his gaze shifted to Naina, way ahead of him as she deftly typed into a document. How was she so unbothered by their fight?

Maybe he ought to cut his losses and follow her lead. If she could play it cool, he could too.

After successfully cheering Dhanush up with a mug of black coffee and a chocolate croissant from the office pantry, Tejas got back to work, deciding he and Naina might as well leverage the power of social media to win this case. There were probably thousands of Kannada film fanatics who knew more about Rohith Pai's life, hobbies, and habits than Rohith's own wife did. Tejas had learned as much after having worked in a Mumbai law firm that often protected Bollywood stars from their stalkers.

He took a sip of his latte and resumed scrolling through Reddit. According to his sister, who was obsessed with Bollywood, there was no better place for celebrity gossip or conspiracy theories than Reddit.

While the r/SandalwoodTea subreddit, dedicated to the nearly hundred-year-old Kannada film industry, had twelve thousand members, the newly created r/PaiMurder subreddit had a whopping 293,000 members. It didn't surprise Tejas that most of the posts in this specific subreddit were against Preethi. They brought up instances of "bad behavior" from her past that obviously made her a murderer, like wearing a skimpy bikini at the beach for her swimwear sponsorship or "enabling" innocent, unsuspecting women to go to the pole-dancing fitness classes she endorsed instead of toiling away in the kitchen, where they apparently belonged.

Tejas's nostrils flared. What a sad, toxic, depressing place the internet was. Blinking away his annoyance, he went through the rest of the r/PaiMurder subreddit, hoping he'd come across something useful.

Forty minutes later, when the words on the page were all starting to blur together in a heinous mix of *knife* and *skimpy* and *home-wrecker* and *blood,* something caught his eye. Half the posts in r/PaiMurder were by one specific user: AllegedlyYourBestTea89. "Huh." Tejas sent Naina the profile link on Teams, then headed over to her cubicle with his laptop.

He noticed the empty chair next to Naina's. "Where's Anil?" he asked.

Naina, who was already going through the subreddit, looked over. "It's lunchtime. He's not going to be back for a while."

Nodding, Tejas pulled out the chair and sat down. His knee brushed against her thigh, and Naina nearly jumped. "Sorry," she mumbled, shuffling away. Tejas would have been offended, but now wasn't the time to think about her indifference to that almost-kiss, to him, to everything they could have possibly shared if she didn't have her guard up all the time.

"This user is definitely shady," Naina said, pointing at the AllegedlyYourBestTea89 profile.

Tejas peered at the screen. Their first-ever post about Preethi was a month ago, on the day they'd created the account, after which they'd posted numerous hate messages about Preethi on the subreddit—nearly one every day. All it said was: Preethi Acharya is and always will be a home-wrecker. She deserves to be locked up.

"Look at the time stamp on this post." Naina pointed to the side of their profile and read out, "Seven forty-one A.M., October 1, 2026."

Tejas's eyebrows furrowed. He stood up and leaned over Naina's desk, noting the way she sucked in a breath at his proximity. "That's the day of the murder. Could it be a mere coincidence that they made their first anti-Preethi post possibly even before it was public news? Or . . ."

Naina bit her lip. "I guess we'll have to find out. I'll look up media archives and see what time the news broke."

Tejas stood, tapping her desk with his fingers. "Good call. I'll see if anyone from IT can track their IP address. Hopefully, it'll be someone connected to our case."

"Or someone the murderer hired to skew the public opinion against Preethi," Naina said bitterly. "I'll go through the rest of their posts. Maybe we can find clues to their real identity. There's bound to be something."

"It's worth a shot," Tejas agreed, just as Anil walked over to his cubicle. "Tejas, hey," he said cheerfully. "Did you have lunch? The cafeteria has a special biryani today."

"I'll head over there soon," Tejas replied just as amicably. "See you, Naina." As he started for his own desk, he overheard Naina say to her best friend, "Where were you at karaoke night after you ditched my ass?"

"Oh," Anil said, his laughter echoing, "having my favorite kind of fun. You should try it too. Maybe with Prince Charm—"

A playful smack sounded, even from the distance. Shaking his head, Tejas returned to his cubicle and switched to working on one of his small-claims cases, this one involving property damage, but his mind was on Preethi Acharya. With India having abolished the jury system decades ago, only the judge would have a say in the matter. Would they be able to prove to the judge, against all odds, against all public opinion, that Preethi was innocent?

Well, with only four days to go until trial, Tejas would find out soon.

Chapter TWENTY-SEVEN

Because Preethi was a celebrity with a reasonable net worth, she was being held in the biggest prison in Bangalore, home to multiple high-profile convicts across politics, entertainment, and sports, where inmates with purchasing power had access to not just expensive booze and cigarettes, but also the latest gadgets and fashion.

Naina and Tejas followed a police officer through the building as he buzzed them into different corridors and hallways. Things were still tense between them, but Tejas had decided to let it slide for now. Preethi's trial mattered more than his complicated relationship (or lack thereof) with Naina.

The cop stopped in front of a visiting room and nodded. "Your client is inside."

"Thank you," Tejas said. He opened the door for Naina, ushering her in first, then shut the door behind them. They sat across from Preethi, who wore jeans and a floral shirt that hung loosely on her bones. Her face was ashen and sickly, and her red eyes were tearstained.

"How are you doing, Preethi?" Naina asked kindly. "I hope no one's been bothering you here. Our bosses requested you be given the best treatment possible."

Preethi smiled faintly. "Everyone's been nice for the most part. They let me wear my own clothes and bring me all the magazines I ask for."

Convicts, even those who weren't proven guilty yet, had to stick to the white plainclothes uniform—a concept meant to dehumanize them, Tejas was sure—but with a few pulled strings, most celebrities on trial could wear what they pleased. Hopefully, Preethi would never have to wear jail clothes.

"On the flip side," Preethi went on, shrugging, "I hate the food here, and I miss going to the gym, not that I have the energy to do anything. The lack of sleep doesn't help."

"We're going to get you out of here as soon as possible," Naina promised. She folded her hands on the table and narrowed her eyes. "Before that, we all need to be on the same page about this case and the trial."

They filled Preethi in on all of their findings and theories from the forensic reports, speaking to witnesses, and Tejas's past experiences with celebrity murder cases. When Naina eagerly brought up that the signs of struggle on Pai's body likely pointed to a male killer, Preethi's shoulders slumped. "I know you mean well, Naina, but my Instagram has a hundred videos of my workout routine and my gym sponsorship deals. And Rohith is"—she cringed—"*was* never one for a fitness routine."

Tejas's stomach sank at the look on Naina's face. He'd brought this up to her earlier, but there was no harm in pointing out the potential inconsistencies.

"About Rohith," Tejas said, biting his lip as he moved on to the next topic. "Do you know why he offered you the lead role after so many years of radio silence?"

"It was curious," Preethi said. "He told me I was the right fit for this role because no other actress in my age group had the build or experience to play a warrior princess—which made sense to me. He said enough time had passed since our breakup and the ensuing fight that we could let the past go, move forward, and be grown-ups about the situation."

Naina's eyebrows shot up. "I'm sorry, I don't know Pai personally, but did that sound genuine to you, coming from him, or were you suspicious at all?"

Preethi fidgeted in her seat. "Honestly, it was both. Logically, I knew he was right, because any other actress would've had to train for months to get to my fitness level. And yet I wondered if there was something more to it . . . and maybe it would finally be my chance at closure."

"Fair enough," Naina said, moving on to the next line of questioning, after which Tejas cleared his throat and asked about the tensions between Gopal and Pai.

"Oh, that was nothing new," Preethi said, dismissing it with a wave of her hand. "It's no secret Gopal hated the idea of working with me because of my reputation. He was distant and cold the entire time we were on set, but he was already contractually bound to the project before they brought me on, so he couldn't do anything except try to fight Rohith on his directorial vision."

"Do you think he could have had anything to do with the murder?" Naina lifted a brow. "Especially since the Krishnans' trailer was right across from Pai's?"

Preethi leaned back in her seat, thinking. "I don't know. He's a big, strong man for sure, but he and Rohith were close. Why would Gopal jeopardize that simply because he hates me? He could have just dropped out and broken the contract if things were that bad. God knows he has enough money."

"Okay." Tejas exhaled loudly, then slid three pages across the table toward Preethi. "Take a look at this."

She flipped through the screenshots of the anonymous hate account, her eyes widening with every passing second. "I knew it was bad enough on Instagram and Twitter, but Reddit too?"

Naina leaned forward and pointed at the date of AllegedlyYour-

BestTea89's hate posts about her. "This was their first post shortly after they created the account. You see the date here?"

Preethi frowned as she looked over it. "That's the morning of the murder. Was this before or after the news broke?"

"They posted it an hour after the official police report, but before the news went viral," Naina said. "Which means this could be someone directly connected to the murder."

Preethi's face blanched. "Even if this is a lead, how would we find out who's behind the account?"

"We've got IT working on it," Tejas said, his jaw clenched. His favorite tech intern had already warned him that it was next to impossible to get someone's IP off just a Reddit post, but Tejas had asked him to try his best.

Naina glanced at her iPad, then asked Preethi, "We were hoping for some character witnesses for you. People who could vouch that you're a good person, talk you up to the judge."

"Oh," Preethi whispered, frowning.

"Anyone in mind? Maybe a close friend, or someone you've worked with?"

She hesitated, then said, "I don't have a lot of connections in the industry anymore, and my family and friends outside of Sandalwood haven't checked in on me since the news broke. Well"—she smiled softly—"except for Sandhya."

That name sounded familiar. Tejas was racking his brain trying to place Sandhya when Naina spoke, her voice hushed. "Wait. Sandhya, Jagannath's daughter?"

"Yes," Preethi said. "She's such a sweet girl. She visited the set with her dad a few times, and we bonded over our love for Pilates. She texted me to check in while I was on bail, but she . . ." Preethi sighed. "She was close with Rohith too, having worked with him while shadowing her father, and who knows what lies Jagannath is telling her about me now. Plus, I doubt he would let her step foot in court. He's very protective of her."

Tejas recalled how Jagannath had spoken to Sandhya during their questioning. Protective? More like controlling. "If we subpoena her—" Tejas started.

"Jagannath's a politician now," Naina reminded him. "He probably has more sway with the court than we ever could. He'll make sure the judge dismisses the order, unless we spring it last-minute."

With a silent sigh, Tejas looked at the iPad in front of Naina. "Anything else to share, Preethi?"

Preethi shook her head, and Naina locked the iPad.

As they stood, Preethi added, "I . . . I'm anxious about the trial, but I feel more confident in the two of you than I was in my previous lawyers." She smiled. "You're good together."

Naina coughed. "Uh, thanks."

Tejas felt his lips widening in a smile before he remembered that Naina disagreed with Preethi's sentiments. She'd made it clear enough that there was no "together" as far as she and Tejas were concerned.

They exited the prison and were welcomed by the late afternoon sunshine and the cooling November breeze that brought with it the promise of a cozy, cuddly winter. "Back to the office," Tejas said stiffly, kicking a rock out of his way with his shoe, his hands in his pockets.

"Yeah," Naina agreed. "Maybe we could head to the archive room and look up old case precedents, on the off-chance this hate account lead goes nowhere."

Tejas gulped. Given the heavy fog of tension between them and the gravitas of this case, it probably wasn't a good idea to be in close proximity to Naina in a dark, isolated room . . . alone.

But hey, maybe this was another chance to confront her and get the closure he needed so they could focus on the case and nothing more. So he exhaled and said, "All right. Let's go."

Chapter TWENTY-EIGHT

Naina couldn't help but notice that Tejas was oddly quiet the entire auto ride back to the office, that he didn't say a word as they headed to the stuffy, dark archive room. He was clearly still mad at her. Well, as long as it didn't affect their work together . . .

Naina flicked on the lights, and they got to work in silence, rifling through old homicide and murder cases. At least for five minutes, after which Tejas spoke, an edge to his voice. "Did it even matter to you?"

Naina forced herself to look up from the May 2010 section as Tejas continued, "Those two weeks. Those perfect two weeks that I never stopped thinking about. Did you even miss me after I left?"

After I left. Naina's left eye pricked with a tear behind her glasses. She thought back to their final night, when he'd touched her like he never had before, almost as though it were his unspoken parting gift to her. If she had realized he would be gone by morning, she would have kissed him for longer. Much longer. She'd have soaked in his scent, relished in the warmth of his skin on hers. She hadn't forgotten the sight of that empty hostel room or the taste of her tears as she cried her feelings into a blanket that still smelled like him. How could she?

But she'd had a flight to catch, a life in Bangalore to get back to, Appa and Anil and AKC to return to. Tejas would never know that she'd faced the window with her silent sobs the entire flight back. That she'd promised herself she would forget about Goa and Tejas and fall back into her workaholic ways because, damn it, that's what people like Naina Shetty did. They married their work, because nobody else loved them enough to stay.

Naina's nostrils flared. "You were the one who disappeared before I woke up," she reminded him.

"Because I couldn't bear the thought of *you* walking away from *me*!" he exclaimed. "And we both know you wouldn't have given me a second glance before leaving."

"You know what?" Naina said irritably as she turned back to the archives. "We shouldn't be talking about Goa right now. We're at work."

Tejas scoffed, and she heard him slam a drawer shut. "Just look at me, Naina."

Naina pressed her eyes shut, exhaled, then whirled around to match his gaze. He stood leaning against the shelf, his muscled arms folded and straining the fabric of his shirt. She remembered those arms, not just from their summer fling, but from the other night. And God, she missed being held by them, feeling the security that only came from someone's solid, warm, loving embrace. No one had held her like that since Goa—well, until Tejas did at karaoke night.

"All I'm asking for is closure," he said, taking one step forward. When she didn't retreat, he took another step. He raked a hand over his tousled curls, lowering his gaze to her lips. "Tell me you don't feel anything for me anymore. Tell me you never did. That I was just some guy you got under to get over your ex. That you never—"

"Stop," Naina breathed through clenched teeth. The first tear slid down her cheek. "We can't do this. We shouldn't. Not now."

"Then when?" he urged. He followed the path of that tear down her cheek, the touch of his finger hot but gentle. "Please tell me what you're thinking. I just need an answer, and"—his voice broke—"and then I'll never bother you about this again. I promise."

Naina looked up at him through her tears as he withdrew his finger from her cheek and stepped back to allow more distance between them. She licked her lips, noticing how his eyes followed the movement. "You want to know what I'm thinking?"

"Yes," he whispered.

She was in a dangerous place, somewhere between stupid lust and soft concern. Two emotions she should not be feeling for the coworker who could ruin her focus *and* break her heart if he wanted to. But feelings were hard to fight—and for the first time in her life, all Naina wanted was to lose. "The only thing I'm thinking," she finally said, "is how I've never been kissed in the archive room."

Tejas's brows furrowed. Whatever he'd expected her to say, this clearly wasn't it. "You've never been kissed in the archive room," he repeated.

"Mm-hmm."

"Do you"—he rested a tentative hand beside her head, dipping his mouth to the side of her face—"want to be kissed in the archive room?"

She didn't have it in herself to process his words; her senses had been entirely taken over by the woodsy scent of his aftershave, the scratch of his stubble on her cheek.

Tejas set his other hand beside her head, pinning her in place. "Naina Shetty," he said, his voice a rumble against her ear, and fuck, her last name had never sounded this hot before, "do you want *me* to kiss you in the archive room?"

Naina couldn't reply with words. Her brain had shut off the moment his breath had tickled her ear. All she could manage was a faint whimper and a tug at his tie, nudging him closer, bridging the gap between them.

This first kiss was nothing like the one from eighteen months ago. No hesitation, no deliberating, no waiting for the other to respond. This was urgent, desperate, borderline needy. Naina's fingers pulled on the front of Tejas's shirt, her tongue moving against his with a ferocity she'd never known she had in her. His hands found her hips, one hand curled protectively over the skin under her shirt, the other holding her steady against the shelf. *Fuck*. Naina wanted—no, needed—more. More, more, more.

Her fingers moved lower to unbutton his shirt, but he broke their kiss abruptly. "No, wait, stop," he said.

"Let me guess," Naina said, sinking into the shelf, "I've been so out of practice that I'm now a terrible kisser?"

Tejas laughed. He brushed a lock of hair off her shoulder, his fingers lingering on her neck. "We're at work, Naina."

Naina lurched away from him, her knees wobbling from the aftermath of that kiss. Fuck. She had just made out with him in the archive room. A first for her, yes, and one that she'd never forget. But certainly there were cameras here? What if she got fired? And oh God, the case—

"It's okay," Tejas said, backing away, arms raised in surrender like he knew what she was thinking. His eyes went to the security camera in the corner, and he added, "I'm sure they don't check the cameras every day."

She wiped her face with a shaky hand. "Tejas, I—I'm sorry. We shouldn't have . . . we . . . I'm sorry."

"No," he said, straightening his tie over his collar again. "We *did*. And trust me, Naina Shetty." His face broke into a smirk that sent shivers down to her toes. "This won't be the last time. I'm not letting you go again."

Naina's heart was beating so fast, she might as well have run a 10K. She ran her sweaty hands along the sides of her shirt and got out a soft "Okay." What else could she say? Her logical brain hadn't quite kicked in yet, and the heat between her legs wouldn't dare protest. If they weren't at work, she would have—they would have—oh fuck.

"I'm going to head back to my desk," she said, trying to avert her gaze from his sexy, disheveled hair. His red mouth, stained from her lipstick. Those sturdy arms that looked as good as they felt wrapped around her—

Stop it, Naina. Without another word, she headed back up the stairs to the main office, her heels loud against the tiled floor. Seconds before she slid into her chair, she changed her mind and tapped the top of Anil's chair. "I need your advice," she said as she took off her smudged glasses and started wiping them with the corner of her shirt.

"Give me a minute," he said. He minimized his browser, put his laptop on standby, and swiveled around. When his eyes fell to her hands, still wiping the glasses, his face split into a know-it-all grin. His voice dropped to a whisper. "You didn't."

She played with the neckline of her shirt, hoping it hid the flush creeping along her collarbone, and put her glasses back on. "Not here, Anil."

He followed her into the elevator lobby, his long legs carrying him faster than hers. They stopped beside the elevator, and Naina blew out a breath. "Okay. Yes. He kissed me."

Anil pumped his fist in the air. *Jerk.* "Tell me you did it in the archive room," he pressed. "The 1990s aisle is especially perfect for—"

"I don't want to hear about your romps with whoever in the 1990s aisle, and no, we didn't do *it*. It was just a . . ." She scratched behind her ear. "A very steamy kiss. To be honest, I'm still turned on."

"Then what happened?" Anil asked. She bit her lip, and he groaned. "Nay, please do not tell me you said you had to work and then ran up here to talk to me, leaving that poor guy all by himself in a dark archive room full of spiders and cobwebs."

"Spiders? Just a second ago you were saying it's perfect for—"

"Nay?" Anil folded his arms, glaring.

"That's exactly what happened," she mumbled. Her eyes fell on his wristwatch, and she jumped at the chance to change the damn topic. "It's almost six! Shouldn't you be heading home?"

"Fine, I'll let you off just this once." He held back a laugh. "Good luck with the case . . . and do something about this thing with Tejas, please. Or maybe just do him. Nudge nudge, wink wink."

Naina cleared her throat. "Thanks. How's *your* life love going, by the way?" she added so he wouldn't bring Tejas up again. "You met a guy at karaoke, right?"

Anil's cheeks reddened. "Uh, we may have gone out a few more times since then."

"Anil!" she whisper-yelled. "What the hell? I need details!"

He adjusted his collar, wincing. "It's still new, and I don't wanna jinx it. See you tomorrow, Nay."

"Fine, see you."

Once Anil was gone, Naina spun around, facing the wall, and raked her hands through her hair. Part of her wanted nothing more than to go back downstairs to Tejas and fuck his brains out. But the other part, the one that knew it would never work out between her and *anyone,* needed to be in control. So she touched up her lipstick with her pocket mirror, plastered on a smile, and returned to work, deciding nothing but Preethi's case would have her attention for the next four hours.

Minutes later, her shoulders straightened at the whiff of Tejas's pine cologne. He brushed past her cubicle, dropping a note on her desk in his wake without a look back at her.

Naina stared at the paper for a whole minute before smoothing it out. Tejas's messy handwriting greeted her. *Meet me tonight. 9 pm. I want to finish what we started.*

Below that message was a home address in Indiranagar—his apartment, probably. Naina coughed and turned around to look at the rest of the office. Thankfully, everyone was focused on their work, except for Tejas, who caught her eye from across the room and lifted a brow.

She held her breath for the smallest of seconds, deliberating, then exhaled. She needed to get him out of her system, and maybe if they just did it once—one final time . . .

Okay, she mouthed.

He smiled and returned to his laptop. Seconds later, her Teams chimed with a message.

Tejas
Could you send me the autopsy report again?

Naina
Sure. [file attached]

Thanks 👍

Her neck prickled, the heat of his gaze searing into her skin even from a distance, but she didn't dare look back. Tejas's note rested beside her keyboard, and the anticipation of tonight—and what it might lead to—mounted as she shuffled in place, adjusting her skirt.

Fuck, she thought. *I'm in trouble.*

Chapter TWENTY-NINE

"Okay, okay, okay," Naina whispered to herself as she stood in front of apartment B-4, her fingers halfway to the doorbell. "You can do this. Hell, you want to do this. You want to do *him*. It's been way too long since Goa, and if it's just this one time, then why n—"

The door opened with a click, and Tejas grinned at her, a towel pressed into his curls. "Talking to yourself, Naina Stark?" His eyes had a playful glint to them, like he'd heard what she'd said.

Her cheeks flamed. God, Tejas looked good. The scent of pine and soap surrounded the corridor, and Naina, like a coat. He wore a loose-knit maroon sweater and dark gray sweatpants that perfectly outlined the curve of his—

"Want to come in?" he asked, and Naina's gaze shot up from his crotch to his face. Fuck, she wanted to wipe that annoying, gloating smirk off his face. And she wanted to do it with her lips.

But she was no longer the fun, charming, sexy woman Tejas had met in Goa. She was just . . . her usual boring self, with her head firmly on her shoulders, a heart caged in her chest, and skin tougher than nails. After an eighteen-month dry spell, she had no idea how to flirt.

Least of all with the man who'd just found her on his doorstep, mumbling to herself.

Naina bit her lip and followed him in, taking her heels off by the shoe rack. His apartment was simple and tidy, a five-seater sofa set and TV unit in the living room, a well-stocked minibar shelf, and a dining table with three chairs by the open kitchen; and . . . was that a quick white blur zooming out from under the couch? It raced into the hallway, which probably led to the bedroom. "Was that Astrid?" She pressed a hand to her heart. "You weren't lying about her footsteps being loud."

Tejas bit the inside of his cheek, studying her. "You remembered that too. Naina Stark, is there anything about Goa you've actually forgotten?"

"Shetty," she corrected him. She propped her work bag against the cream-colored wall, then straightened, fidgeting with her hands. "Nice place."

"Thanks." He hung his towel on a chair and smiled at her, his fingers hooked into the pockets of his sweatpants. "Want something to drink? A beer, or . . ."

"Beer?" Her gaze returned to the minibar, and she gave a sharp shake of the head. "How about something stronger?"

Tejas grinned. He grabbed a half-finished bottle of scotch from the shelf and rummaged in the kitchen cabinet for glasses. "Do you like your scotch with soda?" he asked over his shoulder.

She joined him in the kitchen, leaning her weight against the fridge. "Neat."

"I figured," he said, chuckling. "As for me . . ." He stepped closer, lowering his face to meet hers. She arched into him, pressing her hands to his sweater, waiting for him to close the space between them, but he simply murmured, "Rocks."

"Hmm?" She stared up at him, dazed.

Before she could blink, he wrapped his arms around her waist, lifted her up, and placed her down on the kitchen island like she weighed next to nothing. Then he opened the door to the freezer. "I like mine on the rocks."

Naina nodded, settling her butt onto the cold granite. Damn, he really could put those chiseled muscles to good use. "Right. Sorry, I thought—"

Tejas laughed as he made their drinks, adding one large ice cube to his glass. "What, you thought I called you here to hook up with you?"

"Didn't you?" she shot back, her forehead wrinkling. She might not be the poster girl for casual relationships, but no way had she misread the signs or his note. He wanted this as much as she did . . . right?

He handed her a glass of neat scotch, his gaze softening when their hands touched. "I called you here because I *like* you," he explained. "And I want to finish what we started in Goa."

She forced herself to frown at him, though her stupid heart thudded uncontrollably. "And what exactly did we start in Goa?"

With a clink against her drink, Tejas lifted his glass for a toast. "Us, of course."

Naina let out a small smile and sipped the rich, smooth liquid. "You don't give up that easily, do you?"

Tejas licked his lips. He stepped closer so her knee bumped against his thigh. "Not when I think I have a fighting chance."

"You do," Naina said, shivering at his proximity, "but I can't let anything, or anyone, distract me from my career or my goals." At the downturn of his mouth, she added, "Look, I'm not the Naina Stark you liked in Goa. I'm just Naina Shetty, resident workaholic at AKC—"

"That doesn't change how I feel about you," he insisted, but she held up a finger.

"I don't need a relationship," she finished, resting her hand on her knee, where it grazed against his warm thigh. "My priority is winning Preethi's case with no distractions whatsoever. At least not . . . long-term distractions."

Tejas drank his scotch, his throat bobbing. His gaze was fixed two inches above her head as he seemingly considered her words. "Fine," he finally said, moving away from her. "Then let's brainstorm about the case. You've got your laptop?"

Naina slid off the kitchen island, her mouth dry. The heat between her legs ebbed to a stop. "Wait, what?"

He led the way to the couch, picking up her work bag from the floor and giving it to her. As Naina wondered when and how Prince Charming had morphed into this cocky, breezy version she hadn't seen much of in Goa, Tejas sat down, turning on his laptop that rested on the coffee table. "I went through the autopsy report again," he said, typing on the keyboard while she stood in front of him, her jaw to the floor. "The medical examiner should definitely be on our list of—" He paused and lifted his head. "Is something wrong?"

Naina exhaled and took another sip of her scotch. "Nothing." She plopped onto the couch beside him, switching on her own laptop. "You were saying?"

"I liked your idea of focusing on Rohith Pai's signs of struggle. I'm sure the prosecution will bring up Preethi's crazy-difficult workout regimen, and we have to do our part."

She pulled up their Google Doc. "Great. I already have a few questions I want to ask the medical examiner. Who else?"

"Gopal Krishnan and Jagannath have already been subpoenaed." Tejas pursed his lips. "Pai's wife too. I'm sure they'll play up the 'loyal husband' angle."

Naina switched tabs to the document with Rohith Pai and Preethi's text messages. Between Preethi being cast in his movie and up until the night of the murder, there had been only professional messages. Nothing that insinuated Pai wanted to talk to her in any capacity outside of work. "Whoever framed Preethi must have sent that text, so they had to have been close enough with Pai to know or guess his lock screen password."

Tejas nodded. "I still think it's fishy how Jagannath heard Preethi's screams despite being farther away from Pai's trailer, but

Gopal—whose trailer was right behind the scene of the crime—said he only heard Jagannath's."

"Jagannath's assistant said he usually wakes up early in time for work or with just one reminder call, so he's probably not a very deep sleeper," Naina pointed out.

"Fair enough, but let's not rule either of them out just yet. For all we know, one of them might be behind the hate account," Tejas said as Astrid shuffled back into view from the hallway. She stretched her body into a downward dog pose, then hopped onto the couch and curled up beside Tejas.

"The trial's in two days," Naina said, tearing her eyes away from the adorable cat. "Let's think about potential motives for all our suspects and narrow them down from strongest to weakest."

For the next hour, they worked on doing just that. Gopal had problems with working with Preethi, to the extent he refused to even touch her during filming and had argued with Pai about it. But if he'd had such extreme hesitations, why not back out of the project? His career was stable enough to sustain one hit. Was it because of his long-standing friendship with Pai?

Jagannath had deflected most of Tejas and Naina's questions and hurried to get them out of his house, but he'd also been close with Pai for decades. Could anything have caused enough tension between them for it to lead to murder? And the discovery that his daughter was friends with Preethi was an interesting angle to explore too.

The crew, apart from Jagannath's assistant, had all slept in the same trailer, but one of them could have snuck out and killed Pai. They were all part of his usual film crew and seemed to revere him. Vaishnavi had her own trailer—upon her boss's request—and claimed she had been asleep until the police sirens had sounded, like everybody else.

Tejas shifted in his seat, jaw clenched, and Astrid roused from her nap with a soft meow. "We need to look into Jagannath's background—and his daughter's. Something about him feels off, but I can't put my finger on it."

"And . . ." Naina pressed her palms to her forehead. "We still don't know what made Pai take Preethi on for this project. They hadn't spoken in years, and her reputation was a mess. Was he going to use the controversy to get people talking about the movie? Did he really think she was the right fit for the role? Or something else? We need to figure that out."

"That should be our next step," Tejas agreed, stifling a yawn. He scratched a sleepy Astrid under her chin. "Fuck, it's eleven P.M. Let's reconvene in the morning?"

"Works for me." Naina stood, smoothing out the crinkles in her skirt, and packed her laptop bag, which sat beside Astrid and had three or four white hairs near the zipper. "Astrid is cuter than I remember from the photos," she said, chuckling.

Tejas got up and grinned, his fond eyes on the cat sprawled on the couch. "It's all the extra weight. The vet wants her on a strict diet, but she gives me one sad meow, and I bring out the bag of treats."

Naina sighed as she looked at him, a man who was funny and sexy and so, so sweet. "Sometimes what you *want* isn't necessarily what you need."

"I agree." Tejas patted Astrid on the butt twice, and she made a garbled meowing noise and zoomed into one of the rooms. Then he turned to Naina, his eyes hooded as they fell to her mouth. "Which is why I haven't pushed you up against the wall yet with my hand under your skirt."

A strangled moan escaped Naina just at the thought of it. At the thought of him touching her again.

"But you don't want any distractions." He shrugged, his mouth pulling up on one side. "And I respect that."

Naina could hardly register his words. Her mind was on the barely there dimple creasing his cheek, his woodsy, clean smell tantalizing her senses, and that smoldering gaze, perfectly contrasting with his soft smile. "Fuck it," she breathed as she fisted the front of his sweater with both hands and pulled him in.

His lips moved along hers with a familiarity she hadn't noticed in the archive room, hot and yielding, as he kissed her with the intensity she wanted and the softness she needed. "Fuck," he groaned as she flicked her tongue over his lower lip, a silent plea to give her everything he had. He opened his mouth, his hot breath mingling with hers, and she raked her hands over the wool of his sweater, wishing there was nothing separating them. She walked backward, pulling him with her, until her shoulders pressed against the wall.

Tejas broke away from her, a question in his eyes. "Are you sure?" he asked.

She took his hand, kissing the side of his wrist, and pressed it to her inner thigh. "I'm sure," she said, and then his fingers were exactly where she wanted them, his lips raking over the sensitive skin of her neck as desperate need snaked up her core, begging for release, aching for Tejas to keep going, faster, harder, to never stop—

Stars exploded beneath her closed eyes, and she fell into Tejas's arms, her chest rising and falling with deep breaths. "I—I—oh my God," she whispered, touching her lips to his mouth. "Shit, I can barely stand upright."

"Was that good?" Tejas said, though his grin told her he already knew the answer.

"Yes," she said. "It was . . . just like I remembered it."

His chest rose and fell, the hunger evident in his gaze. The intensity in his eyes was overpowering; she had to look away for a second before speaking again. "Tejas, I want to make you feel that good too."

"Are you sure?" Tejas licked his lips as his eyes fell on the wall clock. "It's late. Your dad's probably wondering where you are."

"I'll be quick," she promised. "I just, I want to taste you again. I . . . I *need* to."

He swallowed, his Adam's apple bobbing, then closed the space between them, his hands curving around her waist. Naina took off her glasses and veered him toward the couch. She pushed him down and straddled him, then moved to take off his sweatpants and boxers. "Is this okay?"

"God, yes," he breathed, shuddering as she kissed a line down his collarbone, his neck, his stomach, until she could finally take him in her mouth. Tejas's hips moved in time with her hands and lips, and Naina closed her own eyes, relishing in the unparalleled joy of making someone feel as good as they made her feel. Eighteen months since she'd seen him like this in Goa, vulnerable and aching for her, and yet Naina remembered it all: biting that sensitive spot on his upper thigh, licking him slowly and gently to tease him, and the loud moan he let out when he came, hard and fast, before pulling her into his lap for a kiss that gave her shivers long beyond the touch of their lips.

It lingered as Naina kissed him goodbye and went downstairs to hail an auto rickshaw home. It lingered as she evaded Appa's questions about where she had been and why her hair looked so disheveled. It lingered even as she hopped into the shower, soaping herself up and wishing Tejas's hands were on her body instead, where they seemed to belong.

Good lord, she was truly fucked.

Chapter THIRTY

The first day of Preethi's trial was finally upon them. Tejas pressed his lips together as he walked up the stairs of the courthouse, Naina and Iqbal flanking him on either side. They all wore the court-mandated uniform for advocates: a white shirt under a black coat, long black pants, and a white band around their neck. Ahead of them was Preethi, handcuffed and accompanied by two female cops.

Ramesh Kumble still thought his iffy advice about finding someone else to pin the murder on, regardless of who it was, was the smartest way forward, but Tejas hoped they wouldn't have to find the killer. The progress he and Naina had made on the case this past week wasn't much, but maybe IT could pull through with the hate account and help them get the charges against Preethi dropped. Everything the prosecution had entered into evidence was circumstantial, which would make it easy for Tejas and Naina to poke holes in the witnesses' statements when they were on the stand.

They were ushered into the courtroom within minutes. Tejas and Naina greeted the public prosecutor, and he smiled at them tightly before returning to his papers.

"All rise, please," the bailiff said.

The judge presiding over their case walked up to the bench. She was an elderly woman dressed in a white saree and a long full-sleeved black coat, her mouth in a thin line. Tejas exchanged glances with Naina. A female judge would more likely stand for justice without any misogynistic bias clouding her decision. At the same time, all of Pai's rabid fans were out for Preethi's blood and eager to see her sentenced. Hopefully, the judge wouldn't let public demands pressure her into making an early decision.

Tejas and Naina probably only had a few sessions in court to prove Preethi's innocence. With India abolishing the jury system in 1973, Tejas had never gotten the chance to win a case by convincing the jury to rule in his favor, and he would never know if it was easier or harder than trying to plead his case to a single judge.

They sat back down once the court was in session, and as the charges against Preethi (culpable homicide) were read out, Tejas noticed Naina had turned to look at their client, who sat behind them with Iqbal. He, too, shifted in place. She was visibly trembling, her eyes closed and her breaths shaky. Being in court, with its stifling tension and eerie atmosphere, was intimidating in itself; Tejas couldn't imagine how much more terrifying it was to be the reason the court was in session. Sighing, he faced the front again, as did Naina. Slowly, hesitantly, Tejas wound his pinky finger against hers for the briefest of seconds. When she looked up at him, he gave her a small nod. *We've got this,* he mouthed.

She nodded back, and he smiled. Over the past two days, they'd spent hours together getting coffee and talking about the case, but neither of them had initiated meeting again for . . . non-work reasons, having been too caught up in the process of figuring out a defense for Preethi. Which meant the last time they'd really spent time together was the night he invited her to his apartment, and Tejas was in need of his next fix of Naina Shetty. He decided that if the first day of court went well, he would ask her out to dinner. A promising day in court might just show her they made a good team as partners . . . and that could maybe extend to a real relationship.

"And how does the defendant plead?" the judge asked, bringing Tejas's attention back to the present.

Preethi exhaled loudly. "Not—not guilty, Your Honor."

The public prosecutor, who was a middle-aged advocate with a graying beard, stood and shuffled the papers in his hand. "Good afternoon, Your Honor, and members of the court. My name is Mohammad Rizwan, and I am representing the state of Karnataka as the prosector on this case of Preethi Acharya v. State of Karnataka. During the early hours of October first, 2026, the defendant, Preethi Acharya"—he shot a glance in Preethi's direction—"brutally killed Rohith Pai, a man who was not only Karnataka's most accomplished movie director but also her former lover, who now leaves behind a grieving wife. This heinous crime of passion must be punished."

A woman's quiet sobs echoed from a few rows behind them. Rohith Pai's wife was on the witness list, and Tejas and Naina had questions to ask her that would hopefully tip the scales in their favor.

After the prosecution's opening statement, in which he described the facts of the murder and the witnesses he would call to the stand, Tejas stood. Naina had wanted to take the lead with their opening statement, but Kumble had suggested Tejas do it, because according to him, male lawyers made better first impressions. It was a horrible thing to say, albeit true in a misogynistic industry like Indian law. Even Naina had grumbled that Kumble's point was valid.

Tejas introduced Naina and himself as Preethi's lawyers, then addressed the court. "Your Honor, this case is nothing more than that of a well-intentioned person being in the wrong place at the wrong time. Like the prosecution said, our client Preethi Acharya *was* found lying beside Rohith Pai's dead body by two witnesses. Her fingerprints *were* found at the scene of the crime, but only because she is a good person and couldn't stop herself from trying—and failing—to save Mr. Pai, despite their long-standing conflict. All she sought was closure, which is what Mr. Pai's text message promised her. And since there is only circumstantial evidence that ties her to this crime, the prosecution cannot reasonably meet their burden of proof." He adjusted his tie over his collar. "Once we put forth our defense, we ask that Your Honor find our client not guilty, because sending an innocent woman to jail for wanting to close the door on a heart-breaking mistake made years ago and move on to a better, brighter future, at long last, would be a travesty. Thank you."

A few days ago, when Tejas had run this "seeking closure from a past lover" angle by their bosses, who were wholeheartedly on board, Naina had pulled him aside to say it might not work. She'd thought people wouldn't buy it, given Preethi's reputation as a home-wrecker and her so-called scandalous brand sponsorships, that they'd assume she went there to hook up with Pai and had killed him when he turned her down. But as Tejas looked around at the faces of the people in court, he knew his strategy made sense. This approach would not only steer people away from their false assumptions about Preethi, painting her in a more positive light, but also appeal to their vulnerability. After all, who didn't want closure from an ex? Who didn't want to forgive and forget so they could eventually find the one for them? Tejas's angle would get people's emotions on their side a lot faster—and hopefully, the judge's too.

Mohammad Rizwan called his first witness: the medical examiner, a thin, nervous-looking man who fidgeted with his hands as he took the stand. After his oath, the prosecutor tapped on his phone until the screen on the wall came to life with pictures of Rohith Pai's dead body from the night of the murder. "Please state your name and occupation for the court," Mr. Rizwan said to the witness.

The man cleared his throat. "My name is Vasanth Kumar. I work as an independent medical examiner in the state of Karnataka."

"Mr. Kumar, what can you tell us about the way Rohith Pai was murdered based on these pictures and your findings from the laboratory?"

Kumar pointed out the signs of struggle, the bruising on Pai's neck, and the fatal knife wound to the stomach. Mr. Rizwan then read aloud an excerpt from the official forensic report about Preethi's fingerprints being on the murder weapon. "Based on these injuries, do you think, in your expert opinion, an altercation could have happened between the victim and the defendant that led to his murder?"

"Yes, it appears the victim was overpowered, despite his attempts to struggle, and then stabbed once, deep in the stomach, which was the fatal wound, and he died shortly after."

"Specifically," Mr. Rizwan said, swiping to the next slide, "do you think this woman—Preethi Acharya—could have overpowered the victim, who was a five-foot-eight man with no background or interest in the gym?"

Tejas sighed silently as a soft gasp escaped the room, as he'd expected. The photo was a collage of screenshots from Preethi's workout footage of her benching and squatting heavy barbells.

"It's possible," Kumar said after a moment of quiet pondering. "She certainly has the height, build, and fitness level to do so. It wouldn't be easy, but it's possible."

"Your witness," Mr. Rizwan said, nodding sharply at Tejas and Naina.

Naina stood, the smallest of smiles on her face. Tejas gave her an encouraging nod when their eyes met. The specific way in which Mr. Rizwan worded his questions had given their strategy a great opening. "Mr. Kumar," Naina said, "you said you believe it is possible for a woman like Preethi to have overpowered Rohith Pai, right?"

"Yes, that's what I said."

Naina clicked through to a different picture from the evidence file: Preethi's mug shot. Her hair and nails, still matted with Rohith's blood, her eyes red and weary, and her face pale as a ghost. "Can you explain to me what you mean by 'overpower'?" she asked.

As Tejas leaned back in his seat, his fingers steepled together, the medical examiner blinked, like he was unsure where she was going with this. "I mean to say that in case of an altercation, this woman, being in the prime of her physical health, would have been able to fight back against Mr. Pai."

"Thank you." Naina pointed to the mug shot. "Mr. Kumar, do you see signs of struggle in this picture of my client taken less than twelve hours after the life-ending altercation she apparently engaged in?"

Kumar scratched the side of his neck. "Well, no. I don't see any bruises from this specific picture—"

"In fact, there were no bruises found on Preethi Acharya's body, or injuries to her fists, when she was initially interviewed by the police or when she was brought into prison last week, as is stated in the police reports in the evidence file." Turning to the stand again, she asked, "Mr. Kumar, how long do bruises typically take to heal after a brutal fight like the one Mr. Rizwan is claiming happened?"

"Uh, one or two weeks, perhaps, with regular care and icing?"

"All right," she replied as she paced back and forth in front of him. "So, Mr. Kumar, if my client did indeed inflict those bruises on Rohith Pai's body, if she had actually overpowered him after he struggled to defend himself, why wasn't there a single scratch on her body? Why wasn't her own blood anywhere at the crime scene?"

Tejas resisted the urge to pump his fist in the air. They'd got him, and based on the prosecutor's wide eyes, he knew it too.

Kumar fell silent. Finally, he said, "I don't . . . I don't know."

"No further questions, Your Honor." Naina returned to her seat as Tejas turned to look at Preethi, who had sat up straighter, color back in her face.

The prosecution brought out their next witness—Pai's wife and childhood sweetheart, Athira, whose face was still damp with fresh tears. "Mrs. Pai," Mr. Rizwan said, "were there any signs that led you to believe your husband was being unfaithful to you in the past year?"

"N-never," Athira said, wiping her eyes with a handkerchief.

"Rohith was a loving husband and my best friend. I've known and loved him since we were kids. He might have gone astray in the middle there"—at this, she shot eye daggers at Preethi—"but after we found our way back to each other again, there was no going back. Decades of our love, six years of a picture-perfect married life, with just one blip along the way . . . until he was murdered." Athira turned to the judge, folding her hands in a pleading motion. "Your Honor, give this witch the punishment she deserves for killing my husband!"

"Ma'am, please direct your communication to the prosecutor, not me," the judge drawled.

While Mr. Rizwan asked Athira more about her relationship with Pai over the years, Naina and Tejas consulted their notes, specifically the page with the details of Pai and Preethi's messages over the course of filming. Finally, Mr. Rizwan addressed the texts from the night of the murder. "Your Honor," he said, gesturing to the WhatsApp chat on the screen, "according to these logs, Rohith Pai allegedly messaged the defendant two minutes before midnight on October 1, inviting her over to his trailer, alone, because he was thinking of her. Why would a loyal, devoted, doting husband—whose wallpaper is a picture of his wife from their wedding day—send a message like that to another woman?"

Although Tejas agreed that the text wasn't Pai's, he still had to hold himself back from rolling his eyes. Doting, devoted husbands didn't cheat years prior, with a girl half their age.

"Ro-Rohith would never have sent that message," Athira agreed, choking on her sobs. "That vile woman must have sent it using his phone to cover her tracks. Rohith didn't believe in locking his phone, and most people in the industry know that."

Tejas and Naina exchanged glances. Good. The prosecution had walked right into their next line of defense: that Preethi was being framed, and that the texts had been sent by someone else who was on set that night.

The judge adjourned the session, seeing as the court was soon closing for the day. The trial would continue on Monday, when they would cross-examine Athira and other witnesses like Jagannath, Bina, and Gopal, who had already been summoned.

As Naina walked out of the courtroom, Tejas smiled at her, giving her hand a light squeeze. "I think this is going really well. Unless the prosecution has some sort of wild card gotcha moment, we've got this."

"I agree," Naina said as they headed toward the exit. "At this rate, we might not even have to dig deeper into Jagannath's possible motive."

Tejas held back a gasp as they stepped outside. People might have called Preethi a C-list actress, but the horde standing before them told Tejas this case was no less high-profile than the many Bollywood cases his previous firm had handled.

Fending off the paparazzi and press outside was a real challenge; they clamored and crowded in front of the courthouse, yelling out questions and shoving cameras in their faces. Thankfully, Naina didn't protest when Tejas wound his arm around her and pushed them both past the mob, Iqbal behind them.

The sun peeked through the clouds like an orange ball in the overcast skies, casting the streets of Bangalore in hazy golden light. Iqbal bid them goodbye, since he had a few things to wrap up at work, and drove off in his car.

Naina checked her wristwatch, which said five-twenty P.M. "Are you going back to the office?" she asked as they walked to an auto rickshaw stand up ahead. "I can't believe *I'm* saying this, but I need a break from work."

"Me too." Tejas hesitated as Naina flagged down an auto rickshaw driver across the street. "Do you, um, want to get dinner tonight?"

Naina fiddled with her thumbs, a blush heating her cheeks. "Like a date?"

A thousand butterflies danced in his stomach as he bit his lip nervously. "Yes. Do you want to?"

She cast a look at the auto, which had pulled up next to them, then smiled softly. "Only if I get to pick the restaurant."

Tejas laughed, putting his hands in his pockets. "The choice is yours. Text me the place, and I'll meet you there at eight?"

Her smile widened. "It's a date," she said before climbing into the auto, and those giddy butterflies in Tejas's belly transformed into something else entirely: *hope*.

Chapter THIRTY-ONE

As Naina unlocked her front door and stepped inside, she didn't quite know how she felt about a dinner date with Tejas. Although she hoped it would lead to him inviting her home, was she ready for anything more than sex? Knowing Tejas and how he hadn't been able to handle a two-week fling in Goa without catching feelings, he wouldn't want this relationship between them, if she could call it that, to stay strictly casual for long.

As much as she wanted to have Tejas's mouth on hers, she also wanted to share a drink or two with him, ask him about his life in Mumbai, even laugh at his cat's shenanigans. Was it a bad thing that maybe, just maybe, Naina's icy resolve to guard her heart was thawing?

She'd find out. For now, the challenge was to tell her father she wasn't coming home tonight without him suspecting she was going on a date or thinking she was in a real relationship. She hadn't been gone for a night since, well, since before her engagement ended.

So she wasn't surprised when Appa had a hundred questions

about where she was going and who would be there. She was prepared with her answers, all of which were white lies.

"Appa, it's just dinner with some colleagues," she insisted, "after which we have to finish a lot of work for the case. I'd rather not come home late and disturb your sleep."

He followed her into her room, watching as she took out her overnight bag and ransacked her closet for a pretty dress. "Wait, are you staying at your colleague's apartment? The same one who's working on Preethi's case with you?"

"He has a spare room," she said, which was technically true. It was a storage room that hosted multiple cat beds for Astrid, though Tejas said she only ever slept on his pillow, curled up beside his head.

"Ah!" Appa's eyebrows shot up. "It's a he!"

She picked out a dress and gave her father a weird look. "You already knew that."

"I did." Appa chuckled as he gestured to the dress, a sleek fiery-red number that was simple at first glance but made Naina's muscly legs look modelesque. "That's a great choice for a work dinner."

"Appa!" Naina scolded. "Get out!"

Laughing, he wiggled his fingers at her in goodbye. "Bring my future son-in-law home sometime so I can judge him. Or"—he paused in the doorway—"judge *you* with him."

She glared until he was gone, the door closing behind him with a soft click. Appa had never been narrow-minded like her friends' parents, but she thought he would have been at least a little upset that she would be staying over at a male colleague's apartment. Then again, nearly two years had passed since the broken engagement. Appa would probably give his left kidney if it meant Naina found someone new to marry.

Once she was dressed, she packed her laptop along with a fresh set of work clothes in her overnight bag. Tomorrow was Saturday, but she had a meeting with Iqbal and Kumble at ten A.M. to discuss her progress and her chances at the promotion to senior associate. With Preethi's case taking up most of Naina's work hours, the weekend was the only time she was available. Hopefully, the promising first day of trial would give her a leg up.

Naina rushed downstairs before Appa could say anything else. Her Uber was already waiting to take her to her favorite restaurant in Tejas's neighborhood. She'd never been there on a date, since her ex didn't drink and was heavily opposed to any music playing at restaurants during meals because it "messed" with his digestion, but she'd gone there with Anil before.

Tejas was waiting for her outside the restaurant, wearing an all too familiar deep violet shirt and a well-fitting pair of jeans. "You look beautiful," he said.

She grinned. "Nice shirt. I love the color."

"I knew you would," he said.

They walked in together, and when their hands brushed, Naina found herself reaching for his warm touch, interlocking their fingers. She didn't let go until the server led them to a cozy table for two in the corner and handed them menus.

"Have you been here before?" Naina asked, settling herself across from him.

Tejas leaned forward so their knees brushed, sending a jolt down her core. "You do realize I only moved to Bangalore last month?"

She frowned. "Tejas, you live two streets away from this restaurant."

"Well"—his eyes twinkled—"I wouldn't have wanted to bring anyone here except for you, and you were playing so unbelievably hard to get."

Naina scoffed louder than the music. "Excuse me! I was focusing on our client, thank you very much."

He rested his chin on his hand, his gaze softening with what looked like fondness. "I know. That's one of my favorite things about you."

The server came by to fill their water glasses. Naina took a sip, chuckling. "What, that I'm such a workaholic?"

"No." He smiled. "Your passion. I saw it even in Goa, how determined you were to get things checked off the list, but today, and all these weeks, seeing you in your natural element . . . I'm more attracted to you than ever."

Naina's cheeks flooded with heat. "Even with my glasses and unstyled hair and boring business attire?"

He reached for her hand, and she gave it to him. "Especially with all of that. I'm grateful I finally got to see this version of you. A lawyer, just like me. I . . ." He exhaled. "Naina, I didn't think we'd ever run into each other again."

She tightened her grasp on his fingers. "Me, neither. I didn't even let myself scroll through the photos from the trip. I knew I would be tempted to find you."

Tejas pressed his lips together and withdrew his hand, tugging on his collar. "I'm not sure how you'll react to this," he said, swiping to the Gallery app on his phone, "but I've looked at this photo more times than I can count."

Naina peered at the screen, her forehead wrinkling. *Huh*. It was a picture of her from karaoke night in Goa all those months ago. She didn't know when he'd taken it, but the far-off, distant look in her glazed eyes was familiar. She clapped a hand to her mouth to keep from snorting. "Oh my God, I was so drunk that night."

"And yet you sang like a pro."

Naina shrugged. "I mean, it is what it is."

He licked his lips. "The night we first kissed, I said that maybe us meeting was fate. Now I'm absolutely sure it was—the hostel, the list, ending up at the same office months after letting each other go—it was all meant to be."

She swallowed, her heart thumping in her chest loud and fast, and when the words slipped from her mouth, she knew she meant them, despite every single reservation she still had about dating and relationships and . . . love. "I think so too."

"I don't want to let you go again," he said, taking both her hands in his.

The server appeared before them, holding a notepad. "Are we ready to order?"

"I'm so sorry, we haven't looked at the menus yet." Naina chuckled weakly, grateful for the interruption, and the server nodded and stepped away. Perhaps Tejas was about to say the three words she'd forced herself not to think, let alone say, over a year ago. But despite their complicated history, this was new, this was uncharted territory, and he was her colleague. They couldn't, *shouldn't,* rush this. Naina didn't want a blazing inferno of instalove with Tejas; she wanted a crackling fireplace to thaw the ice in her heart. And that needed time. "I'm hungry," she said before Tejas could return to the dangerous topic he'd broached. She perused the menu. "What are your thoughts on coastal chicken curry and rice?"

Tejas must have gotten the message, because although he grinned, the smile didn't reach his eyes. "Coastal food? Déjà vu. Let's do it."

♡♡♡

Right as they walked into the apartment and took off their shoes, Astrid came running toward Tejas, her paws thudding. "There's my baby girl," Tejas cooed. Astrid let out an eager meow, and he picked her up and kissed the top of her head. "Did you have a good day? Did you miss your papa?"

Naina's core clenched, an ache between her legs. Was this what people meant about men being more attractive if they were good with children? Sure, Astrid wasn't a human child, and Naina wasn't the most maternal woman out there, but when she looked at Tejas, pressing Astrid snugly to his chest as she purred loudly, Naina couldn't help but smile. "Hey, let me take a picture," she said.

Tejas turned to face her, grinning at the phone camera while Astrid stared lovingly at him. "Text it to me," he said when Naina showed him. "You have my number now, so make use of it."

"Don't tease me," she said, laughing as he set down Astrid, who ambled into the hallway. "I was just trying to stick to our rules in Goa."

"You mean *your* rules, which could have easily been amended," he corrected her. "As they say, if she wanted to, she would."

As a laugh bubbled out of his lips, Naina shoved him. "Fine," she said. "I'll show you what I want and what I'll do to get it."

Tejas's eyes turned molten. He stepped forward, one hand reaching behind her to bolt the front door shut. His other arm went around her waist, and he pulled her flush against him. "How about we show each other?" he murmured.

Naina swallowed. "I'd . . . like that."

In one quick motion, he lifted her up, hooking her legs around his hips. "Bedroom?"

"God, yes," she breathed, pressing her lips to his.

He carried her down the hallway, maneuvering past Astrid, who meowed loudly in protest when he shut the door to his bedroom, leaving her behind. "Will she be okay?" Naina asked, her brow puckered, as Tejas set her down on the bed, which was soft underneath her.

He rubbed the side of his head awkwardly. "She's probably just confused. I haven't had anyone over in a while."

Naina sat up, tugging on his collar until he was leaning over her, pinning her down on the bed. "Define 'a while,' " she teased.

"Ah, fuck." Tejas grazed his lips along her cheek. "Do we have to do that now?"

She pulled his face closer, her breath mingling with his. "We must," she said, sucking on the skin just below his ear.

Tejas groaned, visible goosebumps sprouting along his neck. Then he grinned, settling himself in between her legs. Every graze of his fingers as he scrunched her dress up, inch by inch, was agonizing. Naina let out a breathy sigh when his hand cupped the back of her thigh.

"Eighteen months," he said finally.

"Eighteen?" Naina blinked at him as she did the math in her head. "So you haven't been with anyone since Goa?"

Tejas lifted his head to smile at her sadly. "I tried to. Trust me, I did, I went on so many dates. But I . . ."

Biting her lip, she sat up so they were eye level. "But you what?"

"God, Naina." He pressed his mouth to her forehead. "I couldn't stop searching for your face in every crowd. I found myself reaching for your warmth in my dreams. I never looked you up, out of respect for your rules, but you were on my mind, tormenting me, every day. I—" He paused, then traced his finger along the first tear that fell down her cheek. "Did I say something wrong?"

Naina's lip trembled. "Keep talking," she said, clasping his hands with hers. "Please."

Tejas sighed, squeezing his eyes shut like he was reliving the past all over again. "I couldn't live in a city where I was so brokenhearted—*twice*. So on a whim, I started looking for jobs outside of Mumbai and eventually landed the job at AKC."

Another tear clung to Naina's lashes, on the brink of falling, just like her.

A small smile cracked Tejas's lips. "When I saw you at the office, I felt it for the first time since Goa."

"Felt what?" she asked.

"Like I was alive again. Like fate was on my side and had brought me back to you after I'd nearly lost all hope."

Naina gripped his collar and touched her forehead to his. "Tejas, I . . ." She blinked back the dampness in her eyes. "I've missed you so much."

"I've missed you too." As they kissed, his grin pressed against her smile, and as they undressed each other, their hands roaming, clinging, aching for more and more and more, the faintest feeling stirred inside Naina's heart, its icy exteriors melting as it awoke from its eighteen-month-long slumber.

Tejas took out a condom from his bedside drawer, his gaze steadily on Naina as he put it on. "You're sure about this?" he asked when he got on top, one hand cradling her face.

"I'm sure," she whispered.

He let out a "hmm" sound, a smirk playing on his lips. "How sure?"

Naina groaned. "Please, Tejas, don't tease me. I . . . I need you inside me. Right now, no holding back."

"Good." His jaw clenched, and he slid into her, gently at first, then with more force. Naina moaned, gripping the sheets for support. With every familiar thrust and every familiar kiss and every familiar touch that she had already memorized, the pressure in her core built and sent her over the brink. Tejas gasped and pressed his lips to hers, their shaky breaths in sync. Suddenly, Naina Shetty knew there was no running from the truth anymore. She was falling for Tejas—and she didn't know how to make it stop.

Goddamn it.

"Naina?" Tejas rumbled, her name on his lips softer than the thump of her beating heart.

"Hmm?"

His fingers roamed over the eye tattoo below her ribs, the one she was slowly starting to not regret. "You're staying over, right?"

She snuggled into his chest and closed her eyes. "I am."

His arms tightened over her waist, like he was scared she'd leave if he let go. "You know my one big regret from Goa?"

Naina tried not to giggle as she pressed a kiss to his biceps curled around her. "Ghosting me the morning of my flight?"

"Hey!" Tejas laughed. "I thought we went over that already. It wasn't an easy decision, but I thought it was for the best."

"Mhmm." She looked up at him and bit her lip. "What's the big regret?"

Tejas toyed with a stray lock of her hair, not meeting her eyes.

"That I never got to wake up with you in my arms. Will you let me, Naina Shetty? Tonight?"

She leaned her cheek against his rising chest, hoping that the one tear in the corner of her eye wouldn't fall. "Yes," she finally said. "I'd like that."

Chapter THIRTY-TWO

For the first time since his breakup with his ex, Tejas woke up with another person snuggled tight in his arms. And not just any person—Naina Shetty, the woman he had caught feelings for in Goa, struggled to forget in Mumbai, and fallen back in love with in Bangalore.

He blinked away his drowsiness, trying to adjust his gaze to the sunshine streaming in from the window. It was probably just past nine A.M. Since it was Saturday, neither he nor Naina would have to rush through the morning. Maybe he would make her breakfast in bed again.

Astrid stretched her body against him from his other side, and he twisted his right arm back to pet her. Then he shifted, facing Naina, who was still asleep in his grip, her straight hair splayed over his biceps. The blanket lay in a heap on her feet; she probably ran hot in the morning. Naina had changed into his nightshirt before they turned in for the night, and God, seeing the bare long legs she'd wrapped around him last night made Tejas's heart race. *I love you,* he thought.

He tilted her head up to kiss her cheek, and Naina stirred, a soft smile crossing her lips. “Good morning,” he mumbled. “Did you sleep well?”

Naina looked up at him, stifling a yawn. “Like a baby. That hasn’t happened in months, maybe years.”

Tejas kissed her slow, a light brush of their mouths, then swept a lock of hair away from her eyes. “I had a dreamless sleep too. Going to bed together for a change . . .” He pulled her into his arms again. “It felt right. Didn’t it?”

Naina nodded, her head in the crook of his shoulder. “It did.” Then she blinked, and before Tejas could protest, she sat up and scrambled for her phone on the nightstand. “Fuck. What time is it?”

“Uh, a bit after nine-thirty—” Tejas straightened when Naina cursed loudly and ran out to the living room. Astrid let out a confused meow and raced after Naina, with Tejas following.

In the living room, Naina was rifling through the overnight bag she’d packed. Her hands came up with a pair of trousers and a formal silk shirt. Tejas opened his mouth to ask her where she was going when she pushed past him, back into the bedroom.

“Naina, it’s Saturday,” he reminded her as she tugged her pants over her muscular thighs. “Why are you getting dressed?”

She looked up at him, her eyes wide. “I have a performance review meeting with Iqbal and Kumble at ten. It’s already nine-forty.”

“Okay, breathe.” He reached for her, but she turned to the mirror, buttoning up her shirt. “It’ll be fine,” Tejas said, stepping closer. “My place is only twenty minutes from work. You could blame it on Bangalore traffic. From what I’ve seen, it’s pretty brutal.”

“I don’t like being late,” Naina replied testily. She gripped her straight hair with her fingers. “Fuck, I look like a mess.”

Wordlessly, Tejas handed her a comb from his drawer. “Thanks,” she said, shooting him a weak smile as she ran the comb over her smooth strands. She put the comb down and strode back out, Tejas following in her wake.

“I’ll hail an auto downstairs,” she said, slinging her overnight bag over her shoulder. “It’ll be quicker than an Uber.”

As she started for the door, Tejas pulled her back by the hand. "Hey," he said, and he hated how desperate his voice sounded. "Will you come over after? We could get brunch—"

Naina hesitated, averting her gaze, and he knew before she even opened her mouth that she was reconsidering last night. "I'll let you know," she said, throwing a glance at the wall clock. Nine forty-five. "See you."

And just like that, Naina was gone, the front door ajar, before Tejas could so much as kiss her goodbye.

A confused meow sounded from the floor. Astrid brushed against Tejas's ankle as she peered outside into the hallway.

"I know, right?" he replied. Sighing, he shut the front door, picked Astrid up, and fell back into the couch. He rested his head against the cushions. "Do you think she'll be back, Astrid?"

Astrid said nothing, only blinked at him with her doubtful yellow eyes.

"Yeah," he agreed, his shoulders slumped. "That's what I thought." Sighing, he went through the motions: He filled Astrid's water and food bowls, took a shower, made his usual breakfast, and sat at the dining table to eat his eggs and bread while looking wistfully at the empty seat beside him.

Last night, and this morning, Tejas had seen a glimpse of Naina Stark. Happy, relaxed, at peace . . . with him. And then, in a moment, she had slipped through his fingers.

Naina had needed to rush out for her meeting, and that he understood; he valued time and punctuality as much as any good lawyer would. What scared Tejas, though, was that Naina might take this opportunity to let her fears get in the way of any possible relationship with him.

Tejas put his dish in the sink and returned to the couch, grabbing the television remote. He flipped through the channels until something on the news caught his eye, and he stiffened in place. BREAKING NEWS! the ticker proclaimed. BILLIONAIRE INDUSTRIALIST KAMAL SUBRAMANIAN FOUND **GUILTY** OF FRAUD AND EMBEZZLEMENT ON THREE COUNTS.

"Fuck," Tejas cursed. The court must have released the verdict on a Saturday because of the high-profile nature of the case. With shaking hands, he muted the TV and dialed Dhanush's number. "Hey, I just saw the news," he said when the call connected. "Are you okay?"

There was silence for a few seconds, after which Dhanush spoke, his voice small. "Not really. I'm fucking terrified of what this might mean for me."

Tejas pursed his lips, his heart sinking for his friend. "Do you want to grab a coffee? It might take your mind off things—"

"Thanks, but no," Dhanush said, and a small but weak chuckle escaped his lips. "I, uh, I'm actually not alone, for a change."

"Oh?" Tejas found himself grinning when he heard another man's laugh in the background. "Tell me about it at work."

"I will, once I put out all of these fires. See you."

Tejas hung up just as his phone buzzed again, and he jumped. Was it Naina? Had she changed her mind about brunch? But the caller ID said IQBAL AKHTAR. Frowning, Tejas picked up.

"Hey, Tejas, do you have a minute?" Iqbal said, his words rushed. "Kumble and I just finished our meeting with Naina, and we caught her up on a really big discovery."

Was this about Preethi's case? Tejas's brow furrowed. "Yes, of course."

"My contact at the police station told me that someone tried and failed to visit Preethi in jail last night."

Tejas stood; he clutched the phone to his ear with a trembling hand. "What? Who?"

Iqbal exhaled sharply. "Sandhya Gowda. Any theories as to why?"

"Huh. Preethi mentioned they were on good terms, but that she was also close with Pai," Tejas said, rubbing his chin. "Do you know anything else about her visit?"

"She tried to use a fake name," Iqbal said. "But the jail attendant recognized her and asked her to leave. Plus, she's not on the approved list of visitors, so they wouldn't have let her in anyway."

Tejas paced around his living room. "Thanks, Iqbal. Naina and I will get to the bottom of this."

"You've got this," his boss said before hanging up.

♥ ♥ ♥

TEJAS ARRIVED AT FOURTH WAVE Coffee, where Naina had asked him to meet to discuss this new lead, and spotted her at a table by the window. She was looking at something on her laptop, her forehead wrinkled.

"I'm trying to find a link between Sandhya and Preethi, or maybe Sandhya and Pai," Naina said as soon as he pulled up a chair beside her, their thighs touching. "There's not much except for this." She turned the laptop toward him. It was an old article from a Bollywood news website. EXCLUSIVE: ALL THE CELEBS AT SANDHYA GOWDA'S 21ST BIRTHDAY BASH!

Tejas went through the photos. The party had happened only five months ago at a high-end Japanese restaurant in central Bangalore. Other than Jagannath and his wife, countless other young starlets were in the pictures.

And there, in one of the photos, close to being cut off at the edge, was a middle-aged man with a beer bottle against his lips. He was looking straight at Sandhya, who was dancing with her friends in the center of the frame. Rohith Pai.

"He seems to be the only person at the party who's friends with Jagannath, not Sandhya." Tejas's eyes narrowed. "Why is he there?"

"Exactly," Naina said in a low voice, meeting Tejas's gaze.

Tejas placed his hand over Naina's, nodding resolutely. "We'll figure it out."

Her eyes scanned the café, then she slowly slid her hand out, shifting her chair back a few inches. Tejas's heart sank, and he frowned at her. "You're pushing me away again, Naina."

She put a hand to her forehead, massaging the area. "Look, Tejas, I . . . we shouldn't do this right now."

"You mean you don't want to," he said bitterly.

"I want to. Trust me, I do," she replied, and Tejas noticed the faintest shimmer in her eyes behind her glasses. "But my first priority is and always will be my career. Until we win Preethi's case, I can't make any decisions about our rela—about this thing between us."

Tejas opened his mouth, then closed it as the words died on his tongue. In some ways, he understood Naina's hesitation. Preethi's trial mattered more than anything else at this moment, and if things went south between them, it could affect their work on the case.

And he knew he couldn't convince someone to choose him if they didn't want to. He'd made that mistake with Rahul a year and a half ago. He couldn't in his right mind make it again.

"Fine," he said, crossing his arms on the table. "But I can't take another Goa. I don't want to get physical again until you make it clear where you stand with us."

Naina licked her lips, her eyes raking over his face like she was trying to figure something out. Finally, she gave a slight jerk of the head. "Okay. I get where you're coming from." She cleared her throat and returned her gaze to her laptop. "Let's talk to Sandhya."

Tejas shut his eyes for a moment, then opened them, forcing himself back into work mode. "If we subpoena her, Jagannath might intervene. We'll have to do it behind his back."

"I've been looking at her Instagram," Naina said, showing him Sandhya's page. "She posts about her entire day on her stories, so we might be able to catch her."

"You'd think she'd be more discreet, considering her father's a key witness in a murder case," Tejas said. "I'm surprised Jagannath hasn't put an end to it."

Naina shook her head. "I suppose if she stopped posting all of a sudden, people would speculate why." She thought for a minute, then said, "I'll keep an eye on her stories and figure out where she's going tonight. Maybe I could 'accidentally' run into her."

"I'll join you," Tejas said. "If she's going somewhere on Saturday night, it's bound to be a nightclub full of drugged-up celebrities, and I don't want you to . . ." His voice trailed off, and he hung his head. "Sorry. I know I have no right to worry about you."

Was that a small smile on Naina's twitching lips? "No, you're right," she said as she stared at her phone screen, which had gone dark. "It might be best if you tag along. I'll text you the details whenever she posts about it."

"Good plan," Tejas said, then added, "Also, the IT intern texted me while I was on my way here. He can't get an IP address from the Reddit account without a DM conversation, but he's on it. He said he'll update us soon."

Naina nodded, still not looking his way. "Sounds good. I'll see you tonight, then."

"See you." With a sigh, Tejas stood, his chair creaking, and hailed an auto rickshaw home. Hopefully tonight would bring them more answers than questions.

Chapter THIRTY-THREE

The last time Naina had set foot in a nightclub, she'd called herself Naina Stark. Now, here in Bangalore, the loud electronic beats and thumping bass echoed from inside. Tejas paid the hefty entry charge (that AKC would cover, thankfully) and they flashed their IDs at the bouncer, Naina's head already pounding. Was there a magic switch that had flicked on when she'd turned thirty? Because damn it, this wasn't music, this was pure noise. Why couldn't Sandhya have been an introverted young woman who spent her weekends at a bookstore café?

They entered the cramped nightclub, full of writhing, dancing, horny people, and a memory flashed through Naina's head—Tejas's neon-painted hands all over her, his lips on her neck.

She blinked the dangerous memory away. There was no room in her mind for anything except the case. Her heart, on the other hand . . .

No. Shut up, she commanded herself. *Think about something else. Anything else.*

A drunk man shoved past her, pushing Naina backward into

Tejas. She gasped at the proximity, at Tejas's heady scent invading her nostrils amid the stench of smoke and liquor in the room. "You okay?" Tejas said, his lips near her ear.

She nodded against his shoulder, her breathing still shaky, and he wrapped a muscular arm around her. "Stay close to me, okay?" he said, leading her to the bar, where it was thankfully quiet.

Naina flagged down a bartender and ordered two bottles of ginger ale. No way would they risk getting drunk when the stakes were this high. They sipped their drinks and surveyed the place. Naina scrunched her eyes to see past the pulsating red and blue and green lights. Everyone in the crowd seemed so . . . young. Presumably, they were all rich kids with millionaire parents, trust funds, and hundreds of thousands of Instagram followers. But Sandhya Gowda was nowhere in sight. Nor were her influencer besties, all of whose faces and names Naina had memorized earlier that evening. "She might be on the dance floor," Tejas said. "Let's head there?"

Naina took a big gulp of ginger ale and stared up at him. Dancing with Tejas wasn't just risky; it was dangerous. She might have been entirely in her senses, but just standing next to him, looking at his tensed muscles beneath his shirt and the slight pout of his full lips, with that goddamn cologne in the air—it took everything in her not to pull him in, touch her mouth to his, and re-create that moment in Goa.

But they needed to find Sandhya, and fast. Naina swallowed back her fears and nodded, setting her bottle down. She let him pull her through the crowd to the dance floor until all she could sense was bright lights, torturously loud music, and . . . Tejas's broad chest brushing against hers. His hands rested near her waist, barely grazing her skin beneath her crop top, his mouth in a hard line, his eyes fixed on a spot one foot over her head. He was maintaining his distance, and rightfully so. Naina had set her boundaries, and Tejas had set his own. And she would respect them.

No matter how irresistible he looked tonight in that collared yellow shirt and the same blue jeans she'd peeled off him only last night, his curly hair begging to be tousled and gripped—

Tejas took Naina's hand and spun her so she was facing away from him. Her lips parted when he pulled her taut against his hips, his fingers resting firmly on her skin now. Naina closed her eyes, trying to quell the agony that throbbed low in her belly, but Tejas's rumbly voice in her ear jarred her back to the present moment. "There she is."

Naina sucked in a breath. Sandhya stood mere feet away from them, swaying unsteadily to the electronic music with some friends, a pink cocktail in her hand. Clearly, that wasn't her first drink of the night.

"Should we . . ." Naina said, jutting her head forward.

"No. You see those three dudes there?"

That was when Naina noticed the burly men in unassuming T-shirts and jeans standing close to Sandhya and the girls, their faces grim. *Bodyguards,* Naina realized with a lurch.

Tejas turned her around so they were facing each other again, then he bit his lip. "The only way we could intercept Sandhya is if she went to the ladies' room."

"She's way too drunk," Naina argued, leaning closer so she was audible. "They wouldn't let her go anywhere alone. But maybe if the bodyguards were distracted?"

"So what's our plan?" he said testily. He spun her around again, and Naina noticed two of the girls looking at her—no, at Tejas—before he pulled her back into his arms.

Slowly but surely, an idea formed in Naina's head, one that made her stomach squirm. She didn't know if it would work, or if it was even plausible, given how closely she'd been dancing with Tejas for the past five minutes, but she had to try. *They* had to try.

"You have to go up to the girls," Naina whispered in Tejas's ear. "Act flirty, dance with them, distract the bodyguards while I talk to Sandhya."

Tejas's face went green, and he jerked his head back like he was revolted. "They're kids, Naina."

"They're old enough to drink, and besides, you're only acting. Please," she added when Tejas still looked dubious. "Those girls have been checking you out since we got here. This is our best chance."

His mouth puckered as he considered the plan. Then he nodded. "Fine. I'll do it. Wish me luck."

Naina stepped away from him, giving him a tense smile, and walked to the periphery of the dance floor. She leaned against the rather sticky wall—*ugh, gross*—half out of sight from the dance floor, as Tejas made eye contact with one of the girls, a faint smile tugging at his lips.

Tejas was a pretty good actor, Naina surmised from his easygoing, carefree stature when he approached the group of girls. The way he winked at one of them who had pink hair, then laughed when she said something to him. Naina noticed Sandhya's body stiffen at the sight of him. Sandhya must have recognized him from that day at the Jagan Mansion. To Tejas's credit, he only briefly smiled at her before returning to the girl he was talking to, who was now twirling a lock of her hair around her finger.

Wow, she's really playing up her charm, Naina thought bitterly, folding her arms as the young woman swatted Tejas's biceps, giggling, before letting him spin her around.

Tejas must have sensed Naina staring at him from across the dance floor, because their gazes met. His expression softened, and he flashed his dimple for a split second, until the woman put her arms around him and he resumed dancing with her, pretend-laughing again.

A trickle of heat ran down Naina's back as Tejas shuffled closer to two more of the girls. They flanked him, throwing their hands in the air giddily, and the three bodyguards stepped into the circle, wearing matching glares. Sandhya, meanwhile, was on the edge of the group, her brow knit. She was probably wondering why the hell Preethi's lawyer was flirting with her twenty-one-year-old friends.

It was showtime. Naina caught Sandhya's eye while the bodyguards weren't looking, then subtly tipped her head toward the bathroom in the corner. Sandhya's mouth fell open, then she whispered something to the bodyguard closest to her. He nodded, folding his hands behind his back.

Sandhya moved forward in the direction of the bathroom, her bodyguard on her heels. *You've got this,* Naina told herself, then walked over to the ladies' room, pushing the door open and stepping inside.

With this being a high-end celebrity nightclub, the bathroom was massive, with a mirror hanging over each of the four sinks, five stalls, two of which were occupied, and an attendant who stood in the corner, bowing her head when Naina smiled at her.

Damn, there were too many people here for them to have a proper conversation. Naina washed her hands at the sink glumly. So much for this plan. She was thinking she probably ought to get Tejas away from the girls before one of the bodyguards lost his cool, when the door swung open and Sandhya walked in.

Wordlessly, she took the basin next to Naina's, fluffing up her hair and retouching her lipstick. Their eyes met in the mirror, and Naina opened her mouth, wondering how to broach the topic as two more women entered the bathroom.

"I like your lipstick," Naina said quickly. "Which shade is that?"

Sandhya paused. She looked at the other women, all minding their own business, then said, "Lady Danger, from MAC. But honestly, it would look horrible with your skin tone."

Naina sucked on her teeth. Wow. She hadn't expected that. "Um, thanks, I guess?"

"This other shade will suit you," Sandhya said. She reached for a paper towel from the box, and then, with trembling hands, she wrote something on it with the lipstick. "It's exclusive to the MAC store at the Nexus Mall. Here's their info." She folded the tissue, then gave it to Naina and left the bathroom without another word.

Naina's hands shook as she smoothed out the paper. It said: *Tues 4 a.m. behind Nexus Mall.* Sandhya unfortunately hadn't listed her phone number underneath, but this was still progress. Naina held herself back from pumping her fist in the air. She slipped the tissue into the pocket of her jeans and returned to the dance floor.

Tejas was dancing by himself in the corner, his eyes anywhere but on the young girls, and he looked positively disgusted. "Hey," he said hurriedly when she tapped him on the shoulder. "Did it work?"

Naina tugged on his arm. "Yes. Let's get out of here."

They paid for their ginger ales, and when the cold November breeze ruffled Naina's hair, she nearly melted into the street with relief. "Thank fucking God," she said, letting her eyes close. "That was terrifying."

Tejas chuckled weakly beside her.

"You okay?" Naina asked, frowning at him.

He tugged on his collar, his face still greenish. "While you were gone, that pink-haired girl I was dancing with got a little too close for comfort. She grabbed my face and tried to kiss me."

Jealousy pounded through Naina's veins. "Oh," she said, her voice high-pitched. She cleared her throat and added, "I'm surprised the bouncers didn't rough you up."

Tejas gave her a weird look. "I pushed her away before anything could happen. I don't want to kiss anyone but y—" His chest heaved, rising and falling, and then he ran his fingers through his curls. "Never mind. What did Sandhya say?"

Naina ignored the fluttering in her belly and showed him the note. "It's an odd hour of the morning, but maybe that's the only time she can sneak out to meet us?"

"Tuesday, four A.M. . . ." Tejas rubbed his chin. "That'll be the third day of the trial. Unless the judge makes her decision by Monday."

"She won't," Naina insisted, grabbing his arm to emphasize her point. "We're going to win this. We're so close to winning it, I can . . ." She paused when Tejas's molten eyes fell to her hand curving around his forearm. His mouth parted, his tongue flicking out to lick his lower lip, and he met her gaze. Just as Naina thought he would close the distance between them and kiss her, putting an end to the unbearable tension from the dance floor, he took two steps back, and she released his arm from her hold. "It's late," Tejas said sharply. "I'll call an Uber. You have your car?"

"Parked across the street," Naina said. "I could drop you home—"

"No, I . . ." He lifted his head up to the night sky, his eyes scrunching. "I need to be alone. Let's touch base tomorrow. We still have to figure out if the hate account is linked to the real killer."

"Yeah, all right." Naina shuffled her feet and let out a silent sigh. "I'd better get going."

Tejas walked her to her car, and once she was behind the wheel with her seat belt fastened, he waved his fingers at her. "Get home safe," she called out through the open window.

"You too," he said. "Text me when you're home."

With a nod, Naina pulled onto the main road, her thoughts scrambled. Thank God they'd managed to get to Sandhya without raising any alarms. Naina's plan had worked well, although the mental image of Tejas spinning that girl around still made her nauseous. They were close to a breakthrough in the case; Naina could feel it. All that remained was why Sandhya had tried to visit Preethi in jail—and what her father might have to do with the murder.

Chapter THIRTY-FOUR

The next morning, Naina sat in a corner at the local breakfast café, drinking coffee and going through the r/PaiMurder subreddit and her work emails again while she waited for Anil to join her. They hadn't done a bestie breakfast date in a while, and honestly, Naina needed to tell someone about her not-a-relationship with Tejas before she exploded.

"Hey," Anil said, settling into the chair adjacent to her just as her phone buzzed with a message from Tejas: Facetime at 4? Her cheeks heated until a second message popped up from him. To work, obviously

"Well, well, well." Anil whistled, peering at the messages. "How the tables turn."

Naina glared at him, then sent a quick Sure to Tejas. "Don't start, Anil."

He laughed, resting his arms behind his head. "A lot has happened since the archive room kiss, hasn't it?"

"Okay, fine." Naina covered her scorching face with her hands. "Yes. We . . . did it."

"I fucking knew it!" Anil practically whooped with glee. "Tell me everything. How? When? Where? How many times?"

She looked around, although the tables near them were empty, and inched her chair closer to Anil's. Then she lowered her voice conspiratorially and gave him the rundown of Friday night. "And then in the morning, I was late to a meeting, and I . . ."

"You shut him out," Anil said, his words a statement, not a question.

Naina nodded. "And he said he can't keep doing this until I know for sure what this thing between us means."

Anil smiled at her, his eyes warm. "What do you want it to mean?"

Naina's gaze went to the window, and her heart fluttered when she spotted a stray tabby cat digging through trash outside. If Tejas were here, he'd have fed the cat. Probably given it some pets and scratches too. "I want . . . it to not end," she admitted. "He's so wonderful, and I like him so much. But—"

"No. No buts," Anil said, shaking his head.

"But," Naina pressed on, "I don't want us to break each other's hearts, and if there's anything I've learned from the relationships around me, it's that they end."

"That's bullshit!" Anil exclaimed. The waitress, who was passing by, nearly dropped her tray of milkshakes, and Anil shot her an apologetic smile before lowering his voice. "Just because your ex was an asshole who broke your heart doesn't mean every man will do that. Just because your parents got divorced doesn't mean you will."

"Anil—"

"Look at my parents, who've been together for thirty-five years," he said, listing them on his fingers. "My Ajji still loves Ajja, even a decade after he died. Iqbal's got four pictures of his wife and kids on his desk. And I . . ." He smiled. "I'm trying to be less cynical about dating too."

Something in Naina's heart softened as she sipped her black coffee. "The guy from karaoke night? When do I get to meet him?"

"Oh, um," he stammered, and it was now his turn to have a tomato-red expression, "you've already met him, actually." His eyes darted to Naina's laptop for a split second, which was open to her Teams chats, and everything fell into place.

Naina nearly screamed as the coffee splashed onto the table. She wiped off the coffee stains with a napkin and said, "Oh my God, don't tell me it's Dhanush?"

Anil rubbed the top of his head sheepishly. "Yeah. Beer and forced proximity will do that to you."

She snickered, her arms folded. "I must know *all* the details. How? When? Where? How many times?"

He raked a hand along his stubble. "Well, it started after karaoke night. He's smart. I used to think he was only at AKC because Kumble is his uncle, but he knows his shit when it comes to the law. And well"—he blushed harder—"he really pays attention to what I like, and I don't just mean in bed. He watched three episodes of my favorite K-drama and texted me real-time updates."

Naina frowned. "How's he doing after they lost the Subramanian case?"

"I was with him all of yesterday. He's a wreck, so I'm taking point on the pro bono case now," Anil said, sighing loudly. "I'm glad I can be there for him like he is for me. He loves my catering idea, by the way. He said he has a friend in marketing who could help me with my business plan before I approach more banks."

"Huh." She shrugged, then signaled to the waitress to refill her coffee. "I don't like Dhanush much, or even know him outside of work, but he seems like he's trying to be a good . . ." Her voice trailed off. "Is he your boyfriend?"

Anil switched on his laptop. "Not yet, we're taking it slow." He paused. "Unless you count sex."

"Sounds like me and Tejas," Naina said, chuckling. "Well, at least until he decided to put the brakes on it. For now."

"Oh God." He wiped an imaginary tear from his eye. "I'm so proud of you. My girl's all grown up."

"Haha, very funny."

"In any case," Anil warned as he flipped through the menu on the table, "you'd better not fuck it up with Tejas. He's a good one."

She embraced the flush that crept into her cheeks and along her upper chest. "He really is," she agreed. "And I want to give him a chance. I just don't know how to."

"He's not the one who needs a chance." Anil tapped her on the nose and chuckled. "*You* do, so give yourself one, instead of closing yourself off to good sex and even better love."

Naina studied her best friend. "Do you think I could ever fall in love again?"

The waitress walked up to them, notepad in one hand and a pot of coffee in the other. Once she had refilled Naina's coffee and taken their breakfast orders, Anil leaned forward and whispered, his eyes twinkling, "Oh, Naina Shetty, I think you already have."

"No way," she snapped, although the thump-thump-thump of her heart seemed to say otherwise. "I don't need Tejas. I was perfectly fine before he turned up at AKC, living a perfectly normal life."

Anil smirked. "You don't *need* him," he agreed. "But you *want* him. And I think that's what love is. You know you'll be okay on your own, but every moment would be so much more fun with that person around. You want to do life with them, for as long as you possibly can. Does Tejas make you feel like this, Nay?"

"I . . ." Naina's mouth went dry. "He does. But I'm scared, Anil. You remember how difficult it was for me to focus on work after Santhosh cheated on me."

"And you've come out of it stronger," Anil reminded her with a pat on the shoulder. "I hate that you had to go through a broken engagement, but I'm also relieved Santhosh is out of your life. He was a total loser."

She wrinkled her nose. "He was, wasn't he?"

The waitress brought over their bagels, toast, and scrambled eggs, along with Anil's iced mocha. After she left, Anil said, munching on toast, "It might not be easy for a workaholic like you to balance work and a relationship, but isn't it worth trying on the off chance he's the love of your life?"

She nodded and dived into her bacon-and-cheese bagel. "You're right. But what if being with him distracts me from work? He'll be at the office too. How would I . . ."

"Hold yourself back?" Anil snorted. "Jeez, Naina, you're not an animal. You have self-control!"

Barely, when it comes to Tejas, Naina wanted to say. Instead, she shrugged. "You know how badly I want that promotion."

"Look, as much as I hate to admit it, Dhanush is most definitely out of the running for senior associate after the Subramanian case went south." Anil paused to slurp his mocha. "And based on what you've told me about your case, the prosecution doesn't have any concrete evidence. You'll win it, and with Kumble retiring in five months, they'll decide soon enough."

Naina blew over the top of her coffee, then took a sip. "I guess you're right."

"What I'm saying is, you're a shoo-in for senior associate whether you date Tejas or not. The only question is, will you let yourself have the best of both worlds instead of being an idiot like always?"

Naina's heart thumped loudly in her chest as she mulled this over. The way Tejas made her feel—alive, valued, cherished . . . only one other thing had made her feel the same way. Her job.

Was it really possible? A life that included not just her dream career, but also the man she was falling for? The warmth that spread to her toes at the thought of Tejas's smile, his flirty banter, and the way his eyes softened when he looked at her—that was what told her the answer, plain and simple.

She waited for a beat before saying, "All right. If things go well with Preethi's case, I'll . . . tell Tejas I want to give things a shot."

"Good. Don't go breaking his heart, all right?"

"I won't," Naina promised, and she meant it.

Anil grinned, clinking his iced coffee glass with her mug. "Good."

NAINA ACCEPTED TEJAS'S FACETIME CALL later that afternoon, and her heart skipped a beat when he appeared on her iPad, grinning widely. God, she missed that dimple—but despite what she'd said to Anil, and despite what she was slowly understanding about her own feelings, she had to keep it professional.

For now.

"Why do you look so happy?" she asked.

His video turned off for a second, then he came back on. "Check your email."

Naina's brows furrowed. "Hold on."

She pulled up her email in a separate tab and scrolled through the many unread emails that had come in—including a forwarded email from the IT guy, time-stamped late last night. It said:

> Hi Tejas sir,
>
> Sorry to be emailing you so late on a weekend, but this couldn't wait given the Preethi Acharya trial resumes on Monday. I managed to get a DM back from the Reddit account by baiting them with some fake gossip about the case, which helped me narrow their IP address and location down to this building in Domlur. I don't know which specific apartment it's from, but I hope this helps. Good luck, sir!

A gasp left Naina's lips. "Wait, Vaishnavi lives there! Jagannath's assistant! I remember reading about it online."

Tejas's eyebrows shot up. "Someone must have paid her off to do all of this. Maybe Gopal? Vaishnavi spoke so highly of him."

She shook her head, her heart thudding. "No. It's gotta be Jagannath, especially with Sandhya's connection to this case. I just . . . I have a gut feeling it's him."

"It could be," he agreed. "So, what's our strategy here? Do we confront Vaishnavi with this information or wait for whatever Sandhya has to say?"

Naina sat back and considered it. They weren't meeting Sandhya until Tuesday, and since they hadn't subpoenaed her yet, there was always a chance the judge would make her verdict tomorrow. They might not even get to use whatever evidence Sandhya would give them. Confronting Vaishnavi on the stand would, at the very least, throw some suspicion on Jagannath and shift focus from Preethi's so-called motive.

"We get Vaishnavi on the stand," Naina said finally, lifting her chin up, "and then we break her down until she confesses to the truth."

"I'll let you do it," Tejas replied. "You're more intimidating than me, and I think we need that to crack Vaishnavi."

She laughed. "Yeah, that's a valid point, Mr. Sunshine."

He beamed at her, a softness in his eyes. "Well, then . . . I'll see you in court."

Naina's cheeks flushed as she said, "I can't wait."

Chapter THIRTY-FIVE

Cross-examining Athira on the stand turned out well, since she'd already agreed that Pai's phone password was an "open secret" in the industry. After going back and forth a few times, she finally caved and agreed that someone else could have unlocked her husband's phone too. "I highly doubt it, though," Athira said, her fists balled as she glared at Preethi, whose eyes were downcast. "My intuition tells me that wretched woman did it, and a woman's intuition never lies."

"Unfortunately, a woman's intuition doesn't count as evidence in the court of law," Tejas said, quirking a brow and holding back his smugness. "No further questions."

Jagannath's testimony on the stand was nothing they hadn't heard before. In fact, it was almost word for word what he'd said at his house last month. With little evidence against him, and nothing concrete from Sandhya or Vaishnavi yet, they limited their questioning to Jagannath's relationship with Pai and whether he was aware that Gopal Krishnan and Pai were butting heads during filming.

"They were," Jagannath said nonchalantly, nodding at Gopal, who was seated in the third row, "but eventually, they made peace with it, and we wrapped up the scene. It was nothing but a misunderstanding. Gopal would tell you the same thing."

As predicted, Gopal was in agreement with Jagannath's take on his conflict with Rohith. "Creative differences are common in the film industry," he said. "And I admit I was anxious about getting too close to Preethi. Eventually, I was able to set aside my fears and do what the project demanded from me." When Gopal was asked how he had heard Jagannath's yell for help but not Preethi's, despite both screams having occurred mere feet away from the Krishnans' trailer, he had no answer except to say he was a deep sleeper and was more acquainted with Jagannath's voice than Preethi's.

Since Bina had only woken after the police arrived, her testimony had nothing of note. The prosecution's next witness was Vaishnavi Iyer, Jagannath's assistant. Tejas was on the edge of his seat, wondering what the prosecution was going to ask her. She had no knowledge of what had gone down that night, and the Reddit account wasn't part of the discovery file . . . yet. Naina would put it forth as evidence right before she went up to cross-examine Vaishnavi.

"She looks a little . . . off. Right?" Naina whispered, nudging Tejas.

He bit his lip, trying to gauge Vaishnavi's demeanor. She was blank-faced, though a little paler than usual, and the hem of her sweater was clenched tightly in her right hand. She walked to the stand, her eyes on the floor. Maybe she was just anxious, considering the role she had in spreading vitriol about Preethi online. After her oath, Mr. Rizwan asked, "Miss Iyer, do you recall seeing anything out of the ordinary in the early hours of October first while you were on set?"

Vaishnavi gulped. Her eyes went from the prosector to the judge, then she gave a sharp nod. "I heard footsteps outside my trailer, which was next door to Preethi's. I got up from my bed and saw a woman through the window, walking in the direction of Rohith sir's trailer. She was wearing a maroon dressing gown, and I saw a flash of skimpy pink lingerie underneath."

Multiple murmurs sounded in the courtroom. Tejas squirmed in his seat. Vaishnavi hadn't mentioned this to them when they'd questioned her.

Mr. Rizwan gestured to the screen at Preethi's mug shot, in which she wore exactly the outfit Vaishnavi had just described, the maroon gown and the camisole underneath streaked with bloodstains.

"What else did you notice, Miss Iyer?"

Vaishnavi bit her lip. "It was dark, and I don't remember much because I'd only woken up for a few minutes. I didn't think much of it, I figured it must be Preethi going to use the portable toilets. But in hindsight, I remember hearing a sob. She was crying."

Tejas caught Preethi's eye, and she mouthed, *That's a lie!* Beside Tejas, Naina's hands trembled. He sighed softly, then found her fingers and squeezed them with his own, knowing they still had their chance to get the real truth out of Vaishnavi.

Naina gave him a quick look of appreciation, then said loudly, "Your Honor, this was not part of Vaishnavi's official statement to law enforcement. She didn't mention seeing Preethi leaving her trailer or that she was allegedly crying."

Vaishnavi wiped her eyes, though Tejas saw zero tears. "I was scared to get involved," she said, her voice steadily increasing in pitch. "I didn't want my face all over the news reports. As Jagannath sir's assistant, I work behind the scenes, and it was best for me to stay that way for the sake of my career. Until . . ." She made a choked noise. "Until I realized this is bigger than me. This is about justice."

For a personal assistant, this woman sure was good at theatrics. Tejas held himself back from rolling his eyes in front of the judge.

"Your witness," Mr. Rizwan said, grinning toothily. He sat back down, his legs crossed.

Tejas watched as Naina stood, exhaling softly, the folder of evidence from the IT guy in her hands. Before she could walk toward the witness, the judge spoke up, shuffling her papers. "Unfortunately, we're out of time today. We will reconvene tomorrow at four P.M. for the defense's cross-examination of the final witness and closing statements. The court is adjourned."

"This is fine," Naina said to Tejas as the court emptied. "With Sandhya's testimony, we might actually have a better chance at a confession from Vaishnavi."

"Let's see," he replied as they approached Preethi.

"Were you really crying as you walked to his trailer?" Naina whispered to her. Iqbal joined the group, the confusion on his face identical to Naina's.

Tears fell steadily down Preethi's face. "She's lying," she insisted. "I was determined, not sad. I only got emotional when I walked into his trailer and found him dead." The cops arrived to escort her back to prison. "Please save me," she begged before they took her away.

Tejas whooshed out a breath. "Obviously, someone's paying Vaishnavi to lie. Is it the same person who made her write those things on Reddit? Jagannath, perhaps? Or Pai's wife?"

"Figure it out, and fast," Iqbal said. "I'll see you both at the office."

As they exited the doors, a vicious crowd of people surged forward—paparazzi, journalists, Rohith's fans with their anti-Preethi signage—thrusting mics at Tejas and Naina and screaming into their faces—but Tejas pushed past them, ducking his head, Naina right behind him.

"All right," Naina said, raising her head confidently when they were out of everyone's sight, closer to the auto rickshaw stand. "We'll find out whatever Sandhya has to say, and that'll help us crack this case. As long as she shows up. I mean, we don't even have her phone number."

"I'm sure she'll show up," Tejas said. He reached over before he could stop himself and tucked a lock of her straight hair behind her ear. "You're a good lawyer, Naina. So am I. We have to trust ourselves to win this."

Something shone in Naina's eyes that lit up her face in a way Tejas hadn't seen before. She moved ahead, the heat of her body inching closer and closer to him, and took his hands in hers, smiling. "I trust you, Prince Charming."

Tejas reveled in the touch of her skin against his. He wondered if she knew how badly he wanted to kiss her in this moment, how desperately he needed an answer from her after the trial ended. They were toeing the line between colleagues and lovers, and Naina only needed to take one step forward to meet him where he was. In love.

He smiled back, adoration unfurling in his chest. "I trust you too, Naina Stark."

♡ ♡ ♡

TEJAS NEARLY FELL ASLEEP EN route to Nexus Mall, where they were to meet Sandhya, but he jerked awake when the auto rickshaw driver slammed on the brakes. "You want to stop right here?" the driver asked, his eyebrows drawn in suspicion as Tejas paid him. "The mall doesn't open until ten."

"Uh, that's fine, I have . . . other business here," Tejas replied, grimacing. The streets were deserted this early in the morning, and Tejas had decided to get here a few minutes ahead of time so Naina wouldn't have to wait in the dark by herself. According to the text she'd just sent him, she was still a few minutes away. They would meet at the entrance to the mall, then walk to the back alley together. Hopefully, Sandhya wouldn't bail.

The driver stayed put in front of the mall, glaring at Tejas well after he'd gotten out of the auto. Tejas resisted the urge to glare back. Was this guy an undercover cop or something? Couldn't he just mind his business and drive off?

Just as Tejas considered saying something, a car pulled up across the dimly lit street and Naina got out of it, her eyes narrowed. She was wearing a woolen sweater and faded blue pants. "Hey, is there a problem?" she asked.

The driver said something brashly in Kannada, gesturing with his hands, and Naina argued back until he scoffed and drove away.

"What was that about?" Tejas scratched the top of his head. Damn, he really needed to learn the local language, and fast.

Naina laughed as she started walking toward the alley behind the mall. "He thought we were meeting to hook up. Bangalore, unfortunately, has a lot of unofficial 'moral police.'"

Tejas rolled his eyes. "It's the same everywhere I've been. Well, except for—"

"Goa," she replied, finishing the sentence and breaking into a fit of giggles. "Oh my God, can you imagine going skinny-dipping anywhere else in India?"

"Nope," Tejas said, rounding the corner to the putrid-smelling alley lined with trash bags along the faded yellow walls. "We'd end up splashed on the front page of the news."

Naina smiled as they halted. "That's going to happen anyway, because we're winning this case. Speaking of which . . ." She looked at her wristwatch. "It's a few minutes past four. Where is she?"

"I'm sure it isn't easy evading her family and the security guards manning their mansion," Tejas mumbled. "Guess we just have to wait."

They stood in silence except for the impatient tapping of Naina's feet and Tejas checking on Astrid via his cat camera. She was sipping water, from the looks of it. Astrid had excitedly woken up at three A.M. to the sounds of Tejas getting ready, and he'd been forced to fill her food bowl just so she'd let him leave without protest.

Naina must have peeked at his phone before he stowed it away, because she said, "I never pictured myself as a cat person."

"But?" he said, flicking his eyebrow up.

Her lips twitched. "I have to admit, Astrid is ridiculously adorable."

"She is." Tejas's heart clenched painfully. What he wouldn't give to wake up next to his cat and Naina every morning, give both of them a kiss and snuggle in bed until Astrid's hunger overtook her love for her humans. But despite the warmth in Naina's eyes, she'd given him no clear answer.

And until then, he'd have to put his hope aside.

"Tejas?" Naina said as she wrung her hands.

"Hmm?"

"I . . . I'm glad you're not upset with me."

He snorted, and she blinked in confusion. "Oh, I'm upset with the situation for sure, Naina Shetty. But that doesn't change how I feel about you." Smiling, he added, "We'll save Preethi. I know it. And after that . . . I'll let you decide where we go from there."

Naina smiled, slowly at first, then wider, as she took a step forward. "Actually, I think I've already—"

Footsteps sounded, and Tejas whirled around. A woman stood before them meekly, shivering in the chill breeze. She wore dark clothes and a black dupatta that hid her face, but one look at her small frame told Tejas it was Sandhya.

"Hi," Naina said, walking over to her at a brisk pace. "Thank you for meeting us."

Sandhya's gaze raked over the alley, then at the street ahead of them. "I don't have much time before they notice I'm gone," she said quickly. "But I know who killed Pai, and I can't in good conscience stand by and let Preethi take the fall. I don't have proof, though. Just what I overheard."

"What can you tell us?" Tejas asked, his shoulders taut.

"I'll tell you everything." Her eyes blazed. "And then you'll make things right."

Naina turned to Tejas, a brow raised, and he nodded. "Deal," they both said as one.

Chapter THIRTY-SIX

Later that day, Naina walked into the courtroom with her head held high, Tejas beside her. They finally had a solid defense, and they wouldn't let it go to waste.

Ramesh Kumble was in attendance today, leaving Iqbal to handle things at the office. Naina and Tejas had discussed their strategy with Iqbal already, and he'd agreed it was a solid one. Kumble, on the other hand, was skeptical, given Sandhya's testimony was only what she'd overheard, and not solid proof. But they had a plan to get Jagannath to crack, and Naina was certain it would work. It would land her the big promotion . . . and give her the time and headspace to talk everything out with Tejas.

Speaking of whom—Tejas nudged her as they settled into their row after the judge took her seat. "All the best. You'll kill it, no pun intended."

"I'm counting on it," she said.

Naina rose, her files in hand, and spotted Sandhya in the back row, wearing a plain gray kurti and jeans, her face covered with a dupatta again. Thankfully, Sandhya's father hadn't noticed his daughter walk in. Her testimony would be the grand slam, but they still needed to score more points by getting the truth out of Vaishnavi.

Then Naina walked over to the witness stand. "Miss Iyer," she started, "how well did you know Preethi Acharya?"

Vaishavi shrugged dismissively. "Not well at all. My first time meeting her was in August, when filming commenced."

"And did you interact often while on set?"

She shook her head, though her fingers clenched together. "Only while assisting Jagannath sir."

"Was there any bad blood between you?"

Vaishnavi's mouth opened and closed. Her eyes went to Jagannath, who sat in the front. Finally, she said, "Not from my end. I don't know about Preethi."

Naina tried not to scoff. "And yet you decided to say Preethi Acharya should be 'locked up' the very day of Pai's murder, even before news channels made the announcement? Odd timing, isn't it?"

Vaishnavi's head jerked back, like she had whiplash. *Good*. "Excuse me?"

"Your Honor, I'd like to enter this Reddit profile into evidence." Naina approached the bench, handing the papers to the judge, then switched on the screen to show their findings to the room.

"This isn't part of the discovery file," Mr. Rizwan said, fuming as he stood. "The prosecution was not made aware of any such online evidence."

"Because we only discovered it an hour ago," Naina fired back with a lie. "Your Honor, may I?"

"Miss Shetty, proceed," the judge said.

Naina's eyes went to the stand. Vaishnavi was trembling, her mouth agape. Once again, she looked toward Jagannath, who had also paled. "Miss Iyer, does this profile look familiar to you at all?"

"No, I don't know what this is," she said hurriedly. "I've never had a Reddit profile."

"Then why does the IP address of this profile narrow down to the location of your apartment?"

Vaishnavi looked around the room helplessly. "I . . . I didn't know what else to do."

The judge's eyes widened. She must not have seen this coming. Naina hadn't, either. She'd thought Vaishnavi would act more defensive, deny the whole thing. Now she was risking incriminating herself, and she had every right as a witness to refuse to answer, but it looked like Mr. Rizwan had been too stunned into silence to object.

"I understand," Naina said, exhaling. Time to channel her inner Tejas, and lead with kindness. "It wasn't your fault. You were simply doing what you were told, being a good assistant. Someone *made* you post anti-Preethi propaganda. They also made you lie on the stand. You never saw Preethi that night. But now you're involved in this murder, whether you knew what you were doing or not."

The word *murder* did it. Vaishnavi broke down in sobs. "Please, I—I can't go to jail! I'm the sole provider for my family, I . . ." She turned to the judge, whose brows were knitted. "Your Honor, it's true. That's my Reddit profile. I lied, I . . . I didn't see Preethi the night of the murder. I was paid to lie, to post bad things about Preethi."

Naina smirked as she spotted the flabbergasted expression on the prosecutor's face. "Who paid you, Miss Iyer?" she asked. They had this in the bag. They might not even need Sandhya's testimony—

Vaishnavi blinked back tears. "My boss, Jagannath sir."

Jagannath's fists clenched as he looked around the room. The crowd let out loud gasps, murmurs sounding in increasing decibels. The judge's jaw too had dropped, but she quickly recovered and yelled, "Order in my court!"

As Vaishnavi stepped off the stand, shaking from head to toe, Naina's shoulders straightened, and she continued, "Your Honor, we have one final witness." She caught Sandhya's eye and added, "And she'll help tie up every loose end."

Mr. Rizwan jumped out of his seat. "There wasn't any mention of more witnesses in the discovery file," he said, his eyes going back and forth.

Naina handed the sheet to the judge. "This witness came to us with some crucial evidence this morning. Here's the paperwork."

"Let me see." The judge quirked an eyebrow as she flipped through the papers, curiosity practically dripping from her face. "I'll allow it. Sandhya Gowda, please make your way to the stand."

Loud whispers filled the courtroom. As Sandhya pulled off her dupatta and started forward, Jagannath stood, fists clenched and nostrils flaring. "What the hell are you doing?" he exclaimed, shuffling out of the row toward his daughter. "You shouldn't be here!"

The judge banged her gavel. "Sit down, Mr. Jagannath."

"No! I will not allow my daughter to be caught up in this scandal!" Fuming, Jagannath grabbed his daughter by the wrists as she screamed in protest. The room was in uproar as three cops rushed ahead and pulled Jagannath away. He wrestled to get out of their grip, but despite his broad shoulders and hulking frame, he couldn't overpower three men. His face turned an unpleasant mix of purple and red as Sandhya took the stand.

Once silence fell over the room again, Naina began her line of questioning. "Miss Gowda, is it true that you had a sexual relationship with Rohith Pai?"

"Yes," Sandhya admitted, as more gasps sounded from around them. Her bottom lip wobbled, but she stared straight ahead determinedly. This admission—and the testimony to come—could potentially ruin her career forever, but Naina admired Sandhya wanting to do the right thing, not the easy thing.

"What?" Pai's wife, Athira, stood, a hand clapped over her mouth.

"Order in my court," the judge said as Athira burst into tears. "Mrs. Pai, sit down. Miss Shetty, please proceed with your questioning."

"Did anyone else know about this relationship?" Naina asked. Out of the corner of her eye, she saw Jagannath still fighting to get away from the cops.

"Not at first." Sandhya looked at her father, gulping. "Then . . . then Appa found out."

Naina paced back and forth in front of the witness stand. "How did your father find out about this relationship?"

"While we were together, I'd sent Rohith pictures. The . . . explicit kind." Sandhya hung her head. "Appa saw them on my phone, and then he—"

"Blasphemy!" Jagannath yelled, though the judge seemed like she was too busy hanging on Sandhya's words to even notice.

Sandhya hesitated, and Naina braced herself, knowing what the next phase of the plan was. Even though Sandhya had overheard the full conversation between her parents and knew what had gone down, she would have to play up the heartbroken secret girlfriend act so they could get Jagannath to confess the truth.

"I—I loved Rohith, you know?" Sandhya blubbered, though there wasn't a single tear in her eyes. She'd told Naina and Tejas this morning that she had cried enough. "And he loved me back. He was the one. He said he'd leave his wife for me, and he'd shut the media up if they said anything, and he was even going to ask for my father's blessing—"

"Blessing?" Jagannath spat out. He finally freed himself from the cops' clutches and pointed a finger at his daughter. "That bastard blackmailed me when I confronted him! I was saving you—how can you use that against me?"

"Saving me?" Sandhya laughed, no trace of humor in her voice. Instead, every curve of her face was lined with anger. "By killing Rohith and pinning it on a woman who went through the same thing with him that I did?"

"Any father would have done what I did!" His whole body shook, his voice thundering as he went on. "I was protecting our family's reputation, I was protecting *you*!"

Naina held back a grin. *Gotcha*. That statement was incriminating enough to prove that Jagannath had more to do with this murder than anyone else in the room—least of all Preethi.

"I've heard enough." The judge banged her gavel. "Bailiff, please take this man into custody, where he will be charged with the murder of Rohith Pai. The case against Miss Preethi Acharya," she said, smiling softly at Preethi, "is dismissed."

As the cops took Jagannath away and people filed out of the courtroom, murmuring among themselves, Naina turned in her client's direction. God, seeing the disbelief—and relief—on Preethi's face, knowing it was because of her efforts . . . it was beyond anything Naina had experienced before in her career.

Preethi was shaking hands with Kumble and Tejas, her eyes still big as saucers, when Naina approached her to say congratulations. Trembling with joy, Preethi fell into her arms. "Th-thank you," she told Naina. "I owe you my life."

"We only did our job." Naina grinned, jutting her head toward Tejas. "Enjoy your freedom, Preethi. You deserve it."

Sandhya approached them, nervously as first, but when Preethi shot her a smile, Sandhya's shoulders relaxed. "I'm sorry for what you went through," she said, taking Preethi's hands. "I was the one who told Rohith to offer you the role, because you were such a good fit for the movie. I never thought it would lead to this—"

"Don't apologize," Preethi replied, her eyes shining. "I should be thanking you. You chose to help me over your father."

"He went out of his way to frame you and save his own ass." Sandhya's jaw clenched. "He's as much of a monster as Rohith was."

Preethi nodded dismally. "I hope this won't affect your reputation in the industry."

Sandhya sucked on her teeth. "If it does, then it's not the right place for me anyway."

Naina gestured to the exit. "Shall we?"

They headed out of the courthouse with beaming smiles. Once they were done addressing the press with their statements, Naina pulled Tejas aside by the hand, not letting go even when they stopped at the auto rickshaw stand. He squeezed her fingers reassuringly, his touch warm and gentle, and she was sure he knew what was on her mind.

"Do you want to get a celebratory beer at Madeira?" she asked, licking her lips. "Maybe we could . . . talk."

Tejas's smile grew wide, his dimple peeking out, and Naina's stomach rippled with butterflies that she hoped would never go away. "Just talk?" he teased.

She hailed an auto, and as she slid into it and gestured for him to follow, she said, "For starters."

Chapter THIRTY-SEVEN

By the time Naina and Tejas walked into Madeira, their colleagues had arrived too, heralded by Iqbal and Kumble. Apparently, Tejas had texted everyone well in advance and asked them to come celebrate with them if they ended up winning.

Anil raced forward and picked Naina up, spinning her around until she was dizzy and laughing breathlessly. "Put me down, you fool!" she exclaimed, and he did.

"That's my bestie, y'all!" Anil screamed, lifting Naina's hand up as though they were in a sports competition, while everyone around them cheered. "All right, let's get the first round. Who's buying?"

"Me," Tejas said from behind Naina. As he brushed past her, his fingers grazed her wrist, and he turned once to wink at her. She pressed her hand to her lips, holding back a giggle. She couldn't wait to get a moment alone with Tejas and tell him how she felt. She'd known it since her talk with Anil, but now she was sure. Tejas was it for her.

In some ways, perhaps he always had been.

"Come on." Anil threw an arm over Naina's shoulder and dragged her to the karaoke emcee's station. "You're singing at least five songs tonight."

Laughing, Naina stood beside Anil while he asked the emcee if he had any "bad bitch" victory anthems in his repertoire. The emcee listed off a few suggestions, but Naina wasn't listening. She looked past Anil's shoulder at Tejas, who had rolled his sleeves up to his muscled forearms and was passing out beer mugs to their colleagues. Even Ramesh Kumble, who only ever drank expensive scotch, accepted a mug as he laughed at something Iqbal said.

Even from the distance, Naina could lip-read Tejas asking Dhanush, "Where's Naina?" He followed Dhanush's pointed look, then approached Naina and Anil with two foaming mugs in his hands.

"You can sing later," Tejas said cheekily. "First, gather round for the big toast."

Naina had won a lot of cases in her five years of being a lawyer, but none of those wins had made her feel this proud of herself. Or, she realized, as celebrated.

Tejas stood across from her, with the others piled into the booth, pride and adoration for her flickering in his eyes. "This case was a real challenge," he said, beer mug in hand, "not only because of what was at stake—a woman's freedom and the reputation of our law firm." He smiled at Kumble and Iqbal, who chuckled. "But also because this was my first big case since moving to Bangalore, a city whose local language I don't speak, whose neighborhoods I'm not familiar with, where everyone is a stranger. Thankfully, I had a badass partner who led the way for us to win this case. It's because of her that Preethi is now a free woman. So, everyone"—he lifted the mug, beaming at her—"please raise your glass to Naina Shetty, the most competent and capable lawyer I've ever had the pleasure of working with. To Naina!"

"To Naina," the booth echoed, clinking mugs.

"Wait!" Naina said before anyone could drink. "Tejas doesn't give himself enough credit." She turned to her boss, who grinned.

"Because, Mr. Kumble, you were right. I needed to work on this case with someone who'd help me become a team player. And you picked the perfect partner for me, in more ways than one. Tejas, here's to you."

Their colleagues oohed and aahed at the implication of her words, but Naina only took a sip, her eyes on Tejas's beautiful, perfect, tomato-red face.

The night went on in a haze of drinks, dancing, karaoke, and even two cakes that Anil and Dhanush had brought over. One said, *Congrats, you did it!* while the other said, *We're proud of you anyway.* "I told Dhanush we wouldn't need the second one," Anil explained when Tejas burst into laughter, "but what can I say? He didn't have faith in you."

"Bullshit." Dhanush frowned as Tejas laughed louder. "I was just covering all our bases."

Naina didn't miss the fondness in Anil's voice when he replied, "And I just like pulling your leg." Then he took a big piece of cake and fed it to Dhanush, whose face flushed with a giddy smile. *Hmm.* Maybe type-A Dhanush needed someone like Anil to bring more whimsy into his life.

She approached Dhanush nervously. "Hey," she said. "I'm sorry about the Subramanian case. How are you holding up?"

Dhanush put a hand to his mouth, which was still full of cake. "Kind of okay," he replied, his voice muffled. He swallowed, then wiped his lips. "Hopefully, your win will help take my uncle's mind off of it. But I've lost my chances at that promotion."

Naina shrugged. "You've been living in Kumble's shadow for far too long. Maybe you should start your own law firm instead."

He blinked rapidly. "Huh. Actually, that's not a bad idea . . ." Then he let out a weak chuckle, jutting his head toward Anil, who had just started singing his next song off-key. "I want you to know I like Anil. A lot, actually. I know you aren't my biggest fan, but I think we should try to get along, for his sake, if nothing else."

Naina watched Anil groove onstage as he attempted—and failed at—doing a moonwalk. "Yes," she agreed, nodding at Dhanush. "I'd love that."

"Good." Dhanush finished his drink and returned to the booth.

Smiling, Naina had another bite of cake and looked around. Madeira was quieter and emptier this Tuesday night, except for what seemed like the entire roster of AKC lawyers. And there Tejas was, sitting by the bar, drinking scotch on the rocks. Naina grinned, thinking back to her first time at his apartment, and the tense conversation in his kitchen that turned into a scorching-hot moment. It was funny how just watching him hold that cold glass, his other hand tugging at his collar, made Naina weak in the knees.

Between the toast, her colleagues congratulating her, and the three songs Anil had convinced her to sing already, she'd had no time to talk to Tejas in private. She put her plate of cake away and headed to the bar. "Hey." She tapped him on the shoulder. "Can we talk?"

"Sure," he said, gesturing to the seat next to him. Naina shifted her barstool closer to Tejas's, letting her heels brush against the hem of his pants. His hands rested on his knees, so she took them in hers and interlocked their fingers. "Your toast was really sweet," she said. "I don't normally stop to smell the roses when I win cases, but I'm glad I got to celebrate this with you. Especially after how our last celebration went . . ." She paused, trying to gauge his reaction.

Tejas bit his lip and looked away, perhaps thinking back to that fateful dinner on the yacht. "You were trying to protect your heart, while I was trying to put mine back together," he said, sighing. "We can't hold that against each other."

"And we won't," Naina said firmly. "I know myself, Tejas. There are going to be moments when my walls go up even without my noticing, or when I'll try to push you away because I'm scared of getting hurt. But thankfully"—she touched his cheek, stroking his beard—"I've never been afraid of challenges."

"And I've never been impatient," he replied.

Naina pressed her forehead to his. "You once said I deserve someone who fights for me as hard as I fight for my clients," she whispered, his lips a breath away. "That's you. And if you give me a chance, I promise I'll fight for our relationship every step of the way too."

Instead of replying, Tejas pulled her in by the nape of her neck and kissed her, his teeth tugging at her bottom lip. Naina moaned; she was about to deepen the kiss, not caring that their bosses and co-workers were in the same room, when he stopped abruptly, smiling against her mouth. "So we're in a relationship, huh?" he teased.

Naina pulled away to glare at him. "That's what you got from my grand confession of love?"

Quirking a brow, he said, "I don't recall you saying anything about love."

"You are so agonizing." She rolled her eyes, then let the words out. "Fine. I love you, Tejas. Happy now?"

He threw his head back and laughed, then pressed a quick kiss to the corner of her mouth. "I love you too, though I bet you already knew that."

"I did," she admitted, grinning. "I knew you were in love with me when I stopped you from saying it in Goa."

Tejas fake-pouted. "And how do you plan to make it up to me?"

"Maybe I'll show you how tonight, when we go back to your place. As for right now . . ." She stood, wrapping his arms around her shoulders, her gaze on the karaoke stage. "Let's re-create a different memory from that summer."

Tejas held out his hand. "Deal."

Naina moved to return the handshake, but he tugged her closer instead, his lips meeting hers, moving in time with the karaoke song still playing on the speakers. Naina tasted scotch on his tongue, his pine-scented cologne so familiar yet so dizzying, and when they broke apart, breathing hard, he reached for her. "Shall we?"

Her chest heaved as she took his hand. She'd lost track of the number of times they'd kissed, but somehow, every kiss was better than the last. Every touch woke her up, every dimpled smile soothed her down to her bones. Love did that, perhaps.

They gave the emcee their song selection, and as the lyrics to "Don't Go Breaking My Heart" appeared on the screen, Naina realized she hadn't just won in court today. She'd won in life.

And this was one win she planned to celebrate forever.

Epilogue

Goa, November 2027

"When I told you I like being blindfolded, this isn't what I meant," Naina grumbled.

Tejas laughed, the sound echoing in the wind as he drove through the cramped streets of Goa on their rental scooter. Naina's arms wound around his back, and although he couldn't see her face beneath the helmet she wore, he knew she was sporting her trademark scowl.

After all, he'd decided to take her out, blindfolded, on a surprise midnight drive on the one-year anniversary of making their relationship official. But hell, he'd just had the best year of his life with the woman he loved. She deserved a surprise like the one he'd planned.

He turned right, pulling onto a road by the seaside. The taste of saltwater hung in the air, and the waves roared louder than the scooter's engine. Behind him, Naina stiffened. "Are we driving past the sea?" she exclaimed. "Come on, I want to see the view!"

"Patience," he said. "I promise this will all make sense in a few minutes."

Naina huffed. "Fiiiine. I'll give you the benefit of the doubt."

"Thank you."

As he drove the scooter, Tejas went through the to-do list in his head for the remaining four days of their trip. There was no formal list on this couples' trip with Anil and Dhanush, except for the countless restaurants and experiences they'd bookmarked on Instagram, but considering how busy work kept them, it was a miracle all four of them had been able to make this trip happen outside of the group chat.

Winning the Acharya case had boosted Naina's career trajectory so much that she'd fielded offers from four other law firms before deciding to stay put at AKC as senior associate, landing the partner track mentorship as well. Jagannath had been sentenced to life in prison, while Preethi was slowly but surely regaining her footing in the film industry, with two of her projects set to release in early 2028. One of those projects was to be Sandhya's debut film, a Jane Austen adaptation in which she and Preethi would play sisters. Speaking of sisters, Latika had finally met someone new; she and her boyfriend had double-dated with Tejas and Naina only a few months ago during their trip to Bangalore.

Tejas, meanwhile, was in the process of starting his own law firm with Dhanush, which meant future vacations would be hard to come by. Anil was swamped with his catering business, which he was now expanding to weddings and not just small-scale events. His grandmother was thrilled about all the love her recipes were receiving from customers. And although Anil wasn't out to his family yet, his relationship with Dhanush was thriving.

Along the way, to Tejas's surprise, Naina and Dhanush had become friends, bonding over their chronic work anxiety and their distaste for legal dramas. Life was good, and it was about to get even better.

Smiling, Tejas drove the scooter uphill until they reached their destination. He slowed to a stop, then switched off the engine. "Okay," he said, taking off his helmet as Naina removed hers, "sit tight. I'll be right back."

Naina's eyes widened—or attempted to—beneath the blindfold as she straightened from the scooter. "Wait, you're leaving me here? Alone?"

"I'm only, like, twenty feet away from you," he called out as he jogged, backpack in hand, to the two trees on the left side of the cliff. With a quick click, he turned on the battery-operated lights that Anil and Dhanush had wound around the low-hanging branches an hour ago. He pulled out a Bluetooth speaker from his backpack and placed it under the trees.

"What are you up to?" Naina asked, a chuckle bubbling from her mouth, when the melodies of "Don't Go Breaking My Heart" filled the space. She slowly got up from the scooter, resting her arm on the seat for support. "Do I get to take off the blindfold now?"

"Hold on," Tejas yelled. He readjusted the banner over the tree trunks to make sure it was straight, then returned to the scooter. "There you are," Naina said, sticking one hand out and placing it on his shoulder when he was close enough. She brought her other hand up to her face, but Tejas got there first, hooking his index finger under the blindfold and tugging her closer until their lips met.

Naina let out a hum and kissed him back for a grand total of three seconds before her impatience seemed to win and she pulled away. "Can you remove the blindfold, please?" she asked, her hands clasped together.

"Yes," Tejas said as he felt his pockets to confirm he still had the two things that would complete the surprise. He undid the blindfold with a quick tug of his finger and stepped away. Naina blinked, her eyes adjusting to the darkness lit only by the half-moon, and her mouth fell open when she took in the drop before them, the same sea below the same cliff they'd jumped off from two summers ago. Her eyes, now shining with tears, went to the string of twinkling yellow fairy lights. "Tejas . . ." she whispered. "This is beautiful."

"Do you see what's written on that banner there, below the fairy lights?" he asked, turning her around and pointing to it.

Naina frowned. She took a step forward, scrunching her eyes. "No, it's too dark."

"Maybe this will help." Tejas pressed a button on the small remote in his pocket. The back of the banner lit up, with the words BE MY KARAOKE PARTNER FOR LIFE? glowing in bright purple.

A gasp left Naina's mouth. As she turned to Tejas, pressing her hands to her cheeks, he got down on one knee, holding up the diamond ring that Mr. Shetty had helped him pick out. "Naina," Tejas said, his voice already breaking as he took her hand in his, "I knew you were my person when we jumped off this cliff together. After hitting the water, I realized that I was still falling. And I haven't stopped falling for you since. I love you so much"—he smiled when she mouthed those three words back—"and I find new reasons and ways to love you every single day. Whether it's being in awe of you in court or seeing you take care of Astrid, whether it's arguing over the best karaoke song of all time—you know my vote is still for 'It's My Life'—or spending hours in bed talking and kissing . . . this past year has been nothing short of perfect."

"I love you so much." Naina's voice shook as she held out her left hand. "Just ask me already. Please."

He grinned, blinking back the dampness in his own eyes. "Naina Shetty, will you marry me and allow me the honor of continuing to fall for you, more and more, for the rest of our lives?"

A tear rolled down her cheek. "Yes," she breathed, yanking him up by the collar and kissing him. Her lips tasted like salt and cherry-red lipstick; her hands, threading through his hair, felt like hope and happiness and home. When they broke apart, Tejas put the ring on her finger and pressed her trembling hand to his mouth. "Forever," he promised.

"Forever," she agreed, her lip wobbling. "Oh my God, I have to text Anil." She snapped a quick selfie, holding her hand up, but when she opened WhatsApp to send it to her best friend, she burst out laughing.

"What?" Tejas asked, biting the inside of his cheek. He already knew what to expect when she held up the screen for him to see.

Anil

Soooo

Are you engaged yet, or what? 👀

She smacked Tejas on the arm, squealing. "You told him?"

He kissed her on the forehead. "Who do you think set up the decorations while we were driving up here?"

Naina craned her neck and looked around. "Are Anil and Dhanush both here, then?"

"They went back to the hotel. But," he said, walking backward toward the edge of the cliff, "one last thing before we celebrate our engagement with our best friends." He pulled off his shirt in one quick motion, then unbuttoned his cargo shorts. "Let's re-create another memory."

Naina didn't bat an eyelid. She shimmied out of her floral dress so she was just in her bra and underwear, then took Tejas's hand and pulled him forward with her. They plummeted down, screams echoing from both their mouths as they crashed into the sea.

"Fuck, it's so much colder than I remember!" Naina exclaimed, dipping her head in and out of the water.

Tejas let out an exhale, his teeth chattering. November in Goa was still summer, all things considered, but cold water was cold water. "Guess we'll have to keep each other warm," he replied, tugging her closer.

Naina kissed him, threading her fingers through his curls as a moan escaped her lips. Tejas's arms wound tighter around the woman who was not just his favorite person and co-parent to Astrid, but also his fiancée. Two and a half years ago, when his heart was still battered and bruised, the day he'd first met this unstoppable force of a woman, he'd known she was someone he would never want to shake off, their "wrong answers only" policy be damned.

Now he no longer needed to forget her. Instead, he had the privilege of making her his wife and loving her until their dying breaths.

Despite the long and convoluted journey they had to go through to get to this point in their love story, Tejas wouldn't change a single thing. He had to love her and lose her to know he wanted nobody else. She had to learn to lay her heart bare and trust fate over fear to decide he was the one for her.

Naina was the woman destiny had brought to him not once, but twice. This, he knew, was a life worth fighting for. This was love against all odds; this was love beyond reasonable doubt.

Acknowledgments

I can't believe I get to write the Acknowledgments for my fourth book with Penguin Random House, my second book slated for 2026. I've always wanted to be a two-books-a-year author across YA and adult romance, and with *Love Beyond Reasonable Doubt,* that dream is finally coming true.

The idea for this book came to me very randomly on a trip to Goa a few years ago. My creative writer brain ran with it, wondering, "What's the craziest thing that could happen to two horny strangers who have a 'wrong answers only' summer fling?" And voilà! Second-chance workplace romance, baby! It's my first time writing this trope, and although I was a second-chance romance nonbeliever until recently (you'll find out what changed my mind as you keep reading), I'm so grateful I gave it a shot, in more ways than one.

As always, the first person I thank has to be my superstar literary agent, Rachel Beck. I don't think I'll ever be able to express how glad I am that we found each other, because I'm the writer I am today only because of you.

Thank you to my editor, Mae Martinez, for not just her sharp editorial vision, but also for her kind, encouraging words as I navigated the publishing world for the fourth time with this book. Thank you to the team at Dell, from those in production who spotted the many typos and inconsistencies in early drafts, to the folks over in marketing and publicity for getting the word out about my books, as well as everyone else at Random House who shaped this book and made it what it is today.

To the team at the future of agency, including but not limited to Andrea DeWerd, Amanda Livingston, Saimah Haque, Sarah Mehelic, and Sandra Garcia. Your unbridled enthusiasm for *Love Beyond Reasonable Doubt* means more to me than I can ever say.

As I mentioned above, I've never been the biggest fan of real-life second-chance romances, although I love the trope in books. But in March 2025, someone I fell out of touch with years ago (due to certain romance-novel-esque reasons) taught me that in the end, all you need for a second-chance relationship to work is timing, chemistry . . . and trust. Trust—not just in your partner, but also in yourself—to give your heart to the same person twice. That isn't an easy feat, but Anshuman D Gopi, loving you is the easiest thing I've done. You were my best friend through high school and most of college—and you still are. Except now, you're the love of my life as well. This book couldn't have been written without you holding my hand through it all, and wiping my tears on days when self-doubt and imposter syndrome held me captive. I love you so, so much.

A big thanks to my IRL besties and my author friends, for listening to my rants and to my humble brags alike: Sambhram Puranik, Darshita Agarwal, Amrutha Raja, Anish Ravishankar, Siddharth Jeevagan, Anahita Karthik, Kalie Holford, Ananya Devarajan, Noreen Nanja, Aishwarya Tandon, and Kathryn Harris, among others.

My family is and has always been my lifeline, and I'm forever grateful to them for encouraging my writing career over the years, and even today.

And finally, dear reader: Whether you're new to my work or

have been with me since my debut days, I'm so, so grateful to you for picking up *Love Beyond Reasonable Doubt*. I hope this book brings you joy and laughter and all the giddy feels, but most important, I hope it reminds you that taking a chance on yourself—and on your heart, even if it was once broken—is always the right decision. Trust me on that.

© SANTHOSH NARENDRAN

SWATI HEGDE is the author of *Love Beyond Reasonable Doubt, Can't Help Faking in Love,* and *Match Me If You Can,* a freelance editor, mindset coach, and self-proclaimed coffee shop enthusiast who lives in Bangalore, India. She can often be found at the nearest café with a hot mug of tea, or singing her favorite songs off-key at karaoke night. She looks forward to a long career bringing Indian stories and voices to light.

swatihegde.com
Instagram: @swatihegdeauthor
X: @SwatiHWrites

About the Type

This book was set in Bembo, a typeface based on an old-style Roman face that was used for Cardinal Pietro Bembo's tract *De Aetna* in 1495. Bembo was cut by Francesco Griffo (1450–1518) in the early sixteenth century for Italian Renaissance printer and publisher Aldus Manutius (1449–1515). The Lanston Monotype Company of Philadelphia brought the well-proportioned letterforms of Bembo to the United States in the 1930s.